The Forbidden

(Kelderan Runic Warriors #4)

Jessie Donovan

This book is a work of fiction. Names, characters, places, and incidents are either the product of the writer's imagination or are used fictitiously, and any resemblance to actual persons, living or dead, business establishments, events, or locales is entirely coincidental.

The Forbidden
Copyright © 2019 Laura Hoak-Kagey
Mythical Lake Press, LLC
First Digital Edition

All rights reserved. This book or any portion thereof may not be reproduced or used in any manner without the express written permission of the author except for the use of brief quotations in a book review.

Cover Art by Clarissa Yeo of Yocla Designs
ISBN: 978-1942211693

Books by Jessie Donovan

Asylums for Magical Threats
Blaze of Secrets (AMT #1)
Frozen Desires (AMT #2)
Shadow of Temptation (AMT #3)
Flare of Promise (AMT #4)

Cascade Shifters
Convincing the Cougar (CS #0.5)
Reclaiming the Wolf (CS #1)
Cougar's First Christmas (CS #2)
Resisting the Cougar (CS #3)

Kelderan Runic Warriors
The Conquest (KRW #1)
The Barren (KRW #2)
The Heir (KRW #3)
The Forbidden (KRW #4)
The Hidden (KRW #5 / 2019)

Lochguard Highland Dragons
The Dragon's Dilemma (LHD #1)
The Dragon Guardian (LHD #2,)
The Dragon's Heart (LHD #3)
The Dragon Warrior (LHD #4)
The Dragon Family (LHD #5)
The Dragon's Discovery / Alistair Boyd (LHD #6 / May 2019)

Love in Scotland
Crazy Scottish Love (LiS #1)
Chaotic Scottish Wedding (LiS #2)

Stonefire Dragons

Sacrificed to the Dragon (SD #1)
Seducing the Dragon (SD #2)
Revealing the Dragons (SD #3)
Healed by the Dragon (SD #4)
Reawakening the Dragon (SD #5)
Loved by the Dragon (SD #6)
Surrendering to the Dragon (SD #7)
Cured by the Dragon (SD #8)
Aiding the Dragon (SD #9)
Finding the Dragon (SD #10)
Craved by the Dragon (SD #11)
Persuading the Dragon / Zain & Ivy (SD #12 / 2019)

Stonefire Dragons Universe

Winning Skyhunter (Spring 2019)

Chapter One

Princess Kalahn tro el Vallen clenched her fists at her side and did her best to pack away her emotions as she walked down one corridor and then another, toward her brother's office.

A few hours ago, she'd been part of a video conference with her eldest brother, Keltor, her father, and some family members she'd never known about, complete with a grown niece and three half siblings.

The shock of her new family was bad enough, but the sight of her father's frail body struggling to sit up had only made his mortality that much more real. He was dying, plain and simple.

She'd known, of course, but knowing it and seeing it were two different things. While they had never been close, she still remembered him telling stories about her mother, his eyes lighting up with fondness. Since Kalahn had been young when her mother had died, she'd relied on other people's memories for comfort. Recently, her father had even started to type up and send more stories to her. And soon, she wouldn't even have that.

Tears prickled her eyes and she blinked them away. She wanted nothing more than to curl up inside her quarters and cry. But her elder brother on Jasvar—Kason—had summoned her. And she knew that if she ignored him, Kason would send guards to forcibly retrieve her.

While many would dismiss Kalahn for not only being a female, but especially for being a princess, Kalahn had plans for the future. Plans that required her to somewhat behave and not upset her brother at every opportunity.

She finally arrived at her brother's office, entered, and slammed the door behind her. It was the closest to defiance she could muster without angering him too much.

Her brother looked up with a frown. "Can't you ever act like a normal person and knock?"

With her head high, she strode toward his desk. "I'm a princess. So, no, I'll never be able to act like a normal person. I may as well play the part." Kason grunted, but she spoke again before he could. "One of your guards said you wanted to see me about something?"

He put down his notescreen and studied her. "Are you okay?"

She resisted blinking at her brother's concern. Even a year ago, he never would've bothered to ask her. His human bride really had rubbed off on him. "Honestly? No. Our father is dying and we suddenly have two sisters and a brother we never knew about. Not to mention a niece and nephew only a few years my junior. It's almost as if my entire life has been a lie. However, a Kelderan royal must always put duty above all else and keep their emotions in check. Isn't that what you and Keltor always say?"

Kason stood. "It's just me, Kalahn. There's no need to put on a brave face."

She raised her brows. "Of course I must. Or you'll try to lock me away again."

Sighing, he shook his head. "That was for one day, to ensure you didn't run away before the video conference."

Trailing her fingers along the edge of his desk, she

replied, "I wouldn't run so much if you merely asked me to do things instead of ordering me, brother."

He crossed his arms over his chest. "Taryn keeps saying the same thing."

Taryn Demara was her brother's bride and also the human female leader on Jasvar, who happened to be a highly skilled warrior in her own right. Kalahn admired her more than almost anyone else. "Then listen to her."

"I try, but there are dangers you don't know about, Kalahn. Sit, and I'll explain some of them to you. Maybe then you'll understand my need for caution."

Her curiosity burned to know what he was talking about, so she sat in one of the chairs in front of his desk, while Kason sat on the edge. Her brother spoke again. "I should preface this by letting you know that the information I share can't leave the room. Understood?" At the seriousness of his tone, she nodded. Kason continued, "We've recently discovered a female assassin working for the antimonarchists, here inside the colony."

Interesting. She'd never heard of a female assassin before. Leaning forward, she asked, "Are there others?"

"We're not sure. But while the recent attack on the palace back on Keldera swayed public support in favor of the monarchy, it's not as certain here on Jasvar."

She put it all together. "So that's why you've been so worried about me running away, because you're afraid one of the antimonarchists is here and will try to kill me."

"Yes."

"Putting aside that you should've told me that as soon as you knew, why tell me now? Did Taryn convince you to?"

Kason shrugged. "Partly, but the revelation of our new half sister here on the colony made me realize that if you're going to be looking out for her, you need to know the full truth."

"Does the 'full truth' pertain to everything or just as it relates to my life?"

"How about we take it one step at a time? Like with any job, you learn and train on one thing before tackling another."

"I suppose."

Kason nodded. "Good. Over the next few days, I'll brief you in more detail surrounding the spy on Jasvar and what we've discovered. But for now, let's talk about your current assignment." Kason reached behind him, picked up a folder, and held it out to her. "This is what we know about our sister on Jasvar."

Taking the purple-tinged materials, she barely noted how strange it was to use paper instead of notescreens before opening the packet.

She ran a finger over her sister's name—Kajala Mayven. "You think father would've had some sense and used any other letter but K. With the six of us siblings having K names, plus Keltor's son Kelzal, as well as father, it's going to be confusing and difficult to keep track of everyone."

He grunted. "I didn't select the names. It can't be helped." He gestured toward the papers. "That is Kajala's public record, plus what I could requisition on such short notice from the colony's intelligence arm. I'm sure Keltor will send more information later, but I want you to memorize what's there as soon as possible and burn it."

Frowning, she glanced up at her brother. "I understand burning the information from the intelligence arm, but why also get rid of the publicly available details?"

"Because public records on Jasvar entail paper storage. If you burn it, then there will be some time before another copy appears. The lag will help protect our sister for a while."

She thumbed the twenty-odd pages of information. "I never thought I'd miss technology this much, but computers would've made this easier to sort through."

Jasvar was a low-tech human colony. While part of the agreement between the people of Jasvar and Keldera called for the slow integration of Kelderan technology, it wasn't something that could be done overnight. It could be years, or even decades before Jasvarian resources could be located that were suited to engineer the complex circuit boards needed. It could be even longer before they could design a new composite material for spaceships and other products.

Kason grunted. "Perhaps. But you wished to remain on Jasvar, so this is what we must work with. Let me know when you've digested all the information I gave you. I have men locating Kajala right now. Once we find her, I hope that you'll meet with her as soon as possible."

Kalahn searched her brother's gaze. "That was almost a request. Am I dreaming?" He growled and she smiled. "Okay, okay. I appreciate it, Kason. I truly do." Standing, she clutched the folder against her chest. "It shouldn't take me long to go through this. I'll even remain in my quarters next to yours and not try to slip away."

She turned to leave, anxious to get to work, but Kason's voice filled the space. "One last thing." Glancing over her shoulder, she raised her brows in question. Kason added, "Until we're more certain that the threats are contained on Jasvar, Ryven will be your guard and will help you with Kajala."

Keeping surprise from her face, she asked, "I thought Ryven was going back to Keldera with the colony transport ship?"

"He is. However, there is little for him to do at the moment. Syzel is living onboard the ship, ensuring everything is repaired and ready for the return trip. There are also a few other trainers aboard, keeping the warriors in shape. And since Ryven is one of the soldiers I trust the most, it makes sense that I ask him to help protect our family."

Somehow, some way, it seemed that Kason had never learned of her long-ago kiss with Ryven Xanna. Otherwise, he never would have assigned him as her guard.

And if she protested the assignment, especially since she'd known Ryven most of her life, Kason would deduce that something was amiss.

She'd only just gotten into her brother's good graces and trust circle. She wasn't going to lose her place in either by raising suspicion.

So she bobbed her head. "Okay. He knows where to find me."

Rushing out of the room, Kalahn took a deep breath. Protecting Kajala would be the easy part it seemed. Being in close proximity to Ryven and not being able to kiss him would be the challenge. It may have been years since he'd lowered his head and taken her lips, making her body burn in a good way, but she often dreamed of the male she could never have.

The one who often joked and laughed at her behavior without censure, which was almost unheard of in Kelderan culture. A female wasn't meant to run off and try to seize her own future, let alone stow away on a spaceship and put together a rescue mission for her older brother.

However, Ryven had almost approved of her actions when she'd returned with her brother and his bride.

No. Kalahn wanted change, but she didn't want to waste time on revising the marriage laws of princesses. She'd much rather fight for the right to work and maybe even have a career. Both things that were currently denied to her.

Besides, if she wished to put her plans in motion and

work toward the future she wanted, it was better to remain unattached.

Especially since Kason was finally trusting her with secrets and confidential information, and she wouldn't risk it all by kissing a male.

Not even for a handsome, charming one like Ryven Xanna.

Picking up her pace, Kalahn headed toward her quarters and quickly packed away all thoughts and dreams of Ryven. It was time to prove herself to her brother. With that goal in mind, she should be able to treat Ryven as an old acquaintance and nothing more.

✵ ✵ ✵

Ryven stood outside Kalahn's quarters and readied himself for dealing with the female he had to resist above all others.

Kason assigning him as Kalahn's guard and partner was the last thing he'd expected. His friend's bride must really be rubbing off on Kason; otherwise, he never would've given Kalahn a potentially dangerous task, such as allowing her to protect her sister.

Because until any other spies were located inside the colony and contained, Kalahn could be in constant danger.

Then protect her, he told himself. After all, he would soon return to Keldera and never have to worry about slipping up and doing something stupid, such as pulling her close and kissing her. Years may have gone by, but her eagerness and responsiveness to his kiss back then still haunted his dreams.

But an orphaned warrior wasn't a suitable lord for a princess. It was best for him to remember that. After all, he couldn't protect her from a prison cell, which was where he could end up if he acted on any of his fantasies.

No, the best recourse was to treat this assignment as any other. That meant focusing solely on a successful outcome.

Drawing on years of training, he slowly packed away and contained his emotions and memories. Ensuring his markings were the deep blue of contentment, he raised his hand and knocked on the wooden door.

Kalahn yanked it open after a few beats. "It's you."

He raised an eyebrow. "Why? Were you expecting another male at your door?"

Rolling her eyes, she turned and walked to the plush chair in the room. "This isn't Keldera. I can receive males and females without a chaperone."

He shut the door and faced her. "I never mentioned a chaperone. After all, this is a freer society than back home. I suspect it will lead to many a female dallying before taking a lord."

The second he said the words, Ryven wished he could take them back. He should not be talking about sex with a Kelderan princess.

However, in Kalahn's usual stride, she didn't bat an eyelash and merely raised her brows. "Good. Because a female should be able to try out *everything* before committing her life to another."

Before he could stop himself, he blurted, "Kalahn! You shouldn't mention such things."

"You can take the male from Keldera, but apparently, you can't take Kelderan ways out of the male," she muttered.

Not wanting to debate sexual encounters and the different standards for males and females, Ryven stood tall and clasped his hands behind him. "We're on Jasvar right now, not Keldera, which means our top priority should be protecting your sister. One of my warriors saw her return home not long ago. He and another are standing guard until we arrive."

"Did Kason brief you on Kajala, too?"

He shook his head. "Kason said you would do it."

Surprise flashed in Kalahn's enchanting green eyes, but it quickly disappeared. "Well, the public record isn't as full of information as I would've liked. Most of the file was about her school records, awards, and recognitions. Apparently, Kajala is an engineering genius of some kind."

"Isn't your nephew that way, too?"

Kalahn scrunched her nose. "It's hard to think of twenty-two-year-old Kelzal as my nephew since I'm only three years older than him. But, yes, by all accounts Kelzal is a genius as well, albeit with computers and mechanical items. Kajala focuses more on architectural and structural engineering."

He gestured with his head toward the file in Kalahn's hands. "What else does it say?"

"That she's rarely ventured out of her quarters since arriving on Jasvar." She bit her bottom lip, drawing his attention. Since lingering may give her ideas, he quickly met her gaze again as she replied, "Which is odd because she was apparently quite social when she was younger. However, in recent months, she's quit all her social clubs and started working from home. "

He tucked away all the relevant information. "I think the best way to figure out what's going on is to meet with her. Are you ready?"

Tossing the folder on the chair, Kalahn took a few steps toward him. "Almost. I just want to make a few things clear, first. I'm in charge of watching over Kajala and you are merely here to protect us. I will be giving the orders, unless it concerns our safety. Then I'll hand it over to you."

With Kalahn's head high and shoulders back, it was difficult to believe she was a Kelderan princess. Although

Ryven had to admit to himself that he rather liked Kalahn's straightforward manner. "I agree to your terms." He took a step toward her and leaned forward a fraction. "However, the second there's danger or I sense a threat, you listen to me, no questions asked. I won't have time to argue."

"I can follow orders if need be." He raised his brows and she sighed. "Usually. I will defer to your judgment in the majority of situations. However, no one person is correct 100 percent of the time. I hope that if I have a decent idea, you'll listen."

"I will try, although usually I'm the one giving orders since I train others. It'll take some getting used to."

She smiled slowly, and a warning bell went off inside his head. Kalahn spoke again. "So, does that mean you'll train me in the ways of warriors, too?"

He blinked. "What?"

"I've had some training from the Jasvarian warrior females, but they don't always have time for me. Since we'll be working together to protect Kajala anyway, it could be beneficial for you to teach the both of us."

He opened his mouth to refute the idea but promptly closed it. Kason would probably have his balls for even considering Kalahn's idea. But she did have a point. "We shall see. If you behave, I'll instruct you in some of the basics. However, it may be best to keep this from your brothers for the time being."

"What do you mean if I behave? I'm not about to shirk the first real duty I've been given in my life."

At the affront in her tone, Ryven unclasped his hands and reached out to touch her arm. "I didn't say you would."

Shrugging off his hand, she moved to the door. "I wish to depart. So unless you want to leave me unprotected, you'll follow."

She exited and Ryven cursed. After he caught up to her,

he took hold of her shoulders and stopped them both. "Look at me, Kalahn."

While she took her time about it, she finally met his gaze. "What?"

At the irritation in Kalahn's eyes, the urge to distract her and calm her down flooded his body. The easiest way to do so, and release some tension for them both, would be to kiss her.

His eyes darted briefly to her lips, but he quickly met her gaze again. He couldn't kiss her because if he did, he had a feeling Kalahn would want more. And there wasn't a path forward where that could happen. Neither one of them could afford such a scandal. And given the intelligence Ryven knew about the Kelderan colony on Jasvar, it could set off a dangerous chain of events.

However, a compromise flashed into his head. If Kalahn wanted warrior lessons, he would give her the first one.

Moving his face close to hers, until her hot breath tickled his lips, he stared at her. As the seconds ticked by, heat crept up her cheeks and the runic markings on her neck flashed yellow, the color of unease and nervousness.

He pounced. "That, right there, could cost you your life. While not every enemy is aware that our markings change color with our emotions, enough of them do. Any traitors inside the colony certainly will know. I imagine the information will quickly spread among the Jasvarian humans, too." He moved even closer, and her markings flashed a brighter shade of yellow. "You need to concentrate and keep them a dark blue color."

Her question was a whisper against his chin, "How?"

"Imagine the most mundane situation, one that you do almost every day. That should do it. Now, try it."

At first, her markings flashed between yellow and red—red signaled lust.

Lust? No, he must've imagined the color he wished to see.

Thankfully after about a minute, they turned dark blue, the neutral default of all Kelderan warriors, which signaled calmness of mind and body.

Triumph flared in Kalahn's eyes, which prodded Ryven to push her farther. "The second part of the lesson involves keeping them blue while I push your boundaries. Can you do that?"

She nodded. Ryven raised one of her bare arms into his field of vision, to monitor her marking colors. In the next beat, he moved his lips to her jaw. He gently pressed them against her skin.

Electricity raced through his body at the contact. Only because he had decades of training to draw on was he able to keep his marking a dark blue and not groan.

Training Kalahn would test every last iota of his discipline.

However, the princess wasn't as skilled and the dark blue faded to red.

Maybe she did still find him attractive after all these years.

Pulling back, he cleared his throat. "Containing your emotions and maintaining a neutral color for your markings is your first test. Only once you've passed that will I teach you anything else."

He expected defiance, or even a demand.

Instead, mischief danced in Kalahn's eyes. "So we have to keep doing this until I can pass your test?"

It almost sounded as if she wanted him to kiss her jaw again.

No. To accept that would lead them both into trouble.

He stepped back. "There are other ways to test you, Princess. Surprise is key for any training, so you'll just have to wait and see what else I have planned."

Motioning for her to precede him, he waited for her to move. Her expression turned guarded before she walked ahead of him. Dishonorable male that he was, he couldn't resist watching her hips sway. He swore she exaggerated the movements on purpose, to tease him.

He stood tall and quickly matched her pace. He could never let her know that he'd enjoyed the view, maybe more than he should have.

No, he kept his face neutral and escorted her to Kajala's quarters in silence.

Chapter Two

The entire way to Kajala's quarters, Kalahn tried to push away the feeling of Ryven's lips against her jaw.

She'd always assumed her memories of their kiss had been those of a young female, romanticizing and embellishing an event.

But Ryven's "test" had proved that her memories were truthful. One touch and heat had rushed through her body. She couldn't be sure, but her markings might have even flashed the color of lust.

Get a grip, Kalahn. Even if Ryven weren't flying back to Keldera in the near future, she had no interest in being a bride yet. There was too much to do and few Kelderan males would accept their brides working. Merchants were the only ones who valued a working female, and Ryven most definitely wasn't a merchant.

If and when Kalahn was ready to settle down, her best bet was to find someone in the Jasvarian colony. The males there had no illusions about a quiet, domesticated bride who lived to cook, clean, and raise babies.

Kalahn had nothing against females who wanted that life. But it would be nice to have a choice in the matter.

As they entered one of the temporary living areas carved inside a mountain, Kalahn pushed every thought out of her head except for those related to her half sister. If Kalahn fulfilled her assignment as asked, then she had a chance at future jobs with greater responsibility. She was determined to prove to both of her older brothers that she was mature enough to see a mission through.

Because if she didn't sway their minds, she might never be able to work toward some of her bigger goals regarding change.

Stopping at the living quarters numbered 483, Kalahn nodded at the two warrior guards standing to either side of the entrance before knocking.

For a few seconds, nothing happened, and she was overly aware of Ryven's heat just behind her. Did the blasted male have to stand so close? After all, she'd never seen a warrior stand so near to another female who wasn't a relative or their bride.

No doubt, he was trying to set her off guard with another one of his "trainings." At that thought, she focused on succeeding with Kajala to keep her markings neutral.

A muffled female voice sounded through the door, garnering her attention. "I'm not taking visitors."

"I'm afraid you don't have a choice, Kajala Mayven. I'm Kalahn tro el Vallen, your half sister." When there was nothing but silence on the other side of the door, Kalahn added, "I can easily reach out to our brother Kason and get a key. But I was rather hoping that you'd open the door willingly. You see, I've always wished for a sister to help even the odds against my brothers. I'm impatient to meet you."

A minute passed by before the same voice said, "You can come in, but not the warriors."

Ryven grunted behind her, but she ignored him. "Promise you won't hurt me, and I'll gladly agree."

Ryven whispered into her ear, "I can't allow you to enter alone."

Kajala's voice came through the door once more. "I have no desire to hurt anyone." The lock clicked. "Come in when you're ready."

Placing a hand on the doorknob, she glanced at Ryven. Keeping her voice low, she said, "I'll be fine. I may not know much about my sister, but she's not an assassin. I'll keep the door unlocked so if there's trouble, you can enter straightaway. Is that satisfactory?"

He grunted, and Kalahn entered Kajala's quarters without another word.

As she leaned against the closed door, she zeroed in on her sister.

With her dark blue hair and light teal skin, Kajala looked nothing like her mother. Kalahn had seen Kajala's mother once via a video conference, her golden skin and magenta hair streaked with silver a striking combination.

However, Kajala was striking in a different way. She was tall and willowy, with dark blue eyes that tilted up ever so slightly at the edges.

She was the opposite of Kalahn's golden skin, and shorter, plumper frame in nearly every way; the only trait they shared was dark blue hair.

But as soon as her gaze reached Kajala's midsection, every thought flew out of her head.

Judging by her sister's protruding belly, she was heavy with child.

And according to her records, she wasn't married.

Kajala's soft voice filled the room. "And now you know my secret." She glanced down at her stomach and smiled. "One that I hated at first, but now, I'm glad. It gives me a piece of him."

Blinking, Kalahn gathered her wits. If she didn't pounce

on the opening, Kajala might retreat and never share her secrets. "Who, may I ask, does it give you a piece of?"

"My love, Davrel. He was killed during a space pirate attack eight months ago."

She wondered why nothing had been in her file about a male named Davrel. Regardless, Kalahn put it all together. "He was killed right after you conceived."

"Yes." She met Kalahn's gaze. "We had every intention of marrying when he returned. However, with his death, there was no one to claim me. So I persuaded my mother to talk to our father, and I was allowed to come to Jasvar."

While the humans on Jasvar would think nothing of a pregnant, unmarried female, it was the epitome of shame on Keldera.

She couldn't blame her sister for wanting to leave.

Kalahn took a step toward Kajala. "This is why you've been hiding in your rooms, isn't it?"

She nodded. "Yes. I know those selected for the colony are more open-minded, but many would see me and talk. So I keep to my quarters, and when I do go out, I wear pillows around my sides and rear to make me appear overweight rather than pregnant."

Anger flared. "You shouldn't have to resort to such things." Kajala's eyes widened, but Kalahn pushed on. "Having a child with the male you love shouldn't be a crime. If males could conceive, they would celebrate the accomplishment and most likely throw parties."

The corner of Kajala's mouth ticked up. "Perhaps. Although with a little time, I'm sure we can change things here."

She closed the distance to her sister. "I'm adding that to my list of things to tackle, although I must admit it's getting longer by the day."

Kajala tilted her head. "You are not what I expected for a princess."

She shrugged. "I would give it all up if it meant I could have greater freedom. Alas, it's females in general who shoulder the burden amongst Kelderans." An idea flashed. "Although if two daughters of King Kastor form an alliance, we might be able to accomplish quite a bit."

Kajala smiled. "I'm starting to think that our father kept us apart to keep us both out of trouble. Although, believe it or not, my younger sister is even more troublesome than me."

Taking a chance, Kalahn took Kajala's free hand and squeezed. "Well, I'm the eldest sister so I must set the example." She leaned in and whispered, "And that example is to break as many female-related traditions as possible. Because if I can have my way, I want to be a starship pilot."

"Heights terrify me, so hopefully I don't have to do that, too."

She shook her head. "Of course not. You're already a genius with engineering stuff, or so I heard. The colony is lucky to have you."

For a second, she thought her sister might cry. However, Kajala cleared her throat and motioned toward the small kitchen area. "How about we have some tea? Ever since I learned of your existence, I've envisioned a thousand scenarios but nothing like this. I think we might even become friends."

"Friends. That's something I've wished for but have rarely accomplished until recently. I guess when it rains, it pours, and I'm not complaining."

Kajala headed toward the kitchen area and stirred the fire. As she placed the pot of water on the stove, Kalahn almost wished they had a replicator machine.

To become independent on Jasvar, Kalahn might actually have to learn how to cook.

Sitting down, Kajala motioned for her to do the same. Once they were both seated, her half sister asked, "Will Prince Kason be as accepting as you are?"

"Kason was a general in the Kelderan Army, so he's used to routine." Kajala's face fell, but Kalahn quickly put up a hand. "But he did marry the female leader of Jasvar, so he's learning to be more open-minded. You just have to learn to ignore his grunts and growls." Kajala hesitated, so Kalahn added, "But we can wait a bit before I introduce you to him. I'm sure there's much for you and me to discuss anyway."

Her sister smiled again, but before she could reply, there was a pounding on the door, followed by Ryven's voice. "Kalahn? Are you okay?"

She sighed and whispered to Kajala. "That's Ryven Xanna. He's supposed to protect us. I'm not sure if you're aware, but there are certain threats to the both of us here on Jasvar."

Ryven shouted, "Kalahn, answer me or I'm coming in."

Rolling her eyes, she went to the door and opened it a crack. "I'm alive and well, as you can see. Now, I'm trying to have a conversation with my sister. Or, is that too dangerous for me to do by myself?"

He growled. "Just because there's not an immediate threat doesn't mean there won't be. You've survived mostly on luck to date, but that won't always be the case, Kalahn. You need to let me do my job."

She opened her mouth to tell him a thing or two when Kajala's voice echoed in the room. "Let him in. It's probably the quickest way."

Triumph flared in Ryven's eyes, but Kalahn ignored it. She quickly tugged him inside and whispered, "Don't stare."

"Why would I…" His voice trailed off as he spotted

Kajala a few feet away. To his credit, Ryven quickly cleared his throat and bowed his head. "Kajala Mayven, it is an honor to protect you."

Kalahn was torn between laughing at his formality and moving to stand between him and Kajala.

She blinked. Was she jealous of Kajala receiving Ryven's attention? Preposterous. After all, her sister was still mourning her lost love.

Not that Ryven's affections should matter to her anyway.

Kajala spoke before Kalahn could. "The water should be boiling by now. Sit in the living area and I'll bring the tea and small cakes I made."

As her sister walked away, Kalahn took Ryven's bicep and leaned in. "You need to let me be the one to tell Kason about this when the time is right. Understood?"

※ ※ ※

At Kalahn's stern tone, Ryven wanted to laugh. He was nearly a foot taller than her, and many more pounds heavier with muscle.

However, to Kalahn, that didn't seem to matter when it came to her family. He wished more females were like her.

Before his thoughts could turn toward something he couldn't have, he whispered back, "You're in charge of this mission, and I will try to defer to your judgment. However, if I think your lives are in danger, I won't hold back the truth from your brother."

"Fair enough." She looked toward the door Kajala had exited. "I don't want her to experience any sort of ridicule or shame. That means my mission just became a whole lot more complicated."

"You always protest about your brothers being protective, but you're the same way, Kalahn."

Her gaze shot back to his. "The difference is that I'll listen to what Kajala wants and take that into consideration rather than just make decisions without regard for her desires."

With her face so close to his, whatever sage advice he'd been about to impart fled his head. He couldn't stop staring at the little flecks of gold in her eyes. He could only imagine how they lit up when she argued about something in the heat of the moment.

Or how they turned dark when she cried out his name in pleasure as she came.

Kajala's voice interrupted them. "Everything is ready. Come."

Kalahn instantly moved away from him and walked over to her sister. It took every bit of restraint he possessed not to haul her back to his side. He was a seasoned warrior, for crying out loud. Why he couldn't push away his thoughts and desires for one female, he didn't know.

Well, maybe he knew but he wasn't going to admit it.

Kalahn linked her arm through her sister's. "We have plans to make and details to learn about each other. Let's get started."

Kajala gave one last look over her shoulder at him before escorting Kalahn away.

Alone in the room, Ryven smoothed back his short hair. He only had about a week before he left Jasvar, but if he remained in Kalahn's company, that could be enough to allow him to slip up and shame not only his best friend, but himself as well. He needed to get a grip and act like the seasoned warrior he was.

Once he returned to his quarters, Ryven would go through a series of meditation practices and then spar with some of his trainees. That usually cleared his head. Maybe then he could think of a way to protect Kalahn without constantly thinking about her green eyes or tempting hips.

No, he most definitely shouldn't think about her hips or how he'd like to hold onto them while he did wicked things to her.

By the time he caught up to Kalahn and Kajala, he was mostly back in control. However, as Kalahn met his eyes and flashed him a grin, his gut told him her request was going to get him into trouble.

She spoke overly sweet, which was yet another warning bell. "I'm going to be staying with Kajala for the foreseeable future. Since neither one of us has a lord, it's imperative we learn how to defend ourselves. That means weapons for the both of us, and hand-to-hand combat training for me. We should begin as soon as possible."

He frowned. "You devised this in the time it took me to follow you here?"

Kalahn sipped some tea. "Oh, yes. I know it's tradition to hide intelligence on Keldera if you're female, but I've never been good at that. So you'd better get used to our ideas for as long as you're our guard."

He crossed his arms over his chest. "I can't do such a thing without Kason's permission, and you know it."

She took another drink. "Well, then how about you go find him and garner it? With the guards stationed outside Kajala's door, we'll be fine as long as we stay in here. I even promise not to run away or cause trouble." He quirked an eyebrow and she added, "Well, at least not trouble that takes us out of this room. Depending on how long it takes you to convince Kason of my request, we may have come up with plans to take over and rule the Kelderan colony. So, prepare yourself."

Ignoring her humor, he kept his voice even. "I'm not your lackey, Kalahn. You'd best remember that."

She tilted her head. "So does that mean you're not going to do as I asked?"

He sighed. "Since I agree with you in this particular case, I will. However, remember that I've trained many a defiant warrior in my time. And believe me, if you truly want training, you won't see the surprises I have coming. Nor will I go easy on you for being female."

Before Kalahn could say another word, he bowed toward Kajala. "I'll return as soon as I can, your highness."

Ryven exited the room, instructed the guards to keep a close eye on Kalahn, and went to find Kason. Confronting his best friend wasn't going to be easy, but Ryven had done it before and could do it again.

No, the hardest part would be touching Kalahn and being in her close proximity when he trained her. If her life weren't so important to him, he might consider assigning another trainer the task.

But since he had no idea who to trust outside a small circle of people, Ryven wouldn't risk Kalahn's life by potentially having a traitor train her. At least until he could thoroughly vet and find a suitable replacement for when he went back to Keldera.

Yes, that's right. He only had to endure close quarters with Kalahn for a week. Still, he'd need to undergo some training of his own before giving Kalahn hers. Namely, he needed to learn how to ignore Kalahn's sweet feminine scent and resist her quick wit. Because even if it were only for a week, it would be more than enough to entice him to do what he shouldn't. And Ryven refused to allow it.

As soon as Ryven was gone and Kalahn was alone again with her sister, Kajala spoke up. "You've known him a long time, haven't you?"

Kalahn didn't bother to erase the frown from her face. "Too long. I rarely wish to be thought of as a princess, but sometimes, it would make things easier if he did treat me as such."

Kajala stirred some sweetener into her tea. "Because you fancy him."

Her first instinct was to outright deny her sister's claim. However, Kajala had trusted Kalahn enough to share her greatest secret. It seemed only fair that she started to be truthful as well. "I did, once. But he's leaving soon, so it's not something I care to think about."

"Liar."

Her frown deepened. "You barely know me, so how can you tell that I'm lying?"

"Well, I spent most of my life working at my mother's retreat complex, surrounded by wealthy or diplomatic males and their wives. It was almost my duty to learn when they were lying or not, or we never would've stayed in business. Part of our income relied on gratuities, which were mostly used to persuade us to keep their secrets."

Kalahn took the time to really look at her half sister. Kajala was calm and collected, with intelligence in her gaze. She decided it was time to stop beating around the bush. "Did our father approve of all this?"

Kajala snorted. "I have no idea. You don't know my mother, but she's a strong, fierce female. Kastor may be king, but he never stood a chance against convincing Jalarra Mayven of how to run her business."

Kalahn looked down at her cup of tea. "I didn't really know my mother, so I can't say if she was the same way or not."

Kajala set aside her drink and took one of Kalahn's hands. The gesture was simple, but one she'd yearned to have in her life. She glanced up and squeezed her sister's fingers. Kajala spoke once more. "I've heard bits and pieces about your mother. Mine was never jealous of her and often asked to hear stories. I think my mother truly wanted to meet Kastor's other children and thought understanding his first love would better help her to understand you three. I'm only sad it took so long for our families to come together."

Kalahn placed her hand over their clasped ones. "All that matters is that Father clearly cares for you, Kajala. Not many fathers would've gone out of their way to keep your secret and allow you to travel to a distant colony on your own."

She nodded. "I know. And please, call me Jala."

"Thank goodness. Too many Ka-names were driving me crazy."

Her sister laughed. "My mother wanted to call us Jala and Sarra. But Kastor asked her to follow the naming tradition for the royal family by putting bits of each their names into their children's, hence Kajala and Kasarra."

It was on the tip of Kalahn's tongue to ask about her half brother, Korjal. However, he was missing and the last thing she wanted to do was upset a pregnant female, so she focused on her own brothers. "Kason and Keltor are so much older than me that we never really ran into that problem with too many K-names. I didn't see much of them growing up, if I'm honest. I love them, but always wished for a sibling closer to my own age." She forced a smile. "So it's nice to find I have a sister only a few years my junior. I was isolated from most of the other children, too, growing up, so I usually had to find adventure on my own."

Kajala placed a hand on her belly. "I would join in on some adventure, but I think it may be a while before I can."

"Don't worry, I'll help you with your child, if you wish. I know I sort of forced my way into your home, but I want to do more than help you—I want to know you better."

"Me, too." Kajala adjusted her position on her stool. "Now, you mentioned some changes you wanted to implement. Why don't you start letting me get to know you by telling me a few of them?"

As Kalahn went through her long list of goals for equality, she felt more at ease than she had in a long while. She may have just met her sister, but it was almost as if a piece of her life that she'd been missing had been found.

She only hoped Ryven pulled through and garnered permission from Kason. Because being able to defend themselves was extremely important if Kalahn's plans were to succeed.

And her wishing to start their training had nothing to do with Ryven surprising her with another touch or kiss to further her training, either.

Well, mostly. There was nothing wrong with having a little fun along the way. After all, changing her society's laws was going to be trying, and making Ryven uncomfortable would help ease her stress.

And maybe her curiosity, too.

She'd just have to be careful not to cross a line.

Chapter Three

Ryven stood in front of Kason's desk and tried his best to maintain his composure. "That's quite the deal you've managed."

Kason shrugged. "My brother is king and has sway with the army. If you agree to stay here and help me with finding any spies or traitors, then I'll allow you to train Kalahn."

"I still can't believe the army would give in so easily. I'm not being cocky when I say I'm one of the top warrior trainers."

"Which is why you're needed here. My bride wants you to work with her trainers so that together you can share and learn new techniques from one another."

Ryven grinned. "I knew Taryn was behind this. You've become soft, shuffling bureaucracy and calling in favors to do as she asks."

Pride filled Kason's voice as he said, "She's my bride and carries our daughter. It is the least I can do."

A small part of Ryven was relieved Kason and Taryn's child was female. The Kelderans were still working on a cure for the "doom virus" that killed off most male embryos on Jasvar, but the researchers hadn't yet devised a foolproof solution. "I think it's merely long-term planning so that your daughter will have the best available training when she's old enough."

"Perhaps."

He snorted. "Which is Kason-speak for absolutely. I'm not sure our compatriots back on Keldera would recognize you."

"I don't care for their opinions. The colony must forge ahead on our own path."

"I hope you include Kalahn's future in your statement. She won't marry whichever male you toss her way, Kason, if at all."

He grunted. "I'm aware of that and will handle both of my sisters here accordingly. However, before I can do so, I need you to give me your answer. Will you stay here long-term to help with protecting the colony and give up your official position in the army? Or, will you decline and return? I must admit I'm hoping for the former."

Without hesitation, Ryven stated, "I will stay."

"Good."

He held up a hand. "But only with a few conditions. I'll be busy helping you as well as working with the Jasvarian trainers and can't always watch over Kalahn and her sister. Since she's decided to live with Kajala, it should be easy enough to have guards posted just outside their door and take over some of the duty from me."

Kason studied him for a few beats, and Ryven wondered if his friend understood the ulterior motive Ryven had for the suggestion of additional guards. Because being in Kalahn's constant presence would tempt him, which he had to resist if he indeed were to stay long-term on Jasvar. Things may constantly be evolving in the Kelderan colony, but the laws surrounding the royal council and the requirement of them approving of Kalahn's choice of lord hadn't changed.

Even if Kalahn did decide to marry beneath her station, the council would never approve. As it stood now, their denial meant instant incarceration for the male involved.

And Ryven couldn't protect anyone if he ended up in prison. Given some of Ryven's hidden talents, he might even end up mysteriously dead in a jail cell to protect some of the army's most classified secrets.

Whether Kason saw Ryven's ulterior motive or not, he didn't say. His friend merely nodded. "That is a reasonable demand, provided we both agree on the guards to be used."

He should stop at that, but he couldn't abandon someone he loved. "That's not all. I have one more demand. I'd like for my adopted mother to be in the next wave of colonists to Jasvar."

Kason raised his brows. "You are going to make me test my boundaries with my brother, aren't you?"

Ryven's adopted mother was one of the Barren. However, she was old and lame in one leg, which meant she wouldn't be able to work for her passage, like other Barren had done during the first voyage. "I cannot abandon her, Kason, and you know that. If it takes my entire savings to ensure her passage, I will use it. But I'm not leaving behind my only family."

"Of course not. It would be dishonorable to expect you to act otherwise." Kason leaned back in his chair. "I'll see what I can do. Maybe Keltor and his bride can think of a way to make it less of a scandal to include Barren who can't work or provide any services. As much as I wish we could do as we pleased, we must be careful of the public image surrounding the royal family. I refuse to put Keltor's future bride in danger."

He shrugged one shoulder. "You can handle the politics, as that's not my specialty. But promise me you'll find a way, and I'll agree to stay here and give up my position within the Kelderan Army to join the colony's security forces."

"You have my word. Once you've resigned with Syzel and passed on any relevant information to your successor, then report to Xytor. He's in charge of guard duty and rotations inside the Kelderan colony."

Ryven had worked with Xytor in the past and knew he was an honorable, hard-working male.

However, there was one final issue Ryven needed to address. "Before I do so, will you ensure that I can resign? You know of my classified situation."

Kason tapped his fingers against his chair arm. "Keltor will find a way to make it work, not to mention we need warriors here who can monitor the telepathy plane. I know you've been asked to keep off it for the time being, but once you work for me, I'll be adding that to your list of duties as well. I want to believe there aren't any enemies inside the colony with telepathy, empathy, or even telekinesis. However, I want to be cautious. You'll be my first step toward guarding on that front."

Telepathy wasn't a natural-born Kelderan ability. And since only a handful of warriors had undergone the same DNA-splicing operation as Ryven, Kelderan telepaths were few and far between.

One perk of staying on Jasvar was that he could find and eventually converse with the natural-born telepaths inside the Jasvarian human colony. There was still much for him to learn on that front.

Ryven gave a curt nod and brought the conversation back to his original request. "And what about training your sisters?"

"Fit that in when you can, but find and assign their main guards first."

Ryven made a fist and pounded it over his heart as he bowed his head in acknowledgment. Kason spoke up again. "And ensure my sisters are provided for. I will visit Kajala when I have the chance."

As much as he wanted to explain Kajala's situation to Kason, he'd promised Kalahn he would consult with her first. "I would suggest giving her a few days alone with Kalahn. That way, she won't be overwhelmed with yet another sibling, and an overprotective older brother to boot."

Kason grunted. "She has two of them now, so she will have to get used to it." Ryven opened his mouth, but Kason continued, "I have much to do anyway and will entrust her to you and Kalahn's care for the time being. However, my bride is anxious to meet her, so I can't delay it for too long."

Ryven had only ever had short conversations with Taryn from time to time. "Now that I'm staying, I'll have to get to know your bride better. Then she can understand just how grumpy her lord really is."

"Ryven," he warned.

He winked. "I prefer my females a bit softer, so you have no competition from me."

"Taryn is perfect."

"For you, yes. But if we had exactly the same tastes in females, I don't think we would have remained friends this long. After all, you would've tired of me stealing them all away with my charm and good looks."

Shaking his head, Kason tried not to smile. "Just go. I don't have time for your antics."

"And to think you're going to be stuck with me for the rest of our lives now. Who knows, maybe I'll rub off on you, too."

Before Kason could reply, Ryven laughed at his friend's frown and exited the room.

He may have apprehensions about staying on the colony, but the exchange with Kason reminded Ryven of what he gained with his new home. Kason was his best friend, and the male who knew some of his most closely held secrets, not to mention one of the few people he'd entrust with his life.

He wouldn't fail his friend, either, or dishonor him by flirting with his sister.

Besides, soon enough Ryven would throw himself into his new work and barely see Kalahn at all. That would lessen the temptation and reinforce his priorities. After all, he couldn't take care of his mother if he were in jail. Kalahn was meant for another. End of story.

✵ ✵ ✵

Kalahn paced the length of the living room, snapping her fingers as she went. Staying inside Kajala's quarters was proving harder than she'd imagined. Especially since she wanted nothing more than to go out and find her sister-in-law herself.

Kajala spoke from the cushy chair in the corner. "Taryn Demara is a busy female, and it's gracious of her to come at all. You probably shouldn't have bothered her for my sake."

She stopped to face her sister. "Taryn is busy but has always told me that if I needed help, to ask. So that's what I did. If anyone can help you, it's her."

Kajala shook her head. "She's in charge of the human colony, not the Kelderan one. And since my role in the colony is important, it's not as if I can live in the human settlement."

"That's not what I'm asking for. You saw Ryven's message about our brother wanting to meet you. It's best to prepare him, and Taryn can easily manage that."

A knock sounded on the door. As Kalahn headed toward it, she threw over her shoulder, "It's time to dust off your CEL."

CEL was the Common Earth Language that the humans spoke. Kelderan royals were tutored in the language in case they encountered anyone from the vast Earth Colony Alliance and needed to negotiate terms.

And from their conversations together, she'd learned that while Kajala hadn't been raised in the palace, she'd studied it to help with any diplomatic parties who spoke the language at her mother's retreat complex.

To be honest, Kalahn didn't know how many languages Kajala could speak, but she guessed quite a few to be able to understand and keep secrets.

Opening the door, Kalahn couldn't help but smile at Taryn. She stood in the doorway grinning and rubbing her hands. "I can't wait to find out this secret of yours."

Gently tugging Taryn inside, she shut the door and made sure to position her body to block out Kajala behind her. "If you're expecting a hidden beau who turns out to be a shipwrecked space pirate, then you're going to be sadly disappointed."

Taryn took her hand. "Just tell me what's going on, Kalahn."

Taking a deep breath, she trusted her sister-in-law and stepped to this side. "Taryn Demara, may I present my younger sister, Kajala Mayven."

Taryn didn't miss a beat in closing the distance and putting out her hand. "It's nice to meet another member of my husband's family. After all, our children will be fairly close in age and will probably get into trouble together."

Kajala's voice cracked. "Th-thank you for your kindness."

Her sister looked about ready to cry, but before Kalahn could say anything, Kajala bobbed her head, shook Taryn's hand, and said in accented CEL, "Yes, our children will be close in age. Although given what I've learned of your lord, he will probably keep yours locked up until they reach adulthood."

Taryn let go of Kajala's hand and waved a hand in dismissal. "Leave Kason to me. He may be big and grunt a lot, but I can usually change his mind."

Kalahn jumped in. "I sure hope so because that's the reason I asked for your help."

Taryn looked between them. "Don't beat around the bush, Kalahn. Tell me what's wrong."

"Well, not wrong exactly, but Kason wants to meet Jala soon."

Taryn quirked an eyebrow. "And?"

Kajala spoke up. "And I'm not married. I don't wish to disappoint him."

Taryn's expression turned serious. "He would never be disappointed in you, Kajala. If anything, he wishes to better know his family and try to be a different father to our daughter."

Placing a hand on her belly, Kajala murmured, "You're kind to say so, but I fear for my son."

Taryn stiffened, no doubt imagining the worst-case scenario of the Jasvarian doom virus taking away Kajala's son. "You're having a boy? Have you been monitored closely?"

"Yes, and so far everything is fine. I know the dangers of carrying a male baby on this planet, but it was the only choice I had if I wanted to keep him."

Kalahn growled. "And that, right there, is why we need you on our side, Taryn. I know changing the laws back on Keldera will take time, but something has to be done about the colony. If Jala risked her son's life to come here, she should be guaranteed a future free of fear or shame simply because she had a child without marriage."

Taryn crossed her arms over her chest. "There is a balance, but I think I can manage it. Give me two days with

Kason and we'll have you over for dinner."

Kalahn could all but see the wheels turning in Taryn's head. "What do you have planned?"

"That's my little secret. But trust me on this, Kalahn. And thanks for asking for my help. I never want you to hesitate with me." She uncrossed her arms. "I have to leave for an appointment in about fifteen minutes, so let's make the most of it. I haven't had a chance to talk to you since the video conference. How are you holding up?"

She glanced at her sister. "Fine, but when will we have enough energy to have another one with my father, Taryn?"

"Probably by tomorrow or the next day at the latest. Why?"

Kalahn motioned toward Kajala. "Because Jala needs to talk with Father before it's too late." She sat next to her sister. "We can have it just with Father and your mother, Jala. There's no need to involve Keltor and the others."

Kajala touched Kalahn's arm. "Thank you, but as soon as I tell Kason of my secret, I should trust Keltor as well. He is the king of Keldera after all."

"More than that, his female will have sway with him, too," Kalahn stated. "He and Azalyn may not be married yet, but they soon will be. It's best to involve all the brides if we want to accomplish as many things as possible."

A skeptical looked filled Kajala's eyes. "I find it hard to believe things will change so easily. My mother is a strong female, but that didn't make a difference with our father."

"I'm sure your mother would have changed things if she could," Kalahn replied. "But the difference is that Kason's bride is a human warrior leader and Keltor's worked for a merchant. Both already symbolize change, so in a way, it's inevitable more will come."

Taryn clicked her tongue. "You're better with politics than I would've given you credit for, Kalahn."

She shrugged. "Well, when my father paraded me in front of potential lords, I spent a lot of time inside conference rooms filled with politicians and diplomats. There was nothing else to do but listen to what was going on. At the time, I wondered why he would want to give me to any of those males, but the experiences have come in handy after all."

Someone knocked on the front door, and Kalahn asked the others, "Were you expecting anyone?"

Kajala and Taryn both shook their heads. Before she could go to the door, Ryven's voice came through it. "It's me. Let me in."

As she walked, Kalahn shouted, "Me could be anyone."

"Kalahn, open this door."

Reaching it, she yanked it open. To her dismay, Ryven stood with his markings a dark blue. She'd have to try harder to unsettle him.

He spoke again. "I have permission to train you. You can either come now or wait until the day after tomorrow."

"What about Jala?"

"Jala?" He echoed with a frown.

She rolled her eyes. "Oh, come on. Kajala is Jala. That shouldn't be so hard to figure out."

"So are we calling you Lahn now, then?" he asked, amusement dancing in his eyes.

"Call me Lahn again and I'll slam this door in your face. It'd be a shame if I accidentally grabbed your hand and your arm got caught in the process."

The corner of his mouth ticked up. "You talk the big talk, but you won't feel so confident soon enough."

Taryn came up behind her. She answered in CEL, "Give her time to win against you. After all, I've bested Kason. I'm confident Kalahn can do the same with you eventually."

Ryven looked at Taryn, still speaking in Kelderan. "I have no idea what she said, but she must understand us to comment. How can she?"

Taryn pointed to her ear, and Kalahn explained, "Taryn has a translation device in her ear."

He grunted. "So what did she say then?"

Kalahn grinned. "That given time, I'll win against you. She's beaten Kason sparring before and believes I can do the same."

He raised an eyebrow. "Kason was distracted by his half-naked bride. Are you going to play dirty, too?"

Taryn leaned forward a fraction and replied in broken Kelderan. "I play fair. Dresses are bad."

Ryven's gaze met hers again. "Please let me be there when you tell your brother that you're going to wear one of the skimpy female warrior outfits."

Taryn rolled her eyes. "Warrior outfits useful."

Kalahn jumped in. "How about we stop discussing my wardrobe? I just want to start my training." She peered at Ryven. "Provided you got Jala permission as well."

Ryven nodded. "I did."

Kajala joined them. "You go, Kalahn. I still have work I need to do today. We can go over my schedule later and find a time when we can do it together."

Kalahn knew her sister wasn't rubbing it in on purpose that she had a job, but it still stung.

Ryven spoke before anyone else. "That will work out since I can't teach Jala hand-to-hand combat and defense moves for several months yet because of her condition." He turned around. "Follow me and try to keep up, Princess."

As Ryven started walking, Kalahn glanced at Taryn and Kajala. "We'll talk soon."

Not waiting for an answer, Kalahn half jogged to keep up with Ryven. If she didn't have to wear a blasted dress, she probably could've run and surpassed him.

But since walking around in trousers—let alone the revealing warrior outfits used by the human females—would probably land her in trouble with Kason, she saved the idea for a later date. For now, her goal was to take in everything Ryven taught her and find a way to beat him as soon as possible. Because just imagining his look of disbelief lifted her spirits. She just had to make it a reality.

Chapter Four

Ryven used the walk to one of the secure training areas to meditate as best as he could and prepare his mind for the upcoming session.

Yes, he still needed to ensure Kalahn could keep her markings a dark blue to hide her true feelings. However, an introductory sparring to test her reflexes and skills would provide him with not only the truth of her abilities but also give him the chance to display his own abilities. Because while having Kalahn defy him in front of the Jasvarian leader wasn't the best situation, he didn't want her to do so in front of ordinary colony members or soldiers.

In other words, Kalahn needed a reminder that he was a warrior and not just her brother's friend. Especially since Ryven was staying on Jasvar, he needed to maintain his reputation.

They reached the room Ryven used with the soldiers, opened the door, and waited inside for Kalahn. He'd ensured the room would be empty, so it was merely him standing in a room with a padded floor and the mysterious glowing plants on the walls that served as low-lighting for the Jasvarians.

Kalahn shut the door and stopped a few feet from him. While the slightly greenish light from the walls should make her appear sickly, it instead made her white dress glow brightly.

He wondered if certain food stuffs would do the same and glow in the light. It would be fun to trace a female's markings and slowly lick it off her skin.

His eyes zeroed in on the marking peeking out from Kalahn's neckline. He imagined it winding down to her breast.

Kalahn cleared her throat, and he barely resisted flushing like an adolescent boy.

He most definitely needed to train Kalahn as quickly as possible so he could focus on other duties and forget about her.

Standing tall with his shoulders back and his arms at his sides, he merely stated, "Charge at me."

She raised her brows. "What happened to 'You need to control your markings before I do anything else'?"

"Charge at me and I'll explain."

She took a few steps closer and began walking around him. "I feel as if your order is a trap."

Clever female. "I will reveal nothing until you charge at me."

"Oh, is that so?" She lightly ran a hand across his left shoulder blade and back again, the featherlight touch sending a jolt of electricity through his body. "Then it gives me time to assess my opponent and try to find any of your weaknesses."

Ryven had only one weakness, but not even Kalahn would be bold enough to touch him there.

He repeated, "I will reveal nothing until you charge at me."

Her soft fingers traveled down his spine and up to his other shoulder blade. While he knew it was ridiculous, the contact felt as if she'd left a new brand on his skin.

"Then let me finish and I'll do as you say," she murmured.

As she placed her warm palm against his lower back, he clenched his jaw and willed his markings to stay neutral.

Her hand moved around his side and to his lower abs, the touch light yet confident. He wondered if she knew exactly what she was doing to him. When she traced the marking on the right side of his stomach, he stopped breathing. A few inches lower, and she'd find his weakness. Not even he could keep his wits about him if Kalahn's silky fingers touched his cock.

As if on call, he grew semihard, but Ryven quickly recited the army code inside his head to tame it.

However, rather than move away from his little problem, Kalahn stilled her hand and stared at his lower abdomen. He only hoped she hadn't seen his brief slipup of self-control.

For the first time, he hated the tight trousers that all Kelderan warriors were required to wear.

Yet despite how she affected him, decades of instinct and conditioning couldn't be ignored. He sensed she was trying to unnerve him and make a move, so he dug his nails into his palm to come back into focus.

Kalahn took a step to the right, but then turned and attempted to knee him in the balls. However, Ryven saw the move, grabbed her leg, and flipped her onto her back. Quickly covering her body, he pinned her hands above her head and kept her legs in place with his own. "I commend you for taking your time and trying to outsmart me. However, it will take more than that to beat me, Princess."

"So now I'm a princess?"

"You're always a princess."

Searching his gaze, she lifted her head an inch. "What does that mean?"

The Forbidden

As her warm breath danced against his chin, he was tempted to tell her the harsh reality of her situation—Kalahn would have few choices when it came to finding a lord that had both status and the ability to protect her. No matter what she wanted, Kason was determined to marry off his sister.

But it wasn't Ryven's place to share the information. That role belonged to Kason.

Not that he wanted her for his own anyway. He had many other responsibilities to take care of, and watching over a free-spirited female who lived to test boundaries wasn't one of them.

He focused on Kalahn's eyes. "All it means is that you need to learn how to protect yourself. And I couldn't do that without gauging your skill level."

"So the test is over?"

He wanted to scream no and take a few more minutes to revel in the feel of Kalahn's soft body under his. "Yes."

He released her arms, and they instantly went to his shoulders. Ryven froze.

Kalahn smiled slowly. "I don't think so."

Before he could say anything, she met his mouth and kissed him.

He might've been able to resist if she hadn't probed his lips with her tongue as she dug her nails into his skin.

Whatever restraint he'd been holding onto snapped, and he opened his mouth and quickly accepted her tongue. Kalahn was sweet, hot, and demanding, and completely unlike any female he'd ever kissed before. When she groaned and pulled his body down against hers, Ryven forgot everything but stroking the inside of Kalahn's mouth.

One of her hands went between them and slid down his chest. He moved to stop her, but at that second, she nipped his bottom lip to distract him.

Something primal inside of him roared forth and he lowered his lips and teeth to her neck to lightly bite and soothe the sting.

That was when Kalahn gripped his cock and balls through his trousers and yanked. Hard.

He tried to roll away, out of her grip, but she held on even when he made it to his back. Only when his shoulder blades were on the ground did she release him, but only to put her knee where her hand had been. Leaning all of her weight on him, Ryven moaned in pain.

Kalahn smiled slowly. "So what's my skill level now?"

✷ ✷ ✷

Kalahn wasn't overly experienced with males, but she'd seen enough trysts in the gardens or in the dark corners of the various celebrations inside the palace to know that kisses and touch could drive a male crazy.

She hadn't been sure if it'd work with Ryven or not; attraction played a small part in causing a man to lose all rational thought. While he'd kissed her in the past, Kalahn had never figured out if it'd been because he'd wanted to or as a ruse to distract her.

But when she reached down to grip his genitals, his hardness told her that he was at least somewhat attracted to her.

And that had given her more confidence to continue her plan, even as he rolled onto his back. She silently apologized as she replaced her hand with her knee and leaned her weight into him. "So what's my skill level now?"

He managed to get out, "I think you've been practicing with the human female warriors."

"That still doesn't answer my question."

In the blink of an eye, Ryven had her facedown on the

ground, holding her arms behind her back, with his full weight on top of her. He murmured, "You have a few tricks, but that won't be enough to protect yourself. At least, not until I've trained you properly."

For a few beats, he merely lay on top of her, his hot breath dancing across her ear. She should be annoyed and demand for him to release her.

Yet there was something right about Ryven's hard, muscled body pinning hers. She didn't like to yield often in her life, but she just might do it for Ryven.

No. She couldn't think of him like that. And not just because Ryven was her brother's best friend, either. Kalahn didn't have time for males. They were a distraction she couldn't afford or she'd never see through her dreams in the end.

Putting every bit of royal arrogance into her voice she could muster, she ordered, "Let me up."

Ryven didn't move.

She growled. "I see your point. There's no reason to squish me, Ryven. We're both busy people and don't have time for this."

"I'm trying to make a point. After all, an attacker isn't going to move because you tell him to. How would you get out of this situation?"

She should be thrilled at a lesson, but given how much heavier Ryven was than her and the fact she had no weapons, she didn't want to try. "I can't, okay? Is that what you want to hear?"

Ryven stood, and Kalahn instantly missed his heat and firm body.

Pushing the feeling aside, she sat up and glared up at him. "Well? Are you going to gloat now?"

"No. One of the most important lessons in any sort of defense training is to admit your limitations. Cocky individuals end up dead."

She rose to her feet. "So is that what I'm to expect, then? Lots of time on my stomach with you on top of me, learning my lesson?"

Something flashed in Ryven's eyes that she couldn't identify. His voice was gravelly as he said, "You need to avoid speaking so carelessly without thought. A lesser male would see that as an invitation."

It took her a second to take his meaning. Her cheeks flushed, but she forced her chin high and hoped her markings were staying dark blue like Ryven's always did. "And some would say that a warrior like yourself shouldn't mention such things in the presence of a princess."

He took a few steps toward her, but Kalahn held her ground. "You're either a princess or you're not, Kalahn tro el Vallen. If you truly want to become strong and stand on your own, you need to stop hiding behind your title."

"I would if I could," she murmured.

Moving even closer, he asked, "And if you could, what would you do?"

Kiss you again. What? No. Absolutely not. Ridiculous.

Instead she said, "I would train to be a starship pilot and roam the galaxies."

The corner of his mouth ticked up. "I envision you more as a space pirate captain. You wouldn't be able to follow the numerous rules and regulations required on a formal ship."

"I can follow rules if I must." He quirked an eyebrow and she added, "I can. After all, I never threw drinks at any of the males who attempted to grab my behind over the years."

Ryven's gaze turned fierce. "Tell me their names."

She tossed her hair over her shoulder. "No need. I'm an extremely clumsy dancer and broke a few toes. By accident, mind you. It's purely coincidental that they were the same males trying to claim liberties with me."

Ryven laughed. "There is more to you than meets the eye after all, Kalahn. Just imagine what you could do if you listened to me and worked hard at honing your skills. You have a good instinct, but you need strength and focus to round it out."

Between Ryven complimenting her and not taking her to task for breaking a few toes, Kalahn started to see him in a new light. "You are different from most males."

"I always have been."

For a few seconds, they stared at one another. Not in an awkward silence, but rather one that made her heart rate tick up and heat to course through her body.

In that instant, she wanted to know more about Ryven than the fact he was a warrior or her brother's friend.

But Ryven spoke up first. "And because I'm different, you shouldn't try to defy me at every turn. I want to help you, Kalahn. I honestly do. And that is a good deal more than most males would wish to do. New colony or not, the old ways are still ingrained into every Kelderan here. Add in the fact someone might be out to kill you, and you need to be more careful." He gently took her chin between his fingers. "So, will you listen to me and put your best effort into what I can teach you? Do that, and maybe your brother will loosen the reins more."

She almost nodded, but silly as it was, she wanted to feel Ryven's rough fingers against her skin for a little longer. "I'll try. But I can't completely give up my other plans."

He lightly stroked her jaw, and her heart skipped a beat. It took everything she had to focus on his words. "Tell me what they are, Kalahn. And maybe I can help you with them."

※ ※ ※

Every time Ryven touched Kalahn's skin, he knew he shouldn't be doing so. It was a betrayal to Kason, to Ryven's moral code, and borderline against the law.

And yet, he couldn't seem to keep his distance. Every time he almost regained control, her markings flashed and revealed how much his touch affected her, drawing him back under her spell.

When Kalahn had told him about the dishonorable males trying to touch her without permission, the need to hurt each and every one of them had surged through his body.

He could put that down to being an honorable male looking out for his friend's sister. But when Kalahn explained how she had "accidentally" broken a few toes, he realized there was more to Kalahn than his best friend's sister—she was a female he wanted to know more, maybe even everything, about. Not to mention one he always wanted to protect and have her back.

And that was dangerous.

He needed to banish those kinds of thoughts about her. So he asked Kalahn about her plans, and waited.

Kalahn bit her bottom lip, and it took a good deal of self-control to keep his gaze on her eyes and away from temptation as she replied, "I want to, but I know your first loyalty is to Kason and I don't want to put you in an awkward situation."

At the mention of her brother, Ryven released his grip on her chin. He would help her, but he could never have her. "Provided you aren't going to assassinate him or overthrow King Keltor, I'm sure I can keep a secret."

The Forbidden

She searched his eyes. "But why do you care? You'll be leaving soon enough."

He decided to tell her the truth. "No, your brother has worked it out so that I'm staying on Jasvar permanently."

She blinked. "Since when?"

"Since earlier today. So you see, once the colony is settled and threats eradicated, I'll be quite bored. I could use a few extra tasks to tackle, such as helping you."

She frowned. "Don't be so dismissive. They aren't silly goals."

"I won't know that until you tell me, now, will I?"

As indecision flashed in Kalahn's eyes, he wondered why he kept pushing her. He had zero right to demand her secrets.

And yet, he wanted to know them all.

Yes, he was definitely headed into dangerous territory, but he wasn't going to rescind his offer of help now.

She finally spoke up again. "I want to be useful. Not in a 'take care of a niece or nephew' kind of way, either. I want to help our people on this planet. Females in particular came here for freedom. I want to make that promise a reality."

"Have you discussed this with Kason or Taryn?"

She searched his gaze. "You're not going to dismiss me as being naive for wanting such things?"

He raised his brows. "Why? I want to see better treatment of the Barren, which is maybe even more difficult. Vala has made a start, along with her lord, but it's not enough."

"Why do you wish to do that? Not that I don't agree that it needs to be done, but why?"

Ryven could count on one hand the number of people who knew the reason why, but he didn't hesitate to make Kalahn another one. "My mother is one of the Barren."

He waited to see if Kalahn comprehended the significance of his words, and her eyes widened. "You were orphaned and taken in by one of the Barren citadels."

He nodded. "My parents, like many others, were killed toward the end of the Brevkan wars. The Barren took me in and one of them adopted me as her son."

"Is she here?"

"Not yet, although I'm trying to secure her passage on the next colony ship."

Kalahn stood tall. "Tell me her name and I'll pester my brothers to make it happen."

The corner of his mouth ticked up. "I appreciate the support, but so far I have things under control."

"You'd be surprised what Keltor and Kason will do for me, which means she could get here sooner. After all, your mother should be here if you are."

He knew Kalahn had lost her mother young, which was why she was so quick to offer assistance—she believed everyone should spend time with loved ones while they still could. "If I need help, I'll ask. I promise. But it's better to save your goodwill and favors with your brothers for something that truly requires it, such as equality for females. I suspect you have a list of what you wish to do?"

"Of course I do. I don't want to forget anything. But you're changing the subject. We were talking about your mother."

Sighing, he clasped his hands behind his back. "I didn't realize this was an interrogation."

"It's not, but if I don't ask now, I'm not sure if I'll ever have the chance again."

An idea struck. "Work hard to pass my first levels of tests, and I'll allow you to ask me anything you want for twenty minutes."

"Anything?"

"On my honor, anything."

At the devilish glint in Kalahn's eyes, Ryven's stomach dropped. She was going to make the most of those twenty minutes.

Too bad she didn't know he was good at answering without giving the full truth. Every warrior learned how to do that during their initiation training, to ensure they could resist if captured.

Kalahn grinned. "Okay, then let's get started."

"Fine. Drop down and do this."

Ryven went into a push-up position. "I want five like this."

He lowered slowly and pushed up. He most definitely wasn't showing off to Kalahn. She needed to increase her strength to impress her brother.

When done, he jumped up and clapped his hands. "Ready?"

A skeptical look filled her eyes. "How is a push-up going to help me defend myself?"

"You said you would listen to me, and I promise this is important. Now, get down."

He expected Kalahn to grumble, but she followed his order without another word. As she struggled to complete the exercise, a new training regime ran through his mind. True, he wanted to help Kalahn, but he also needed the distraction. Otherwise he'd watch her soft, delectable behind as she moved, and that would lead to even baser thoughts. Ones he should never have about a princess.

Chapter Five

Two days later, Kalahn groaned as she shuffled to the kitchen area of Kajala's place. "Damn Ryven and his exercises. It feels as if my arms are going to fall off."

Kajala chuckled from her perch on a stool next to the counter. "You've been doing extra ones yourself, so you can't blame only him."

She shot Kajala a glare. "I thought you were on my side."

"I am, but I also believe in the truth."

"More like you just want a distraction."

Kajala's hand went to her belly. "That, too."

Kalahn suddenly felt insensitive. "I'm sorry, Jala. You shouldn't worry. Kason will welcome you, just as Keltor will. Besides, you get to speak with Father later today, too."

"We'll see."

Wanting to distract her sister, Kalahn sat beside her. "If that weren't exciting enough, Kason's going to give me a briefing of what he's found out so far from that assassin woman. While it won't be as interesting as seeing her in person, it's a huge step for him to even think of sharing the interrogation information with me."

"I know it excites you, Kalahn. However, the fact an assassin exists only makes me more worried about my future."

She waved a hand in dismissal. "Nonsense. We're all going to stand with you and help protect your son. I dare anyone to try and harm him."

Kajala touched Kalahn's arm. "Thank you. Although I'm not sure if you'll want to stay here once he's born. Newborn babies cry a lot."

Kalahn opened her mouth to refute moving out, but someone knocked and Ryven's voice came through the door. "Let me in."

Standing, Kalahn took her time to brush out her skirts. While she knew Ryven was busy with other duties, she hadn't seen or heard from him in two days. It was almost as if he wanted to delay her training so as to not allow her to pass her first level tests and ask him twenty minutes of questions.

But she was nothing if not determined.

Reaching the door, she opened it and let him in. Ryven bowed his head toward Kajala. "Good morning, your highness." He looked to Kalahn. "Are you ready?"

"Good morning to you, too." She motioned toward the door with her head. "I would take charge and leave, but I don't want you to worry about some booby trap that's miraculously appeared in the last ten seconds."

He grunted. "You shouldn't be so flippant about your life."

Kalahn was tempted to growl, but restrained herself. "I'm not. But to be overcautious about every aspect isn't good, either. Stop stalling. I'm anxious to see Kason and hear what he has to say."

Ryven looked at Kajala. "The guards posted outside are some of my most trusted warriors. Don't hesitate to ask them for anything."

Kajala lowered her head in acknowledgment. "You're too kind."

"It's my honor, your highness."

As Kalahn watched the pair, she wanted to roll her eyes. There were times for diplomacy and formality, but the present wasn't one of them.

Ryven finally opened the door and exited, and she followed.

She struggled to keep up with him, but it wasn't long before they arrived at the conference room being used by Kason for some of the most delicate issues surrounding the Kelderan colony.

Inside, sat Kason, Syzel, Thorin, and a male she recognized by face only. She quickly sat next to Kason and raised her eyebrows in question.

When he didn't scold her behavior, Kalahn knew something was amiss. Thankfully Kason didn't beat around the bush. "There's something special about the female assassin we captured."

"I thought this was a briefing?" she asked. "Shouldn't you start with her general information first?"

Kason patted a folder in front of him. "Everything you need to know is here. However, I asked you here for another reason."

Kalahn looked at each person in the room in turn, finally settling on her brother again. "Everyone seems rather serious in here. How about you tell me what's going on? I wouldn't be here if you didn't need my help, so dancing around the issue is a waste of time."

Her brother sighed. "Sometimes I wish you'd be a little more formal."

"If so, I doubt you'd have me here at all. So, what's going on?"

"You're right that there's a specific reason you're here." Kason nodded at the male she recognized by appearance only. "I'll let Merctor explain."

The Forbidden

A vague memory about Merctor being a scientist popped into her head, but she quickly focused on what he said. "The female assassin is not purely Kelderan. Judging by her DNA, she's part Hirlanzian."

Shaking her head, she murmured, "I've never heard of Hirlanzia, so I'm not sure why that's important."

Kason grunted. "Merctor's not done yet."

Sensing that her brother might be losing his patience, she bobbed her head and waited.

Merctor continued, "While one of her parents must be Kelderan due to her looks and genetic code, the other is not. The Hirlanzians are known telepaths, and the trait is dominant, meaning she possesses it too."

Kalahn's attempt to remain silent failed. "As in she can read minds?"

Ryven shook his head. "She can only read minds of other telepaths. Or, at least those who don't have their minds properly shielded."

Her brows drew together. "I'm not sure I follow. Kelderans don't have telepathy, so she shouldn't be able to read our minds."

"You're correct that Kelderans aren't born with the ability," Merctor stated. "However, they can be given the ability through a specific DNA splicing process."

Kalahn put out a hand. "Wait, what are you talking about?"

Kason spoke up again. "Thanks to the splicing procedure, we have some Kelderan telepaths inside the army."

Ignoring the vast number of questions she had, she focused on Kason. "You were in the army. Have they done this to you?"

Her brother shook his head. "It's something done rarely and usually to someone with a lesser profile. I've always been a highly sought-after target since I'm a prince. In case

I was ever captured, we couldn't afford to let any of our enemies know about our advancements."

She leaned forward. "But are there telepaths inside the colony on Jasvar?"

Ryven shared a look with Kason, and her brother gave a slight nod. Ryven met her gaze. "Yes. In fact, I'm one of them, as is Syzel."

Ryven was a telepath. She'd had no idea.

Maybe she didn't know him as well as she thought she did.

Kalahn didn't know how long her jaw dropped, but she finally closed it and asked, "If you have telepathy, Ryven, are you reading our minds right now?"

He shook his head. "It doesn't work like that. I can only communicate with other telepaths. There may be other species who can communicate with anyone and read random thoughts, but the Kelderans have never encountered them. As I mentioned, since the female assassin is part Hirlanzian, we're almost positive that she can only read another telepath's mind, too. Although Taryn is reaching out to the Earth Colony Alliance to confirm our suspicions since they have more information about the Hirlanzians than us."

She had a feeling that Ryven was barely scratching the surface of what he and other Kelderan made telepaths could do. However, she would corner Ryven and ask him more later. For the moment, she wanted to know why Kason would invite her here and share such sensitive information. "You're telling me this why?"

Ryven's voice was tight as he said, "They want to make you a test subject, not caring about the danger it could lead to."

Kason shook his head. "We've argued this for the past two days, Ryven. She is one of the few who we cannot only trust implicitly, but who would be underestimated at first glance."

Ryven slammed a hand down on the table. "She hasn't even cleared her first level of defense training yet you want to put her in a room with a trained assassin."

"She will be trained thoroughly and also will be heavily protected when it comes time for her to help with the assassin," Kason stated.

Kalahn stood and put up her hands. "How about you talk to me instead of about me? What *exactly* are you wanting me to do?"

Merctor was the first to answer, no doubt to prevent Kason and Ryven from arguing some more. "The Kelderan Army has spent decades researching ways to give warriors extra abilities, in case there's another war with alien enemies that possess them. Especially since the Brevkan rage was a huge advantage to our enemies during the last war. In the decades since the end of the Brevkan war, we've discovered a way to slightly alter a person's genetics to give them abilities such as telepathy or telekinesis. Prince Kason proposed that we splice your DNA to give you telepathy."

Ryven growled, "Tell her the part where it's irreversible."

Kason flashed him an annoyed look. "Give us a chance to get to that."

"You're building it up without providing all the facts. I don't like it," Ryven stated.

Kalahn looked pointedly at Ryven. "I trust my brother. He's not someone who jumps in without thought and lots of planning. So, putting aside that I'm not highly trained, are there other reasons you're so set against it?"

His gaze darted to Kason, and Kason waved a hand. "Inside this room, speak freely. That way you can't say I was unfair or duplicitous."

Ryven moved next to Kalahn and took her shoulders, making her face him. "What they aren't telling you is that we have no idea what other abilities this female might possess. While her Hirlanzian side shouldn't have other abilities, she might have telepathy tricks we've never encountered. For starters, she could possibly kill you without a weapon."

"How?"

He shook his head. "That is part of what we don't know and why I think Kason shouldn't have mentioned this to you yet, if at all."

Questions raced through Kalahn's mind. Despite the access she'd had to her father's meetings and listening in on his conferences with politicians, there was a lot she didn't know about her own planet.

Ryven had been given telepathy, for one thing.

The image of Ryven being strapped to a table and screaming in pain flashed into her mind. Before she could stop the question, she blurted, "Does the process hurt, Ryven?"

He grunted. "Truthfully, not more than a really bad headache. But that's not the point. Once it's done, you can't undo it. And for all we know, giving you the ability could open a door and allow the female assassin to more easily kill you."

"Have you seen her yourself and tested any of these theories?" she asked.

Kason spoke up. "Both Ryven and Syzel have, but the assassin has always been guarded. There are only a handful inside the Kelderan colony who possess the ability, but they are all male and cause the same reaction. A female telepath that the prisoner could underestimate may be our only chance to learn what our enemy knows. Only then can we stall their actions and protect the royal family."

"And if it fails?" Kalahn asked.

Kason studied her a moment before he replied, "You are much calmer about this information than I had expected."

She stood taller. "It involves our family and their safety. I may not be male, but I care just as much as you do, Kason."

For the first time Kalahn could remember, approval flashed in her brother's eyes.

Determined to impress him further, she asked another question. "Putting failure aside for now, how did the female even get here? As far as I know, everyone onboard the colony ship was thoroughly vetted. Someone who wasn't full-blooded Kelderan would've caused a red flag."

The light-blue skinned warrior named Thorin spoke up. "There are ways around it. I am only half-Kelderan myself."

She scrutinized his features. "But even if you look Kelderan, I know enough about genetics to know your DNA would reveal your true heritage."

Syzel jumped in. "Yes, but I recently discovered some weaknesses in the storage database encryption software. That weakness could've been discovered and exploited, meaning the records could've been altered."

She looked at each male in turn. "In other words, we could have a hundred enemies within the colony and not even know it."

"Precisely," Kason said. "That's why the female we captured is so valuable. She may have slipped up and been caught, but others might not be. I don't risk your life lightly, Kalahn. But I believe you are the best female for this job, provided you can train well and Ryven clears you."

She focused back on Ryven. "The bigger question is whether you'd ever do so?"

Ryven narrowed his eyes. "I may not like the suggestion, but I would do my duty. It's better for me to train you properly than to let someone with less experience handle it."

She tilted her head. "You're clearly dead set against it. But I ask you one thing—if your mother's life were at risk, would you do it?"

"That's not the same."

She raised her hands, palms up. "Isn't it? In order to overthrow the monarchy, there is a plot to murder my entire family. So I ask again: if it were your family at stake, would you do it?"

"Yes," he said without hesitation.

Kalahn nodded and moved her gaze to Kason. "I want to know as much about the process as possible beforehand, as well as everything you know about the female assassin. Provided you meet those conditions and the explanation doesn't scare me away, I'll do it."

Kason paused a second before replying, "Merctor will give you a presentation about the process, and then I'll give you a day to think about it."

She closed the distance to her brother. "No, I'll make the decision right after I have all the information. At this point, I'm leaning toward doing it. After all, the longer we delay, the greater the chance any of us could be killed. Believe in me for once, Kason. Let me try to protect our family for a change."

Thorin grunted. "If she volunteers and you deny her, I suspect it will only cause trouble. Given your bride, you should know that."

"Be more respectful of my bride," Kason bit out.

"I'm not being disrespectful," Thorin stated. "Taryn is the leader of a planet, and she has a strong connection to and influence upon your sister. I'm merely being wise about the situation."

Kalahn clapped her hands to garner their attention. "When can Merctor give me the presentation? The longer we delay, the greater the risk it poses to our family."

Kason stood and put a hand on her shoulder. "As long as you promise me that after you listen to Merctor's presentation, you voice any and all doubts to me without hesitation." She bobbed her head and he added, "You are brave for a princess."

Ryven jumped in. "She's brave, end of story."

She met Ryven's eyes from across the room. His overprotectiveness reminded her of too many years of her brothers and father trying to keep her isolated from the world. But then he went and stood up for her like that, saying she was brave.

Ryven might end up being different from other males, but now wasn't the time to think about it. Kalahn looked at her brother again. "Maybe now you'll realize that there is more to me than merely being a princess. Let's get started."

✹ ✹ ✹

Ryven stood at the back of the conference room, only half listening to Merctor's detailed description of the DNA-splicing process. He paid enough attention to know that Merctor wasn't sugarcoating it, but he mostly watched Kalahn's face.

He still didn't agree with Kason's decision, but two days of arguing hadn't accomplished anything. While on the surface Ryven agreed that a weak-looking female would probably lower the assassin's defenses, he would've preferred it to be one with a greater ability to defend herself.

And preferably one who he hadn't kissed thoroughly scant days before.

However, with the pool of highly trusted females being so small, Kason had decided Kalahn would be the best fit. Especially since she was looking for a way to prove herself and would probably not back down.

Merctor finished his presentation. Kalahn didn't waste a second to say, "Now that I know all of that, I still want to go through the process."

Ryven stepped forward. "There is one last thing you should know, Kalahn. Something only a person who's undergone this procedure can tell you." All eyes moved to him, but he didn't care. "Until you're fully trained, your thoughts will be an open book to any other telepath. If you train with me, then you will, in essence, be allowing me to see your most hidden and forbidden thoughts. I won't be looking deliberately, but I guarantee you will unknowingly broadcast them to me."

For a second, indecision flared in her eyes. But it was gone as quickly as it had arrived. "I've known you most of my life, Ryven. I trust you not to use my secrets against me."

Kason grunted. "If he does, he'll answer to me."

Ryven rolled his eyes. "Stop with the threats, Kason. Of course I'm not going to hurt your family."

Kalahn clapped her hands. "Good, then it's settled. When can we get started?"

Merctor motioned toward the door. "Straightaway. Everything we need is aboard the colony transport ship."

Kalahn turned toward her brother. "Since I'm not sure how long this will take, make sure Jala gets to the video conference with Father and her mother later today. And no matter what happens, you vow to look after her in my absence and let her know I'll contact her as soon as I can. The more truthful you can be about what I'm doing, the better. I don't want her thinking that I've tired of her so easily."

Kason didn't argue, but stood, made a fist, and pounded it over his heart. "I vow to protect all of our family, but I will personally take care of Jala until you've recovered. I shall also pass along your message."

She nodded. "Good. Then I'm ready."

Kalahn gave her brother one last, long look before she picked up the folder with all the assassin-related information and left the room. Ryven was tempted to follow her, but Kason's voice stayed him. "I need you here, Ryven. Syzel will go."

Syzel made a fist and pounded it against his chest. But rather than speak aloud, he said mentally, *I will look after her. I'm more delicate with freshly spliced individuals than you.*

There were many things Ryven wished to say, but he merely replied, *I trust you.*

Thorin sighed. "I wish you two would speak so we could hear you as well."

Syzel shrugged. "Ryven and I must practice every once in a while to stretch our mental muscles, so consider it training."

With that, Syzel left.

Kason's voice garnered his attention. "I will soon be entrusting my sister's sanity into your hands. Don't screw up."

"I don't intend to."

He and Kason stared at one another, an understanding passing between them.

As Kason and Thorin discussed strategies and timelines regarding the assassin, Ryven's thoughts kept straying to Kalahn. He'd wanted nothing more than to put distance between them as soon as possible. However, it looked as if they would soon be more intimate than ever before.

The question was whether he would be strong enough to help her, probably learn some of her deepest secrets, and walk away in the end. He could do it easily with his warriors, but he already had dreams of Kalahn naked and in his bed every night.

Training her telepathy was going to be his toughest assignment to date.

Chapter Six

Kalahn woke up and immediately put her hands to her pounding head. It was as if tiny people lived there and were using hammers to batter her brains to nothing.

She must've made a sound because Merctor's voice filled her ears. "Are you awake, your highness? If so, take as long as you need to open your eyes."

Attempting to do so, the light caused the pain to intensify tenfold and she shut them, covering her eyelids with her hands.

Merctor spoke again. "The pain will fade soon enough, and I wouldn't ask if it weren't vital, but Syzel is going to touch your mind. It may hurt, but if the procedure failed in any way, now is the time to know. Otherwise, you may suffer irreversible damage."

Kalahn had heard all of that in his presentation, but it was still hard to concentrate with the banging noise inside her brain.

She only hoped it was normal.

A male voice filled her head. *It is.*

Taken aback, Kalahn sat up and promptly fell off the bed.

The voice was softer this time. *Princess, this is Syzel. Please try to respond. We need to know if everything is fine and that the procedure took.*

Each syllable sent a fresh wave of pain down her spine.

Gritting her teeth, Kalahn dug on every iota of strength she possessed to stand up to the discomfort. If she couldn't succeed with this trial, she'd never be able to help her family later. No doubt she'd have to suffer far worse during her upcoming training exercises.

She used the rhythm of her breathing to focus. The message coming in had felt like a gentle push. So maybe sending one out would require a similar push.

The male voice said, *Yes. Imagine sending out your thoughts, or maybe even tossing them. Later, you'll learn how to target one person. But for now, I'm the only one in range who can hear you.*

Kalahn took another few seconds to contain the pounding in her head and imagined her mental voice shouting out, *CAN YOU HEAR ME?*

Yes. The voice switched from a mental one to one she heard with her ears. "The procedure was successful. I heard her and she heard me, clearly both ways."

Merctor replied, "Good, then I can administer the final serum. It should help with the pain and stabilize your DNA."

Slowly, Kalahn blinked her eyes open and managed to keep them that way.

She was sitting on the floor of a small lab, with Merctor to one side and Syzel on the other. Syzel nodded and said, "You have a strong voice. I think you took to the procedure well, your highness."

Despite her mouth feeling like cotton, she muttered, "I normally have a strong voice, so that doesn't surprise me."

Merctor turned around with a syringe full of a purple-colored liquid. "You may want to lay down on the bed. This serum will leave you unconscious for a couple days, to allow your body to fully heal and adjust to your new programming, to put it in simple terms."

She had questions, but even without the serum, Kalahn's muscles complained as if she'd just run around the entire main continent of Jasvar. She'd never felt so tired in her life.

Syzel's mental voice came through. *It's okay, your highness. Your body has been through a lot and needs rest. You will feel better when you wake up. Ryven should be there and will begin instructing you straightaway.*

Despite her exhaustion, she managed a weak response, *I need help up.*

Syzel relayed her message and Merctor helped her up and onto the bed. "The serum will take effect almost immediately. However, one last thing—when you next wake up, you need to let Ryven know right away if anything is painful or feels wrong."

"Yes," she murmured.

Merctor put the serum into her IV and administered it.

Kalahn struggled to keep her eyelids open. "Tell Ryven…"

Before she could finish that thought, the world went dark and mercifully silent.

❈ ❈ ❈

No matter if Kajala Mayven stood or sat, her lower back always hurt. The only time it didn't was when she moved, which was why she currently paced the room where she waited to meet her half brother Kason and his bride.

She wished her mother, younger sister Kasarra, or even Kalahn were in the room with her. While she hadn't been a coward before getting pregnant, ever since she'd been too afraid of someone finding out her secret and stealing her child. So much so that she tended to avoid people. New people, in particular, always made her nervous.

Mostly because she couldn't stand when someone looked at her with pity. Or worse, disgust.

Rubbing her belly, she whispered words of love to her son. While not the ideal way to become a mother, he would always be proof that Davrel had been real.

Davrel. Tears prickled her eyes at the thought of what a band of space pirates had done to him.

The door opened and Kajala quickly wiped away her tears. Pasting a smile on her face, she turned around and spotted two people—her brother and his bride.

Her brother Kason reminded her of their father, albeit from his younger days. While pictures of Keltor had shown that both of her older brothers were tall, with dark blue hair and golden skin, Kason was a bit stockier, just like their father had been before sickness had wasted him away.

It was the human female at his side—Taryn—dressed in tight trousers and form-fitting top, who smiled and came at her with arms open. She spoke in CEL. "It's good to see you again, Jala."

Before she could say anything, Taryn wrapped her arms around her and squeezed gently. Once she released her, the human stepped back and waved Kason over. "Come say hello to your sister."

At Kason's stern expression, Kajala expected him to grunt and stay put. But to her surprise, he came and put out a hand. "Nice to finally meet you, Kajala. I hope that in time you will learn to trust me. I take family seriously."

She held her breath and waited for him to make a remark about her pregnancy. However, no pity or other negative emotion filled his eyes. It could be because he was a former general and was skilled in hiding his emotions, but a small flame of hope flickered inside her chest. "I hope it doesn't become necessary to ask for help, but thank you all the same."

Taryn nudged her lord. "Ask."

Kason released her hand. "Until Kalahn returns from her current project, you should stay with us."

"You still won't tell me what's going on with Kalahn?" Kajala asked.

"No," Kason stated.

Taryn jumped in. "It's not because we don't want to, but it's a delicate thing. Once it's safe to tell you, we will. So, how about it? Will you stay with us? I could always use another female around to side with me against Kason."

Kajala murmured, "I don't wish to be an inconvenience."

Taryn waved a hand in dismissal. "You're family now. It's almost your job to inconvenience us."

When Taryn winked, Kajala couldn't help but smile. "I shall remember that."

The human female hugged her again. "Good. Please remember that Keltor is your brother, too. So don't worry about him being king. I find that being informal works better with him anyway."

Kajala wasn't sure she could do that considering King Keltor was a stranger to her, but from her recent interactions with Taryn, Kajala knew it was easier to nod than to argue.

As the human chatted about how she could show Kajala around the human settlement, she wondered how she'd gone from a recluse hiding her pregnancy from the world to being surrounded and so easily accepted within a matter of days. At one time in her life, she'd have rejoiced at the ease. However, things had seemed easy with Davrel, too.

And that hadn't ended well.

Since even just thinking about her former love made her cry, Kajala instantly pushed her memories aside. She had a son to think of. Learning about her half siblings and garnering their protection would help him more than anything.

Yes, focusing on her son's future would keep her busy. Then she wouldn't have time to think of how things could go wrong later.

Kason finally spoke, but in their native tongue of Kelderan. "I hope you will take our offers seriously, Kajala. I learned about the male who fathered your child and read the reports of his gallant sacrifice to save his crew members. He was honorable, and I believe he would've married you as soon as he returned. I won't allow anyone to shame you."

"I—" Her voice cracked. Clearing her throat, she continued, "Thank you. I didn't expect such a welcome."

"Things are different on Jasvar. Remember that," her brother stated.

Something beeped and Kason switched to CEL. "That's the five-minute reminder of the video conference. Come. We must hurry to reach the secure transmission room in time."

She hesitated a second before asking, "So I can be prepared, how bad is Father?"

Kason frowned. "He doesn't have long."

Sadness squeezed her heart. "Thank you for telling me the truth."

"I believe truth is better than lies."

Taryn rolled her eyes. "He says that now. He was all for keeping things from Kalahn until recently." Taryn threaded her arm through hers and continued before Kason could say a word. "Come, we should go. If we're late, you'll lose precious time with them. And I imagine Keltor will be there with Azalyn, so you'll have to go through introductions with them, too."

As Taryn and Kason guided her out of the room and down a special set of corridors, Kajala steeled herself for the video conference with her father. She hadn't known it at the time, but him pulling strings to send her to Jasvar had probably set her on the best possible path for her life.

And all too soon he wouldn't be around anymore.

The thought of him not being nearby was too much for her to handle. So Kajala focused on her new family members and tried her best to smile. For her, smiling was armor as much as anything else. Maybe one day she could do it freely and not use it as a mask. However, that day hadn't come yet.

And to be honest, she didn't know when it would.

Chapter Seven

Four days later, Ryven paced just outside of Kalahn's room and resisted hunting down Merctor to demand some answers.

Most of those who went through the same procedure would sleep for maybe two days before waking up. Kalahn had been out for almost four.

Sure, Syzel had assured him that the procedure had taken and she now had telepathic abilities. But none of that mattered if she never woke up again.

Maybe he should've fought Kason harder. But since he couldn't change the past, he would have to focus on the present.

There was one thing he could try, but he'd resisted because it was a violation of Kalahn's privacy.

However, as the computer chimed the hour, he knew he had to attempt it. Because if she didn't wake up after five days, her chances of doing so again were slim to none.

After rolling his shoulders and stretching to release some of his tension, he entered Kalahn's room and went to her bedside.

It was unusual to see her still and motionless, except for the gentle rise and fall of her chest. From the first day he'd met her, when she'd been a child and he a teenager, she'd always been moving or talking. Everyone had suspected that Kalahn would grow out of it eventually, but everyone had thankfully been wrong.

It was now up to him to bring her back.

He took her cool hand in his and closed his eyes. Ryven usually had a barrier up around his mind, to keep others from invading it. He carefully dismantled one section, layer by layer, until he had a small opening.

Without hesitation, he reached out to the invisible threads of consciousness he knew would be flowing around Kalahn. Until she learned to construct even a crude barrier, any telepath would be able to take what they wanted from her. It was why her room was reinforced to prevent anyone outside of it from reading her thoughts and dreams.

He mentally brushed against one tendril and a video-like image flooded his brain.

Kalahn swam at the bottom of a waterfall, wearing scraps of cloth over her breasts and groin that he'd seen the Jasvarian humans use before.

In other words, she was as good as naked by Kelderan standards.

Ryven tried his best not to gawk, but as she turned to float on her back, he couldn't help but linger on the slopes of her breasts, her rounded belly, and her shapely thighs. The pieces of wet material hid little, and he swore he could make out her hardened nipples.

A male popped his head out of the water and playfully dunked Kalahn under the surface. In the second before she emerged once more, Ryven noted that the face of the male in the water with her was a blur.

The nameless male form could be his way of reaching her.

Ryven imagined the male form taking his head and shape. As the features became defined, he ignored the guilt that tugged at his heart. He would never willingly try to control someone else's thoughts or dreams unless it was a last resort. And in this case, it was.

When he finished the manipulation, Kalahn opened her eyes and immediately splashed him. He waited to see if she'd notice his intrusion and flee.

However, Kalahn merely laughed. "I was hoping you'd finally come play with me." She swam up to him and looped her arms around his neck. "Why don't you show me what else you have in store?"

Even though it was a dream, the heat and playfulness in her eyes, combined with her soft, wet body against his, made Ryven want to kiss her and live out one of his own fantasies.

But then he remembered the reason he was here. Removing her hands from his neck, he shook his head. "This isn't the time to play. I need you to listen to me and listen carefully."

Confusion filled her gaze. "I don't understand. Aren't we here to have fun and relax?"

A seasoned telepath would realize he was reaching out to her, but Kalahn was green. "We can relax later. Do you remember that you now have telepathy?"

"I..." She closed her eyes and pushed away from him. "What's going on? There's now a thundering noise inside my head that's drowning out my thoughts."

"That's because of me. You need to wake up, Kalahn. And now. Or you may never do so."

She searched his gaze. "What do you mean the noise is because of you?"

He swam a little closer. "I had no choice but to invade your mind. The longer I'm here while you're unconscious, the more it will hurt. That's why I need you to wake up."

"Even if I wanted to do it, I don't know how."

"Do you trust me?"

She paused before answering, "I think so."

That was going to have to be good enough. "Then I'm sorry for what's about to happen."

Gathering all of his mental might, Ryven shoved against Kalahn's mind as hard as he could.

Her instinct kicked in, pushed back, and tossed him out.

He instantly opened his eyes. Kalahn lay in a curled ball on the bed, moaning.

"Kalahn, I'm so sorry."

She bit out, "What did you do to me?"

The pain in her voice was a stab to his heart. Before he could reply, he heard her thoughts.

Why would he hurt me? The pain is too much. I think I'm going to die.

His first instinct was to smooth her hair from her face and whisper soothing words. If there was a way for him to absorb her pain and endure it for her, he would. But there wasn't.

Not even touching her was his privilege to claim. It was his duty to train her and ensure her mental health. Nothing else.

Dismissing Kalahn felt wrong, but he pushed past it and spoke again. "You've been unconscious for four days. To date, anyone who underwent the DNA-splicing procedure and didn't regain consciousness by day five never did so. I needed to wake you up."

She opened one eye and gave the best one-eyed glare he'd ever seen. "By bruising my brain?"

"Merctor and his assistants tried everything else they could, and nothing worked. So this was our final option."

She closed her eyelid. "Don't ever do it again."

The hurt in her voice went straight to his heart. However, there'd been no other way. Hopefully Kalahn would acknowledge that with time. "Unless your life depends on it, I vow never to harm you." Against his better judgment, Ryven laid a hand on Kalahn's bicep. "Will you allow me to help you erase the pain?"

Every minuscule movement caused an explosion of hurt inside Kalahn's brain.

To be honest, it put everything in her life into perspective. She'd thought she'd endured trying times in the past, what with her mother's death and her father's terminal illness. But nothing compared to when merely breathing made you want to scream in agony.

The only question was whether she could find the strength to push past the stabbing sensation and focus on anything Ryven tried to teach her.

When he spoke again, his voice was closer, almost at her ear. "I've always sensed a great strength inside you, Kalahn. You can do this. Not only to help yourself but to also help protect your family."

At the mention of her family, an image of Kajala holding her newborn baby came to her. She hadn't known her sister long, but Kalahn took being the eldest female sibling seriously. No matter her actions, Kajala deserved a happy future.

It was, indeed, her turn to protect those she cared about. "Tell me how to get rid of the pain."

"You must protect your mind and shield it from outside noise. That will take away most of the discomfort as well as give you privacy. I will instruct you on the process, but before we put your shields up, I need you to reach out to me mentally and use your telepathic abilities. I wouldn't ask unless it was necessary, but Merctor needs reassurance that the final serum did its job without any serious side effects. Thoughts escaping is one thing, but controlling them is another. I need to confirm the latter."

While the task should be simple, Kalahn's brain was muddled. The last time she'd felt this way was after having a high fever for a few days.

Ryven murmured, "You can do this, Lahn."

Irritation flared at the name. She imagined throwing out her words, *Don't call me Lahn.*

He mentally chuckled. *You're fine. Now, try this.*

She wasn't exactly sure how he did it, but Ryven sent the equivalent of an instructional video, showcasing each step necessary in order to construct a crude barrier. Once it finished playing, he asked, *Can you do that?*

Leave me alone and I'll try.

The warm, masculine presence evaporated. She wondered if she'd feel the same way if anyone brushed against her mind. With everything that had been going on, she couldn't remember how it'd felt with Syzel.

All she knew was that having Ryven touch her mind while awake was far more pleasant than when she was unconscious.

While she had a million questions to ask, she pushed them aside temporarily and began building her shields.

Layer by layer, she encircled her mental space. With each addition, some of the pain and background noise lessened. By the time she reached the tenth layer, there was silence inside her head once again.

Inspecting her wall, it was uneven in parts and bulged here and there, but no amount of prodding revealed any gaps.

Pain and noise free, she slowly blinked her eyes open to find Ryven's face a few inches from hers. After he searched her gaze, he murmured, "You look better."

"Excuse me for not looking my best after someone all but punched my brain."

"I said I was sorry. Now, stop with the guilt-tripping. We have more important things to do."

He eased back to standing, and Kalahn managed to sit up. She only wobbled a second before she regained her balance. "I guess this is instructor-mode Ryven."

The corner of his mouth ticked up. "Oh, you haven't met him yet. Once you do, you'll know."

"That sounds a little foreboding."

His eyes turned fierce. "This is no joking matter, Kalahn. If I don't prepare you properly, what I did to you will seem like a stroll through the gardens compared to what the female assassin might do. She kills for a living. Remember that."

Her confidence faltered a second. "Maybe I was too cocky about my abilities. If I can't keep you out, how do I stand a chance with her?"

Lightly taking her chin between his fingers, his voice was steely as he said, "You have already done better at this stage than most of my students in the past. Few could construct a gap-free barrier on their first try. And yes, I had to check it to ensure you were protected. But the point is, I think your strength of character will aid greatly in your training. A meek female wouldn't stand a chance at succeeding, but you're not a meek female, Kalahn."

At the protectiveness in Ryven's voice, some of her uneasiness faded. "So, for once, being different is a positive trait?"

He leaned in. "It's always been a positive trait in my eyes."

With his heat and scent so close, flashes of her dream, with Ryven holding her close in the water, came rushing back. She wondered just how much he'd seen. Because before the swimming at the foot of the waterfall, she'd asked him to kiss her.

Since she would essentially be trusting Ryven with her life, she blurted, "Am I broadcasting now?"

"No," he murmured as he brushed a stray hair behind her ear. "But your cheeks and markings tell me plenty."

A quick glance showed her markings flashing red, and she quickly imagined them a dark blue.

She rarely had trouble keeping her composure. Why Ryven had such power over her, she'd never understand.

Liar. She knew full well why.

However, she didn't have time to worry about a male or how much she wished she could just hold him close and claim him as her own. Shaking off his fingers, she sat up taller. "Then what do I do next, oh wise teacher?"

"You rest." He took a few steps away from her bed, and she almost reached out to grab his hand. Somehow she refrained, and Ryven continued, "After you sleep, your first task will be to wake up and immediately check your barrier. Eventually you will be able to maintain your shields as you sleep. But until then, your greatest task will be protecting both your mind and your thoughts from others."

"What about if I want to allow someone in?"

He took another step back. "We'll get to that as soon as I think you're ready. Now if you'll excuse me, I need to report your status to Merctor and your brother."

Ryven exited the room.

Kalahn sighed. Her brain was jumping and she constantly checked her shields to ensure there weren't any holes. Not to mention she was curious about what she could do with her new abilities. Being able to have a conversation without anyone listening in would have its benefits. Of course, she didn't know exactly how many people around her had telepathy. That was something else she'd have to discover when she had the chance.

Thoughts and questions continued to swirl and she wondered how she was supposed to fall asleep.

But after an hour of trying to better shape and fortify her mental walls, exhaustion took over and she drifted off.

Chapter Eight

Ryven exited Kason's home office and all but ran into Kajala Mayven. He managed to catch himself in time and took a step back. "My apologies, your highness."

The tall, willowy, and heavily pregnant female studied him for a few seconds before speaking. "Why do you do that? Call me 'your highness'?"

"Because you're the daughter of King Kastor."

After studying him a second, she asked, "May I speak to you in private for a few minutes?"

He had no idea what the female wanted, but he motioned toward the room Taryn used as an office when home.

Once inside, Kajala closed the door and laid her hands over her belly. "What are your intentions with Kalahn?"

He blinked. "My intentions?"

"It's obvious that both of you fancy each other, and yet you fight it. As someone who hesitated and put off claiming my love as I should have, I don't understand why you're doing it."

Kajala was either overly perceptive or he hadn't been as good at hiding his feelings as he'd thought. However, he didn't think Kalahn had noticed, which was all that mattered. "There's a difference. Kalahn doesn't fancy me."

The corners of her mouth ticked up. "She does. But I

find it interesting that you don't deny you're interested in her."

Ryven didn't know Kajala well, but she was definitely clever to catch his omission. He'd have to be careful around her. "Right now, I'm simply helping Kalahn with a confidential project and nothing more."

"Liar."

He frowned. "If you were a male, I might challenge you for calling me a liar."

"It's the truth, though." Kajala took a step closer. "I'm also not a male, and you won't. I know hearing the truth can hurt, but I'm just trying to help you."

Ryven should bow and walk away, but her words piqued his curiosity. "Help me how?"

"Well, I spoke with Keltor and his future bride privately. They told me they are working to change things so that any member of the royal family can marry whomever they wish. Well, provided they aren't a traitor, enemy, or some other such extreme."

He frowned. "Why would they do that when there are more important issues for them to focus on?"

She tilted her head. "I have my suspicions, but does it really matter?" She turned toward the door. "Don't make the same mistake I did, Ryven, because living a life of regret is not something I wish on anyone. That's all I wanted to say."

With that, she left him alone inside Taryn's office.

Rubbing his hand through his hair, Ryven tried to process what had just happened. He had no idea why Kajala would pull him aside like that, but it didn't change anything. Because even if her words were true, he and Kalahn had bigger issues at hand than whether or not to give in to attraction.

Such as working to end the threats against Kalahn and her family. Oh, and keeping them alive.

Brushing the strange encounter aside, he left Kason's quarters and made his way to the secure, reinforced area where Kalahn was being kept. After nodding at the guards stationed in the hall and knocking a few times, he entered to find Kalahn thumbing through one of the rare notescreens the Kelderans had brought to Jasvar.

She looked up. "I'm not sure how I'm supposed to learn all of this so quickly."

"You had numerous tutors growing up and you speak two languages fluently. I think you can handle a few more lessons."

"How do you know about my tutors?" she asked.

"You went on about them endlessly when you were young."

She rolled her eyes. "Yes, yes, I know. You're over a decade older than me. I'm surprised you remember, old man."

He grunted. "I prefer to be called experienced."

"Okay, experienced one, explain how something that usually takes at least six months will be accomplished in less than one?"

He sat on the edge of her bed. "I already told you that you're more skilled than most of my former telepath trainees. I have faith that you will continue to progress quickly."

"Why? Most people dismiss me as a frivolous, spoiled princess."

"You can be spoiled at times..." She glared and he laughed. "Well, it's true. But I've known you a long time, Kalahn. Whenever you wanted to do something, even if it was something as stupid as sneaking aboard a ship and stowing away without being detected, you put your mind to it and accomplished it. I think if we channel that rebelliousness toward your newfound telepathy, you can achieve great things."

He waited for another quip or look, but it never came. Kalahn murmured, "Thank you for believing in me."

Judging from her tone, few had done so in the past. Irritation flared at all those who had dismissed her. "It's your past actions that formed my opinion. Thanking me isn't necessary."

"It's nice to see you like this."

"Like what?"

"Not always changing the subject with a wink or smile. That side of you is fun, but I must admit I like the serious side too."

The longer he was in Kalahn's company, the more at ease he felt with her. Ryven could easily see himself relaxing completely in the near future with her, which was a big deal to a seasoned warrior trainer as himself.

One of the first rules of being a trainer was to always project strength, control, and stability. Showcasing faults wasn't an option.

But with Kalahn, he wouldn't mind showing her some of his faults.

Kajala's words from earlier, about Keltor trying to change the laws for his family, came back to him. If there was no legal barrier, would he pursue Kalahn?

A resounding yes echoed inside his brain.

"Why did your marking just flash purple?" she asked.

Purple was the color of happiness.

Glancing down, he was relieved to see them a dark blue. "It must be the lights inside the room playing tricks on your eyes."

She leaned forward and touched his arm. The light sensation sent electricity through his body.

Kalahn searched his gaze. "I know what I saw."

He tried to think of how to respond, but a few seconds later, he heard her mental voice, *Don't lie to me, Ryven.*

Her mental voice was softer and more like her own voice when compared to earlier. He answered, *The truth is unwise.*

In that second, he knew if he kept trying to partition his thoughts and ignore the female in front of him, he wouldn't be able to train her properly.

He should tell her the truth.

She might want nothing to do with him afterward and demand a new trainer. Part of him hoped for that.

And yet another part desperately wanted her to wish for the same.

Tightening her grip on his arm, she spoke aloud. "Considering I will probably reveal a lot about myself in the coming weeks, even if unintentionally, it only seems fair that you share some truth with me willingly. I should know the male who will all but shape my mind."

He leaned closer. "But you may not care for what I have to say."

With her eyes half-lidded, she murmured, "Then show me."

A more honorable male would resist such an invitation. But with Kalahn's proximity and the recent intimacy of her mental connection, he didn't want to fight it anymore. He would just have to trust that her dream portrayed what she wished as well.

Cupping her cheek, he pulled her face close and kissed her.

✸✸✸

Kalahn's heart beat double time as she waited to see if

Ryven would kiss her or not.

However, when his firm lips pressed against hers, all worry fled her mind. With each nip and nibble, she started to believe it was real and not just another dream.

And to be honest, having Ryven so close in real life was better than any dream.

All too soon he broke the kiss and kept his face a few inches away from hers. At the desire in his eyes, it took everything she had not to crawl into his lap and take another kiss from him.

His voice was husky as he said, "You didn't try to stop me or push me away."

There were many reasons why she should laugh and pretend she didn't want to kiss him again. But she didn't believe any of them. "Because I've wanted it for a long time, Ryven. Ever since you kissed me years ago, back on Keldera, when you were sent to retrieve me from my latest escape."

Moving his hand, he lightly traced her jaw. "As I remember it, you kissed me as a distraction."

"Regardless of who initiated it, I've thought about it often since then."

Ryven's markings tinged red before moving back to dark blue. "Don't lie to me, Kalahn."

She shook her head. "I'm not lying. At first, I thought that kiss was a girlish fantasy, one I'd built up in my mind. However, once you kissed me again, it was even better than I remembered it."

He groaned. "That may be, but if we do it again, it will only lead to more trouble."

"You say that as if to deter me."

The corner of his mouth ticked up. "You most assuredly shouldn't do it again."

For his cheekiness, she closed the distance and kissed him.

Unlike last time, she took the lead, following his example earlier of worrying his bottom lip. Ryven moaned and opened his mouth.

She tentatively tasted him, and it sent heat through her body and between her legs. What she wouldn't give for more than a kiss. The image of Ryven kissing his way lower, to her nipples, flashed into her mind.

With a growl, Ryven stroked her tongue one more time before he pulled away. She leaned forward, but he shook his head. "You're projecting and it's tempting me."

She should be embarrassed, but instead, she used her mind to reply, *Then why did you stop?*

While she expected to feel Ryven's warm, masculine presence brush her mind, he spoke aloud instead. "There are many reasons as to why this is unwise."

"Is this the part where you go on about duty, loyalty, and other excuses?"

"It's more than excuses, and you know it."

Kalahn sighed. Maybe Ryven was like all the others after all. "And yet another male refuses to listen to what I want and believe what I say."

Ryven searched her gaze and remained silent a few beats before he asked, "Then tell me, why are you so persistent? Is it because I was the first male you ever kissed?"

"That has nothing to do with it."

She hesitated. She didn't want him to think she was crazy.

Ryven murmured, "Tell me."

This was it—no turning back now. "Well, for one thing, you treat me as a person rather than as a princess. At least, most of the time. Not to mention my antics don't drive you crazy, or make you start yelling."

"I have thought about scolding you from time to time."

"Don't joke right now, Ryven. This is hard for me."

He put up a hand in apology. "Sorry, it's out of habit. But I can't be the only one who accepts you. There has to be more you aren't telling me about why you want me."

"There is, but it's hard to explain. Although I'll try." She took a deep breath and continued, "When you were inside my mind, there was pain, yes. But it also felt...right. As if your warmth accentuated my own, helping to chase away the negative emotions. Not to mention each mental brush from you feels as if you're touching my skin, leaving fire in its wake. Even now, I crave more of it." She bit her bottom lip before she blurted, "Is that normal, to want someone to be inside your mental space or to only talk telepathically?"

Brushing her hair behind her ear, he answered, "No. Usually it's uncomfortable and you learn to tolerate it through training."

Placing a hand on his chest, she reveled in the hard muscles under her fingers. "Will you..."

She trailed off, but Ryven caressed her jaw again. "Tell me."

Taking a deep breath, she let it out. "I wonder if it'd feel the same for you if I was inside your mental space."

Ryven hesitated. He'd never done that with her, meaning he was trying to figure out a way to politely refuse.

She pushed aside her disappointment. Maybe it would be better to forget she'd ever asked. "You don't have to, if you don't want to. I'm sure I'm being inappropriate again."

"It's not you, Kalahn." His eyes glanced down to her kiss-bruised lips and it was as if he were kissing her all over again. "I never want you to hold back with me. Besides, I'm curious now. Let's try it."

Her heart leapt at his words. She tried her best to contain her excitement. "How?"

He met her gaze once more. "You must've taken a small section of your shields down earlier, to speak with me. You need to do that again and then reach outward, toward me."

"I'm not sure I understand."

"Telepathy is almost like another plane of existence. Each person has a unique signal, and if someone goes searching on that plane, you can find a specific person. Well, provided you've met them before and can recognize their unique signature. A telepath's signature is like a face—everyone has one, but they're each slightly different from one another."

She tried to imagine what he spoke of, but struggled. "What's mine like?"

He paused and then smiled. "Like an exotic purple flower with thorns, swirling in a fierce rapid." He took her hand and squeezed. "Soon, you'll see mine. I know everything will be overwhelming, but try your best to memorize my signature. Because I want you to be able to reach out to me whenever you like."

"Whenever? Are you sure you want to say that?"

His eyes turned heated. "Yes, whenever."

Her cheeks flushed. If he was this sexy after one kiss, she could only imagine what would happen if it ever went further.

"Focus, Kalahn."

At his commanding tone, she said, "I can't concentrate with you so close."

He lightly ran a finger along her jaw. "That is something else we'll have to work on."

Ryven's confidence was addictive. After being paraded in front of one brown nosing politician or another over the last few years, it was refreshing and welcome.

And probably why her father had tried so hard to keep her away from the warriors. No doubt, he knew she'd be drawn to them. After all, they were the males who could better handle her personality.

Although she'd gamble everything she owned on the fact that Ryven was unique; she wouldn't be attracted to just any warrior. Their kiss was probably just the first step. The fact they both had telepathy was yet another thing that would probably tear down any sort of boundaries.

Ryven moved to a chair against the wall and crossed his arms over his chest. "Let's set a challenge, then, seeing as you like them. I won't speak again until you reach out to me mentally."

Closing his eyes, he feigned sleep.

It was on the tip of her tongue to ask for more guidance, but she restrained herself. Kalahn had solved problems and new issues before. Between what she'd read and what Ryven had taught her so far, she was confident she could figure out how to find Ryven's signature.

To help block out everything else, she closed her eyes. There was a small section of her shields that she'd rebuilt to allow a small opening when needed. Since it was currently patched over with multiple layers, Kalahn slowly peeled them away. A faint buzzing filled her head, much like it did every time she created an opening. She'd have to ask Ryven about that later.

She peeked out of the opening and took her first real look. However, all she saw was darkness, meaning she had to leave her safe place to look for Ryven.

Taking a deep breath, she imagined gliding through the opening and outside her mental space. Turning slowly, she finally noticed a small light in the same direction as where Ryven sat inside her room. Maybe that was a connection—a person's physical presence also affected their location in the telepathy plane.

As she approached, the intensity of the light increased and also became more defined. When she was almost there, she finally made out Ryven's signature. A wild, light green

Kelderan feline roared atop a mountain peak. The green cat was as big as she was and called a *cerrak*. While fierce, they were also protective and loyal of others in their social groups.

It was fitting, but Kalahn wondered why she had a flower when he had a fierce beast.

Ryven's warm voice answered, *You see a flower, but I see much more.*

Free of her shields and so close to Ryven, she found speaking easier. *Then tell me already.*

He chuckled. *It seems your impatience transcends methods of communication.* She thought about turning back, but he added, *Enough teasing for now. The flower is surrounded by thorns. I suspect they're to keep others away, because in reality, you're unique but delicate inside. And swirling in the rapids is akin to you struggling to find out where you belong.*

I'm not delicate.

You can be, although you hide it well with attitude and quips.

She hated how well he knew her. Kalahn had always resented how much stronger physically her brothers were than her.

When she didn't respond, he added, *No need to become upset. Signatures can change as a person does. So who knows, maybe one day mine will be a* supak *munching on grass, complete with a flatulence problem.*

A *supak* was a four-legged Kelderan animal that smelled of old cheese. *I hope that's not how you envision yourself when you're older.*

Probably not. But your mental signature reflects who you are. It is, unfortunately, one of many weaknesses telepathy brings to the table. There are ways to distort and hide the image for a brief span of time, but that is further along in your training.

While interested in details, Kalahn sensed exhaustion setting in from overstretching her mental muscles. It was time to bring things back on topic. *I'm here. So will you allow me into your mental space?*

Follow me.

She couldn't exactly see him, but she sensed his presence moving toward his signature. When he entered via a small entrance hidden in the feline's mouth, she smiled. Of course he would put it there, to test out who was brave enough to approach.

Well, that and the area inside the feline's mouth was shadowy, making it harder to spot the temporary vulnerability. She'd have to think of a more strategic place to put her own opening.

Since Ryven would never hurt her, Kalahn followed him without hesitation. The second she was beyond his shields, she was engulfed in his warmth. And maybe she was crazy, because she swore his scent was everywhere, too.

The space was filled with a soft glow, but nothing else. *Are all mental spaces like this?*

I don't know. I've only helped with training and have never violated someone's space once they were established.

The primal part of Kalahn was glad. Mentally touching someone was intimate, and she wanted to keep Ryven all to herself.

Not wanting to think too hard about how easily that thought came to her, she asked, *So? Is me being here like everyone else? You mentioned something about it being uncomfortable.*

Something swirled around her before he answered. *If I speak the truth, I have a feeling it may change things.*

I never put you down as a coward.

I'm not. His warmth circled around her again. *But training you is of the utmost importance. Are you sure you can take another distraction?*

Ryven, just tell me. I've spent my whole life surrounded by people hiding things from me, and I don't need any more of it.

After a beat, he finally said, *You being here is the furthest thing from being uncomfortable. If I'm honest, I want to keep you here forever.*

Her heart rate kicked up. She tried to figure out how to respond, but Ryven spoke before she could string her thoughts together. *However, I sense your presence flickering and it won't be long before you snap back into your own space. I need you to retreat and patch your defenses again.*

She wanted to argue, but it was becoming more and more difficult to reply to him. *Okay, but we'll discuss this later.*

Reluctantly she exited his space and headed back to her own signature. She couldn't get inside fast enough, and she struggled to apply the necessary number of layers to block out the noise. As soon as there was peace, she forced her eyes open.

Ryven was next to her bed, his gaze boring into hers.

Any doubts she had about him putting up barriers between them vanished when he cupped her cheek. Trying to raise her hand, she failed. Her limbs were as heavy as boulders.

Ryven's soft voice filled the room. "Sleep, Kalahn. I'll be here when you wake up again."

Her eyelids kept drooping, but she managed to keep them open. However, Ryven began to sing a lullaby created by the Barren. Each verse made it harder to keep her eyes open.

As he promised safety and love, she slipped away, wondering why he'd selected that song to sing to her.

Chapter Nine

Ryven stared at Kalahn's sleeping face and wondered what it'd be like to see it every day.

Her stepping into his mental space had felt unlike anything he'd experienced before. Almost as if she brought light and warmth into what once again felt like an empty, lonely space without her.

There was much the Kelderans didn't know about telepathy, but he wondered if certain people were destined to stir such feelings of acceptance and warmth as he'd felt with Kalahn. Or perhaps it was merely an echo of his subconscious.

However, before he thought too much more on the idea, one of the guards came into the room and said without preamble, "There's been an incident, sir. Someone tried to poison Kajala Mayven's guards while she was temporarily inside her quarters. One of the warriors managed to take out the threat, and while injured, he received medical attention in time."

Kajala had been staying with Kason, so the timing was extremely telling. "And the other?"

"I'm sorry, sir. The amount of poison he received was fatal."

Ryven cursed. "And Kajala?"

"She was on a conference call with some of the colony's developers, which was how she asked for help. She's a little shaken, but unharmed."

Considering the use of most of Kelderan technology would be almost nonexistent within a few years, the threats would only grow more dire if something wasn't done. Reading the female assassin's thoughts and learning her knowledge was more important than ever before.

When the warrior didn't salute and leave, Ryven knew there had to be more information. "Since Kason and Xytor are in charge of coordinating increased security and not me, there has to be another reason you're still here."

"Yes, sir. Prince Kason believes it best that we move the princess to a remote, secure location. The sooner, the better."

Ryven couldn't agree more. "What of Kajala? Will she be coming with us?"

"Being so close to her delivery date, she must remain near the colony so that she has access to the medical staff. The prince didn't say where, but only that he has two locations in mind—one for Princess Kalahn and one for her sister."

Ryven caught the lack of the honorific for Kajala. However, the guard's omission was the least of his worries. "I know he's busy, but I need to speak with Prince Kason as soon as he has the chance. Tell him it's related to the princess's medical condition."

The cover story was that Kalahn had undergone intensive treatment for a Jasvarian sickness that was only contagious through touch. The mysterious illness would keep most away, which was necessary since sometimes new telepaths picked up latent telepathic thoughts and had trouble focusing.

The Forbidden

Making a fist, the guard thumped it against his chest. "I will deliver your message to the prince straightaway. For the time being, I'd suggest staying in this room. There is extra security arriving as we speak. Ask them for anything else you may need."

Once Ryven nodded, the guard left.

Alone with Kalahn, he tried to think of how to handle the situation. Knowing the princess as he did, she'd demand to stay by Kajala's side. However, keeping the targets in separate locations would be best. Not just for their respective medical issues at the moment, but also to lessen the chance of a double blow.

Just the thought of someone poisoning the guards outside Kajala's doors and then getting inside to her made his stomach drop. He was reluctantly agreeing that giving Kalahn telepathy and training her to do undercover telepathic spy work was a good decision, especially given her strength and affinity for the skill.

However, he and the others had underestimated the immediate threats to the royal family on Jasvar. Clearly the female assassin was only one of many, just as they had postulated.

Because of the timing of the attack, Ryven suspected there was a mole somewhere in the higher ranks of the guards. Kajala had mostly been using secret tunnels to navigate between her quarters and Kason's. Only someone on the inside would know that she was supposed to be in her quarters at that specified time.

As he tried to go through and figure out who it might be, a knock on the door snapped him back to the present. Kason entered and promptly shut the door.

After a quick check to ensure Kalahn still slept, Ryven stood and motioned for his oldest friend to go into a side chamber. Once they were out of Kalahn's earshot, Kason spoke up. "I don't have a lot of time, so just listen. You and Kalahn will be moved to a remote location that only Taryn and her closest advisors know about, and you will leave as soon as possible. All of the guards I'm sending with you are males I trust with my life. But it will be up to you to protect Kalahn in the ways that matter now."

In other words, her mind. "She won't go easily without her sister."

"That's why Merctor will be along shortly to administer a sedative. Kalahn will be moved while unconscious."

"She's not going to like that," he drawled.

"It doesn't matter. The threats are much more serious here than we thought. I won't risk any of my family's lives. If that means angering them in the short term, so be it."

"You do know that once you hide away your two sisters, you will become the main target, right?"

Kason grunted. "I'm counting on it." Ryven raised his brows and Kason added, "I won't tell you anything else. Not because I don't trust you, but rather anyone could be listening and I don't want anyone to know my plans ahead of time."

He nodded. "I understand, but promise me you'll look after yourself, too. I have a feeling your bride would be upset if her lord were injured."

"For that reason, Taryn will be helping me."

Ryven wanted to voice his concerns outright about a traitor within the warrior ranks, but took Kason's warning about someone listening to heart. Instead, he spoke in a sort of code—shared experiences. "This reminds me of alpha team days."

The alpha team days referred to a set of warrior training exercises from their teenage years. Kason and Ryven's team excelled until they suddenly started losing every time because the other teams predicted their actions. Not just a few of the teams, but all of them. It was only after a few weeks they figured out one of their fellow team members had sold them out in exchange for vintage weapons to add to the male's collection.

Kason nodded. "I agree, and I'm looking into it. But I do trust those who are going with you."

"So when do we leave?"

"Merctor will be here within the next few minutes. I'm afraid you can't take anything with you beyond what I provide. Given that the traitors are from Keldera, they could have all types of technological spying tools at their disposal."

"I agree. Will everything be provided or will we have to forage?"

"Foraging will be necessary, to help keep your exit a low profile. However, there will be a Jasvarian accompanying you who will train you two on how to survive on this world. I'm afraid it's going to be similar to our survival training days, and Kalahn isn't going to like it."

Kason's dismissal of Kalahn didn't sit well with Ryven. "Kalahn is stronger than you think. And considering I helped teach the survival classes back home, I should pick up everything quickly."

"Just remember that this is a different planet, with different challenges. Until you have learned everything you can from the Jasvarian, your life will be in the Jasvarian male's hands."

"Male?" Ryven echoed.

"Yes, male. You'll meet him at the rendezvous point later." He gripped Ryven's shoulder. "Take care of Kalahn. There's no one else I would trust with her life."

Guilt threaded his heart at Kason's words. After all, Ryven had thoroughly kissed Kason's sister not that long ago.

Pushing the guilt aside, he made a fist and thumped it over his heart. "I will protect her until my last breath."

Kason squeezed his shoulder and released. "I'm glad you stayed, Ryven. It seems life on Jasvar isn't going to be boring and having the best warriors around me will greatly aid in protecting both my family and our fledging colony."

Ryven winked. "Well, I did beat you in the last sparring session. So I may be the best one on all of Keldera to have on your side right now."

Kason's lips twitched. "Don't remind me." His friend moved to the door. "Communication will be restricted, but if matters devolve, you know what to do."

Meaning Ryven would have to reach out to one of the few telepaths among the colonists. "Of course."

With a nod, he followed Kason out of the side chamber. His friend exited the room and Ryven looked back at Kalahn's sleeping face.

Even now, all he wanted to do was cup her cheek and wake her with a kiss. But if he ever wanted the chance to do so, he needed to focus on her training. The sooner she was prepared, the sooner they could try to learn more about their adversary and what was coming. Because only then could they neutralize the threats and go about their lives once more.

Until her training was complete, kissing was off the table.

But once the threat was vanquished, he wouldn't hold back any longer. Between danger revealing to him how he felt about Kalahn, as well as their shared mental discoveries, he couldn't imagine another female at his side. He'd just have to find a way to win her and then change the laws.

The Forbidden

❈ ❈ ❈

Several hours later, Ryven was in Jasvarian attire—leather trousers, loose linen shirt, and a wide-brimmed hat. The materials of the clothing weren't uncomfortable, but it reminded him of a Kelderan farmer's garb from several centuries earlier, when clothing had been made by hand.

Readjusting his hat, he did another cursory sweep of the area. He currently stood in a dense patch of forest, next to a narrow wooden carriage. Inside it was Kalahn's unconscious form and the supplies Kason had mentioned.

It had taken over an hour to zigzag through various pathways to get to the meeting point. Taryn Demara herself had shown them the way.

But she'd left them not long ago. The Jasvarian survivalist and their warrior escorts should've arrived already. While he had Kelderan weapons hidden inside the billowing folds of his shirt, he was anxious to get moving.

Keeping his ears open, it wasn't long before Ryven heard the snap of a twig. A female with pale blue skin and silver hair came out of the brush. While Ryven hadn't interacted much with the female, he knew she was one of Taryn's trusted advisors and friends. "Nova Drakven."

She grinned. Her Kelderan was broken as she said, "At your service." Moving closer, she whispered, "I share my secret."

Considering Nova hadn't spoken any Kelderan that he knew of, she must've been studying it. His first instinct was to demand details about what was going on. Nova was a battle strategist for Jasvar, meaning she was too valuable to serve as Kalahn and Ryven's companion.

A male's voice murmured behind him in perfect Kelderan, "You should be more careful."

Turning around, Ryven studied the teal skin and black hair of the male. Considering he'd snuck up on him without making a sound, Ryven suspected that the male was the one who would be showing them how to survive off the land. After all, a noisy hunter would starve. "You're Kelderan."

"I was Kelderan. Jasvar became my home ten years ago."

The timeline clued him in on the male's history. "You were one of the scientists who disappeared a decade ago."

He grunted. "By choice. My name is Orvar. Nova is here to guide us to the secret location. Once there, I'll take her back to this starting point while you settle in."

He studied the tall male. "For a scientist, you're accustomed to giving orders. What was your role on the former exploration team?"

Ignoring him, Orvar turned toward Nova and spoke in CEL. Ryven only had a basic grasp and couldn't follow along.

It seemed Orvar wasn't going to be a friendly addition to him and Kalahn.

Nova finally met his gaze again. "Come."

Ryven spoke to Orvar. "Aren't there supposed to be warriors accompanying us?"

"They will be shown after the fact, via a different route. Every precaution is being taken."

He nodded. "I understand that." Ryven glanced at the vehicle containing Kalahn. "I hope the way we're going is accessible to this carriage."

Orvar grunted. "The princess is just a female. You could carry her."

There was another reason Kalahn had to stay inside the carriage—it was fortified with extra materials to protect her mind.

Not that Ryven could share that information.

Nova said something to Orvar. The male then studied Ryven. "She senses concern and worry. Why?"

His gaze shot to the smiling female. "She's an empath?"

Orvar answered for her. "Only a low-level one, due to her half-human heritage. Her father is a full-blooded empath with more skill. Nova only senses strong emotions. And no, she can't control it."

Since humans didn't have blue skin or metallic silver hair, Ryven reasoned those were from her father's side as well. He'd have to look into what species of alien her father was later. "You seem to know a lot about her."

"I make it my priority to know everyone I encounter, including you."

Ryven raised his brows. "I sense there's more."

"Perhaps," Orvar stated. "I'll find out the cause of your concern later, because we need to get going. We don't want to be stuck in the wilderness after dark."

Questions rushed into his brain about what happened once the sun set, but he ignored them. "You two lead the way and I'll bring up the rear."

Orvar said something to Nova. The female gave a thumbs-up, and she walked down a barely visible path. The Kelderan male took the reins of the great pack animal and followed her, the carriage rumbling along.

As he brought up the rear, Ryven now understood the narrowness of the vehicle. The paths Nova took were meant for walking. However, considering the Jasvarians had had the narrow carriage in storage, Ryven surmised that this wasn't the first time someone had needed to disappear into the wilderness.

Ryven did his best to keep his eyes and ears peeled, even though he didn't know as much about Jasvarian animal and plant life as he'd like. Hopefully Orvar could teach him quickly. Because the longer the male was around, the greater the chance he'd learn of Kalahn's telepathic abilities. Taryn and Kason must trust him or they'd never have sent Orvar to help, but Ryven didn't want to risk anyone else learning about Kalahn's secret that didn't absolutely need to know it.

After several hours of turning down one path and then another through the endless miles of purple trees, Nova motioned to the side. Orvar interpreted, "Just over there."

It took a few seconds for Ryven to spot the hidden structure. To the untrained eye, it looked like a clump of dense, blue bushes. But he noted a few wooden supports, as well as patches of ground surrounding it that looked unstable. They had to be booby traps—probably deep pits—to keep invaders away.

While he'd admired Taryn Demara's ability to lead her people, he realized that even without advanced technology, Jasvarians still thought of effective security systems to protect their own. Maybe if the Kelderans and the Jasvarians worked together, they could make improvements.

Nova walked in a specific pattern, pointing to which areas to avoid. She stopped in front of the bushes and asked him something. Orvar spoke. "Why aren't you following?"

"I've memorized the pathway. However, I won't leave Princess Kalahn unprotected."

Once Orvar conveyed the message, Nova tilted her head. He had a feeling she was reading his emotions.

He quickly packed away any thought or feeling beyond protection. Nova blinked.

Good, he must be a mostly blank slate now.

The female turned away and toggled something inside the foliage. A second later he heard the creaking of a door opening. Nova stated in her accented Kelderan, "Bring Kalahn."

Orvar spoke up. "I'll watch the carriage while you do so. As it is, I plan on sleeping out here instead of in there."

Since the Jasvarians mostly lived inside the mountains, it was odd for Orvar to speak as if sleeping inside was torture.

Opening the side door of the carriage, Ryven checked inside to find Kalahn unconscious on her back, just as he'd placed her hours ago. He carefully lifted her out and held her in his arm, keeping her body close against his chest.

He wanted to probe her shields to ensure they held, but didn't want to risk intruding on her dreams. Especially not with a low-level empath nearby.

So he quickly constructed a temporary shelter over Kalahn's mental signature, just so she wouldn't broadcast her emotions to Nova.

Ryven carefully walked in the same pattern the female had done and approached the mostly concealed door. Ducking inside, he blinked as his eyes adjusted to the low glow emanating from the plants on the wall.

Nova's metallic silver hair reflected the light, making her almost burn like a star. She motioned with her hand. "This way."

She took him down a long hallway and through several sets of doors before they entered a tunnel carved out of stone. He prepared himself for another cave-like dwelling at the end of the corridor. However, they soon stepped out into the fading sunlight.

It took a few seconds for his eyes to adjust, but several structures made from wood and stone slowly came into focus. Only then did he notice they were entirely surrounded by a high rock wall that extended above them; it was almost the length of a Kelderan starship fighter.

Nova said, "Dead volcano."

He nodded, and she moved toward the largest structure inside the area. She pointed. "Home." Then she pointed to the far wall. "Bath." And at a smaller structure. "Water."

To the several small buildings apart from the rest, she said, "Temporary home."

He had no idea what she was talking about when she said "temporary home," but he would explore the compound once Kalahn was settled.

Readjusting his grip on Kalahn, he motioned his head toward the biggest structure. "Home?"

"Yes. Come."

He followed the female inside and to one of the rear rooms, which contained a large bed on one side and a wall of hooks fashioned out of wood on the other. Ryven gently laid Kalahn down on the mattress and resisted smoothing the hair away from her face.

"I keep secret." At Nova's voice, he looked at her and frowned. She winked. "I promise."

Since he had been careful to keep his feelings guarded, as well as Kalahn's thoughts, he had no idea how Nova could sense anything.

Because of the language barrier, he couldn't demand answers anyway. So Ryven murmured in CEL, "Thank you."

She bobbed her head and replied, "I go. Orvar. Now."

Nova left without another word and he sat next to Kalahn on the bed.

He quickly removed his temporary barrier and checked Kalahn's mental walls.

After a quick search and plenty of poking, he was confident they held. However, he wouldn't be able to judge if the sedative had given her some sort of adverse effect or not until she was awake.

One of the downsides to the DNA splicing process was that it changed a person's reaction to a variety of things, never working the same way twice for people.

Gently brushing her cheek, he noticed her cool, dry skin. At the lack of sweat, she couldn't be having too bad of a dream then.

Tempted as he was to curl up at her side and maybe help keep bad dreams at bay, Orvar shouting from the entrance to the extinct volcano prevented him.

Ryven lingered one second longer before going to meet the male. He needed to get as much set up and prepared as he could before Kalahn woke up. Her training was second only to her safety.

Hopefully, in the isolated location, he could speed up her training regime and truly push her to her limits. He wouldn't dare try it in a high-traffic location such as the colony settlement. However, in the wilderness, there was little to possibly harm or attack her on the telepathy plane, especially since Ryven had probed Orvar thoroughly and knew he wasn't a telepath.

Of course, he had another motivation for completing her training quickly. Ryven could almost still feel her warm, soft body against his chest as he'd carried her. He may delay kissing her again, but he wasn't going to give up on her. He sensed there was a reason her presence inside his mind was a comfort rather than an irritation and he was determined to find out why.

Chapter Ten

Kalahn opened her eyes to find an unfamiliar wooden ceiling above her where there had previously been one made out of rock.

She hadn't had a chance to even sit up before Ryven's voice came into her mind. *You're awake. Don't panic. I'm here.*

Looking over, she saw Ryven sitting at a table, leafing through what looked to be an old-fashioned bound book. "Where are we?"

He replied telepathically. *Check your shields and reinforce them first.*

Ryven went back to reading his book.

Since she'd get answers faster by completing the task, she didn't argue and looked inward. She took her time layering the cracks she found. One was almost the entire height of her mental wall, so she spent extra time reinforcing that section. When done, she opened her small communication passageway and projected out in Ryven's direction. *I'm done. Will you answer some questions now? Or am I supposed to merely lay here and admire you reading a book?*

His voice was tinged with amusement. *I need to finish this book anyway, but you admiring me along the way will make it that much more enjoyable.*

Ryven!

He turned his body toward her and spoke aloud. "Your telepathic voice is stronger, which is a good sign."

After quickly retreating into her safe mental space and closing the opening, she replied, "The more I do it, the easier it gets to control it."

He nodded. "Good. I'll make sure to practice enough with you to push your limits, but not mentally exhaust you. Your next main task will be reaching out to talk to me privately so that even if another telepath is nearby, they can't hear your thoughts."

She scooted to the edge of the bed. "Before we attempt anything else, tell me where we are."

"It's easier to show you." Standing, he reached out a hand to help her up. Kalahn took it without hesitation, and ignored the thrill of his fingers closing around hers. He tugged. "Come on."

She noted the painted wooden walls as they walked, as well as the wooden floors. "Unless someone has been redecorating while I was asleep, we're not inside any of the mountain settlements."

He pointed toward a window. "I would think that would be the first clue."

"We only just turned the corner. I may be telepathic now, but I can't see through walls."

The corner of his mouth ticked up. "Good thing, as you'd probably peek at everyone changing or bathing."

She managed to keep her markings a dark blue and her cheeks from flushing. "Maybe that's what you'd do. I, however, am a princess."

"Which means you're even more likely to rebel. You've never been prim and proper, Kalahn. So don't even try to pretend you were."

"Sometimes it's irritating that you've known me so long."

He winked. "Blame your brother. For whatever reason, he started a fight with me that day long ago. When I kept avoiding his punches and instructing him on how to do better, he never left me alone."

She was about to mutter a few choice words about her brother Kason when they exited the structure and she forgot what she was going to say.

There were numerous buildings scattered inside a circular rock formation that went high into the pink-colored sky. Light filtered down from the opening, with birds diving in and out of the area. The long, flowering vines creeping down the sides of the walls completed the picture. "Where are we?" she breathed.

"Somewhere safe. There was an attempt on Kajala's life and we needed to move you somewhere remote. Kason's bride knew of this place, and so here we are."

Her gaze shot to Ryven's. "Where's Jala?"

"She's fine, and safe at another location."

"Why isn't she here?"

"I understand you wanting to protect her, but Kason has one of his most trusted warriors looking after her. Concentrating any of you in one location is unwise until we know more about our enemies."

As much as she wanted to see Kajala for herself and give her sister a hug, Kalahn knew Ryven was correct. "So it's just the two of us here?"

He shook his head. "No. Since I'm unfamiliar with the land, there's someone here to teach me how to forage and hunt the Jasvarian animals. He returned not long ago with the two warriors who are now watching the front entrance."

She motioned toward the creeping vines. "Someone could come from above."

He smiled. "Yes, they could. But I do have a few skills under my belt, and watching for any large humanoids descending from the sky is one of them."

Sighing, she tried to walk toward one of the other structures but Ryven tugged her back and kept one of her hands in his. He stated, "We go together or not at all."

"With guards at the entrance and you using your mighty skills of observation to watch the skies, what do you expect to happen? For someone to tunnel up from the ground?"

"There could be escape tunnels we haven't discovered. The best I can tell, this area isn't used often and the original construction plans have been lost for quite a while. It could take months or even years to check and determine if any secret entrances exist."

Damn Ryven and him being able to snag her curiosity about why he thought the place wasn't used often. "Are you going to tell me more about our temporary home or are you going to make me drag it out of you?"

His mental voice brushed her mind. *There are a few training exercises you need to do today first.*

"And I will happily complete them later. After all, I won't be able to concentrate if I keep wondering about this place and what it was used for."

Sighing, he murmured, "Using logic to best me, just like your brother."

She grinned. "Thanks for letting me know how to sway your opinion in the future."

"Kalahn," he growled.

She put up her free hand. "Okay, okay. Enough teasing. Tell me a little about what you found out and I promise to try my hardest at whatever exercise you throw my way."

Squeezing her fingers in his, he motioned around them. "The book I was reading is a journal and the best I can tell, this place was used as a transition location."

"Transition for what?"

"The alien males the humans tricked to land on their planet and then subsequently captured."

Her curiosity piqued. "If so, wouldn't a lot of people know where this is?"

An unfamiliar Kelderan male's voice answered, "No, because the males were both drugged and blindfolded when being brought here and when being taken away."

Turning her head, she noticed a Kelderan male with teal skin and black hair. His lanky frame meant he wasn't a warrior. And since Ryven wasn't surprised at his appearance, the male must be the one teaching Ryven to forage. "How would you know that?"

He walked up to them, carrying a large dead bird of some sort. "Because I was one of them." He tossed the bird down, and then untied the small sack on his belt and threw it down, too. "Those are for your dinner. I'm hunting until Ryven can do it himself, but I'm not your cook. So it's up to you to do it."

"Wait—"

Kalahn didn't get to voice her questions because the man walked away and disappeared into a tunnel on one side.

Looking back at Ryven, she raised her eyebrows. He explained, "That's Orvar. He was with the exploration ship of Kelderan scientists who disappeared a decade ago. I don't know much else about him except that Taryn and Kason trusted the male enough to have him help us survive out here."

Given what she knew of how the Jasvarians lured alien males to their planet, Kalahn guessed Orvar had married one of the human females. Maybe he was grumpy and curt because he missed being away from his bride.

THE FORBIDDEN

As curious as she was about Orvar's history, her temporary home was more important. Picking up the small sack, she motioned her head toward the bird. "Take that. I hope you've found a kitchen, because until I eat something, I'm not sure I'm going to be able to concentrate on any sort of mental task. Besides, you can tell me more over dinner."

"You and your logic again." He picked up the bird. "But just know that it won't always work, Kalahn. So use your weapon wisely."

"Another challenge? You know what I do with those."

His gaze turned heated. "And I plan on using it to my advantage many times in the future."

Gulping, she avoided looking at his lips. "Be careful. An overly confident male can get himself into trouble."

"Perhaps." He tightened his grip on her hand. "Come. I'll show you around our house."

As they walked back toward the main structure, Ryven's words of "our house" kept replaying inside her head. Of course they wouldn't live here forever. And who knew if she'd ever get more than a few kisses from Ryven. But for now, she liked to pretend it was real.

Because for the first time in her life, she could be herself without everyone judging her. Ryven accepted her as she was. And to a woman constantly trying to live up to society's expectations and failing spectacularly, it was a gift. One she didn't want to take for granted.

❉ ❉ ❉

Most would call Ryven a fool for holding Kalahn's hand and flirting with her. But free of judgmental eyes, he found he didn't care what others would say.

He'd always dismissed his attraction to Kalahn since their first kiss as him merely wanting the forbidden fruit—

she was not only his best friend's sister, but also a princess. However, as they walked hand in hand and eventually began laying out the ingredients for dinner as if they did it all the time, he thought maybe there was more to it.

Kajala's words earlier, about King Keltor looking for a way to ensure all his siblings could marry whom they wished, started to mean more to him.

Interrupting his thoughts, Kalahn mentally said, *I can't cook.*

Careful to keep his tone light, he replied, *I've eaten grubs before. Whatever we make can't be any worse than the crunchy, gooey center of those things.*

She gasped and said aloud, "I didn't consciously reach out to you. Did you hear me?"

Finally releasing her hand, he put the bird on the preparation table and began plucking the feathers. "The bigger question is whether you wanted me to hear, or are your walls failing?"

After a short silence, Kalahn shook her head. "Everything is fine inside my head. No cracks or holes to be found."

"Then it merely means you trust me completely. Be careful, because when you're around me, it means you might start broadcasting on a regular basis."

"Of course I trust you. But there are some thoughts a person wants to keep to themselves."

He paused in his task. "Such as?"

Rolling her eyes, she dumped out the contents of the small bag. "If I want to keep it quiet, then why would I tell you?"

"Because I'm ruggedly handsome? Charming? Amusing?" Kalahn tossed a small root vegetable at him, but Ryven caught it. "Let's add superior reflexes to the list, shall we?"

She growled. "Let's be serious for a second, okay? If I'm broadcasting because I trust you, then why don't I hear you? Do you not trust me?"

He hated the uncertainty in her voice. He met her gaze, wanting her to see the truth to his words. "I trust you, Kalahn. That was solidified when you rescued Kason and brought him and his bride back alive."

Moving around the vegetables in front of her, Kalahn murmured, "I just wanted to help my brother."

"Now you're being modest?" He dipped his hands in a bowl of water and quickly dried them off before taking hold of her shoulders. "I trust you, Kalahn. But I've learned to keep my thoughts private out of necessity. When training others, I can't risk broadcasting some of my memories."

"Which memories?"

While Kalahn was trying to be sly, Ryven didn't outright deny her. He could brush off the question, as he'd done with others many times before. However, a small part of him wished to share some of his past.

After all, there would be no future for them if he kept hiding what had shaped him.

So he answered calmly, "Mostly ones from when after my parents died, but before the Barren took me in."

Searching his gaze, her voice was soft as she asked, "Why? What happened?"

"How about instead of me telling you, I show you?"

Confusion flashed in her eyes. "What do you mean?"

"Telepathy isn't limited to speaking with words. We can do it with images, too."

"Like you did with the wall-building instructions."

He bobbed his head. "Exactly. But it requires you allowing me inside your mental space. Will you?"

She didn't hesitate. "Of course."

Her absolute trust in him did something to his heart.

Not wanting to broadcast his emotions when he stepped inside her mental space, he quickly packed them away.

He guided them both to a set of chairs and they sat down. "Then create an opening and show me where it is."

Retreating to his mind, he went in search of Kalahn's signature. As he stared at the flower swirling in the rapids, he waited until Kalahn's presence brushed against him. *Follow me.*

Careful to keep contact with her telepathic presence, he followed her into one of the rapids. *I approve of the entry point.*

I didn't ask for your approval.

He wanted to snort, but restrained himself. *Too bad, as it matters. Only I can say when you've completed your training.*

Well, then hurry up and get started, Mr. Trainer. I'm waiting.

He did chuckle at her dry tone. *All right then, let's begin. I'll play out the memory. However, if you speak up during it, it will interrupt the transmission. So save your questions for later.*

Before Kalahn could make a quip, he focused on projecting his memories.

※ ※ ※

Thirteen-year-old Ryven peeked around the corner of a composite building, never taking his gaze from a certain merchant male. Every day the food merchant would leave his stall unattended for thirty seconds to shout a regular customer's special order inside, and the merchant fool thought nothing of the obvious routine and opening.

And if not for the half-starved children back at the abandoned building, Ryven would tell the merchant his mistake. However, Ryven needed the food. The Brevkan had attacked yesterday, and all the people in the capital city were staying inside, afraid of more laser attacks or bombs, and unwilling to risk opening a door to help a homeless child.

Not that he could blame the fear. One such attack had stolen his parents from him.

Still, he hated the growing number of orphans flowing into the streets, having to take care of themselves because of the chaos. No one else would help them, so Ryven had formed a loose alliance and taken it upon himself to feed as many little ones as he could manage.

Jobs were scarce for young males such as he, so stealing was his only option.

The merchant went inside right on time and Ryven raced to the stall, scooped up as much fruit and bread as he could carry, and raced back to his hiding place. When the merchant returned, he barely paid attention to the missing pieces. Mostly because Ryven had taken the ones he couldn't see from a vantage point behind the stall.

Not wanting to stick around since the merchant's regular customer would arrive any minute and notice the missing food, Ryven raced down the alleyway. He'd barely taken a dozen steps when a female's voice was strong and clear behind him. "You shouldn't steal."

Panic raced through him, and he pushed his body to run as fast as possible, doing his best not to drop the food. After zigzagging down at least a dozen side streets, he finally stopped and looked around to see if the female had followed him.

However, all he saw were the crumbling houses and former shops. Not even a dog was in sight.

At the empty street, he breathed a sigh of relief.

He scanned his surroundings a few more times before

he darted inside one of the abandoned buildings and up the stairs. Entering the large room he and the other children used to sleep in, he counted the inhabitants to ensure no one had left. As he handed out the fruit and bread to each child, careful to break it up into portions so everyone could eat, he catalogued their health.

A few of the younger ones coughed or complained of pain Ryven couldn't fix. They needed to see a doctor, but that was tricky. While there were some free clinics not too far away, they required thumbprint scans to verify identities. Ryven had learned early on that if there was no listed family, the children would be seized and sent to the outlying areas for who knew what reason. He suspected they were sent to labor camps disguised as orphanages.

And he wouldn't allow his charges to be sent to those hellholes. Ryven would just have to find a way to help the sick ones, like he always did.

Which meant breaking more laws.

Since his current haul wasn't as large as some days, Ryven gave all the food to the other children and kept none for himself. He'd just have to find something to eat later.

As he went to check on the youngest orphan, a little girl no more than two, the female voice from earlier spoke. "What's going on here?"

He turned and readied himself for a fight. However, at the sight of a thin female with purple hair, light blue skin, and an intricate tattoo on her forehead, he blinked. "You're one of the Barren."

The woman raised an eyebrow. "Indeed. But that still doesn't answer my question." He hesitated, trying to think of how he could get the woman to leave. However, her voice was gentler as she added, "I won't report you for stealing, if that's what you're worried about."

One of the young girls came up behind him and hid. He

murmured, "It's okay, little one. I'll protect you."

He wasn't sure how, but he'd find a way.

The Barren spoke again. "My name is Gosarra. Is everyone here an orphan?"

Ryven hesitated. If he said yes, he had no idea what she'd do. He doubted she'd help them all out of the kindness of her heart.

Nearly two years on the street had taught him not to trust easily.

Gosarra clasped her hands in front of her. "I suspect they are. If so, I can help all of you."

Adults often made promises they couldn't keep. Ryven decided to test her.

Since he knew the Barren helped with healing sometimes, he motioned toward a bedridden little boy. "Then help him first. He's been sick for weeks."

Whether the Barren knew it was a test or not, she didn't blink as she made her way to the sick boy's bed. After a quick examination, she took a small injection device from her pocket and looked Ryven in the eyes. "This will help with his fever and congestion. Will you allow me to give it to him?"

"Why would you ask me? Adults don't ask children for permission."

Well, at least no one had since his parents had died.

The Barren replied, "I believe that you're in charge here. Since you've been their caregiver, it makes sense I ask your permission."

He stood taller. "I'm their protector."

"Then as their protector, please let me help this boy."

Please was another word adults didn't use with him anymore. And for the first time in a long time, he wanted to trust an adult, even if it were for a short time. He nodded. "Then help him."

The Barren injected the sick boy. Within seconds, the boy's breathing became less ragged and his little body relaxed against the pile of blankets for the first time in days.

The female stood and faced him again. "Did I pass your test?"

"How did you—"

She smiled. "I've worked with many orphan boys over the last ten years or so. Trust doesn't come easy, nor do I expect it to for some time. But if I pass the first test, I usually have a shot at earning it in the long run."

The two-year-old girl walked over to the Barren and tugged on her brown skirts. Without missing a beat, the Barren picked her up and held her on one hip. As the adult female tickled the little girl, Ryven started to wonder if maybe the Barren could help them.

Because all of the children he'd protected deserved better than to live in a dirty, abandoned house, never knowing when their next meal would come.

Lowering his arms, he cleared his throat. The Barren looked at him and waited patiently until he spoke. "How could you help us?"

"I'm sure you know that the Barren citadels take in orphans and raise them?"

"Yes, but usually only the orphans of the wealthy."

Gosarra shook her head. "Not true. We often go looking for orphans on the streets to take in. And in your case, someone tipped me off about your activities."

He frowned. "My activities? You mean stealing?"

"Yes. And while you've done well for a young male, you aren't a warrior or guard, and someone noticed you and reported you to the authorities. When it comes to crimes committed by orphans, provided they aren't severe, the Barren are often given the first opportunity to collect the

The Forbidden

reported orphans and take them back to the citadel."

Ryven had never heard of that before. Not that he'd gone out of his way to learn what the authorities did in certain cases. "And if I don't go?"

"Then the guards will find you the next time and probably take you to a juvenile rehabilitation facility."

"You mean they'll put me to work until I'm of age," he muttered.

Gosarra shrugged one shoulder. "I have no control over what certain agencies do. However, I can control this situation. Say yes, and you will come to my citadel."

He studied the female for a second before asking, "I don't really have a choice, do I?"

"You always have a choice, child. I've given you two options—to come with me or stay here and take your chances with the authorities. So which will you choose?"

Ryven didn't like being backed into a corner, but the Barren had been kind to him and the other children so far. And the thought of having a regular place to live for more than a few weeks at a time was more than he had hoped for in a while.

Not that he'd agree so easily. "We'll go, but I won't make any promises."

She tilted her head. "That's a challenge for me, then. Because I'd like to adopt you as my own."

He frowned. "But you just met me. Why would you want to do that?"

"Stick around long enough and I'll tell you the reason." The Barren motioned around the room. "Help me get the children ready to go. I'll make a quick call and have some of my colleagues come here to help, too. The quicker, the better. I want to get everyone out of here before the next Brevkan attack."

As Ryven helped the Barren gather the children and

what meager belongings they possessed, he tried to ignore the emotion in his heart. Because for the first time in years, he had hope.

Hope that maybe he could protect the other children without having to commit dishonorable acts.

Not to mention hope that maybe someone wanted him again.

Hope that he could be loved.

***

Once the memory ended, Kalahn opened her eyes and tried her best not to cry. Not trusting her mental abilities, she used her voice. "Ryven, I had no idea."

He shrugged. "You were quite young when the war finally ended. But for years, what you just saw with me and the other children was all too common."

Reaching out, she took his hand. "I'm sorry that happened to you. It couldn't have been easy to fend for yourself and so many other at such a young age."

"I wouldn't be who I am today without those experiences. Besides, Gosarra did become my mother. And as much as I loved my birth mother, I couldn't have asked for a better second chance."

Kalahn had wanted to bring Ryven's mother to Jasvar before, but now it was almost imperative she did so. Without Gosarra's kindness, Kalahn may never have met Ryven at all. "Then once everything settles down, I'll make sure she comes here on the next spaceship. I know you said you will manage her transfer yourself, but I insist."

"At one time, I would've refused your help again, until I knew I couldn't do anything. But I'm not that young male any longer, out to prove I can do everything myself. I'll take your help on one condition."

Searching his gaze, she asked, "What?"

"That you agree to meet my mother when she arrives."

She nodded. "Of course. I would've asked to anyway. I have to admit I'm curious about the female who took in a wild teen and shaped him into a wonderful grown male."

Ryven cleared his throat. "I'd like to think I was a wonderful person before then, too. I only did what I had to do to survive."

"I agree, but I'm sure your mother influenced you as well. I'll just have to judge for myself when I meet her. I'll also have to pry out all the embarrassing stories she knows about you, too. I'm sure there are some good ones."

Shaking his head, he said, "We'll see about that. Knowing my mother, she'd want something in exchange, such as a secret for a secret. Come to think of it, it could be amusing to watch her negotiating terms with you."

Kalahn raised an eyebrow. "I can negotiate as well."

He grinned. "We'll see how well you do." He motioned toward the food on the counters. "Now, let's hurry and get dinner made so we can get on with your training."

Ryven released her and went back to plucking the bird. As she remembered the images of him as a thin child, clearly undernourished, Kalahn vowed she'd do her best to cook an edible meal for him. Someone with his honor and integrity should never go hungry again.

Returning to her pile of vegetables, Kalahn only recognized one that was some kind of root vegetable. If only she'd taken up the cooking lessons some of Taryn's friends had offered.

She needed help if she were to make Ryven a good meal. Glancing around and noting all the unexplored cupboards, she said, "If you found a journal, then I bet there has to be a cookbook around here somewhere."

"I didn't look for one, so go ahead. Although I'll repeat

that I eat almost anything, so don't worry about it."

Merely being edible wasn't good enough by Kalahn's standards, so she rummaged through the cupboards, trying to ignore Ryven's silence. She could feel his eyes on her as she moved about.

Not that she was embarrassed. Kalahn bent over a little more than she needed to in order to check a lower cupboard. If Ryven were staring, she was going to make a show about it.

Something flittered against her mind, but quickly vanished. The signature had the same warmth as Ryven's had earlier.

She debated reaching out to him, but quickly forgot about it as she spotted an old, worn book. Taking it out, she read the title written in CEL: New Jasvarian Cooking.

In the next second, Ryven's heat was at her back and his voice low at her ear as he said, "I can't read the title. But I'd like to think it's a book full of secrets."

She rolled her eyes and looked over her shoulder. "In a way, it is. You need to work on your CEL."

His voice filled her mind. *When you master your telepathy, then you can teach me the language.*

Teachers often make the worst students, so I'll have to be quite strict.

His telepathic voice was husky. *I look forward to it.*

Aware that she could be broadcasting, Kalahn quickly pushed aside the image of him giving orders to her when they were naked and in bed.

Whether he heard or not, Kalahn had no idea. But his voice was more distant as he spoke aloud. "For the present, however, I'll gladly listen to your instructions for dinner."

She turned around to face him. "Good. Then finish preparing the meat."

Making a fist with his fingers, Ryven pounded it over his heart. "As you wish."

As he turned and went back to his task, she couldn't help but smile at his obsequiousness. Kalahn had never imagined she'd want to cook anything, but it seemed doing any task with Ryven was more fun than when she'd done the same before in the past.

Of course, she wanted more than just fun. All the man had to do was stand behind her and her heart rate kicked up.

In that moment, Kalahn made a decision. She didn't know how long she'd be staying in the remote location with Ryven, but she was going to make the most of it. Yes, she'd work hard on her training and do her best to excel so she could help her family. However, she also planned to kiss Ryven many more times, too. Because it was all too easy to envision cooking with him fifty years in the future, when they both had laugh lines around their mouths and at the corner of their eyes.

Life with Ryven would never be dull, nor did she think he'd try to change her into a different kind of female. Since her eldest brother, Keltor, had married a merchant female, why couldn't she marry a warrior?

Kalahn had lived her life pushing boundaries, and she was about to test one more.

Chapter Eleven

Ryven was in trouble. The more time he spent near Kalahn's mental presence, the harder he found to stay away. Hell, when Kalahn had bent over to look inside a cupboard, he'd unintentionally reached out to her mind. Thankfully he'd realized it before she could sense it. Or, so he hoped.

And yet, it took every iota of strength he possessed not to reach out again to feel her warmth.

What was known about telepathy on Keldera was mostly related to those spliced with the ability. There were a few natural born telepaths in the Jasvarian settlement, thanks to the humans bringing aliens into their society. Ryven would need to track one down and fill in his knowledge. No trainee he'd talked to or record he'd read had mentioned something similar to his current craving for Kalahn on the telepathy plane.

Since he couldn't attempt to find a natural born telepath for some time, he focused on watching Kalahn attempt to chop vegetables. Some might think her simple, yellow linen dress would lessen her beauty compared to her elaborate princess gowns, but Ryven thought the yellow made her blue hair stand out more. Not to mention it softened her face.

She was beautiful.

Kalahn looked up at him and raised her brows. He kept still, waiting to see if she'd heard him.

"If you've finished your task, you could help me, you know."

The corner of his mouth ticked up. "Maybe if you said please."

Sighing, she replied with an overly sweet voice. "Would you please assist this helpless female, who can't seem to manage without a male explaining everything?"

He snorted. "Stop it. That sort of request doesn't suit you."

When he moved to her side, Kalahn looked up at him. "Why are you so accepting of my behavior? I've always wondered about that, especially since everyone else has tried to change or correct me from the moment I could talk."

He shrugged. "I spent many years living inside a Barren citadel. Things are done differently amongst them when no one is watching. The vast majority of the residents are female, and the citadels don't run themselves. The Barren Mother is almost the equivalent of a politician or even a king. To me, it seems natural that females can do more than what the current law allows."

He reached for a knife, but Kalahn stilled his hand. "Do you think if others were given a chance to visit the citadels or even stay for a week or more, opinions would change?"

"I'm not sure, both concerning the Barren and the citizens. The Barren have peace when the outsiders aren't around, and to subject them to strangers constantly being underfoot would be unfair. At least until they have more freedoms everywhere."

Kalahn sighed. "It was just an idea."

"And change starts from ideas, so don't stop proposing them. Besides, given what I've heard of Azalyn Sulani, she will try to change things as well. After all, she worked in the merchant business, which is the most open-minded when it comes to what females can do and/or accomplish."

At the mention of Azalyn, Kalahn plucked at her dress. "I wish I could know my soon-to-be sister-in-law better. I heard stories of Keltor falling for and losing his love as a teen, so I'm glad he found Azalyn again. I think she and I would get along well. But as selfish as it is, I think my place is on Jasvar."

Placing a finger under her chin, he gently forced her to meet his gaze. "It's not selfish to want to stay somewhere you feel useful. I, for one, am grateful you're here." He leaned down a fraction. "And not just because you seem to have an affinity for telepathy."

As they stared at one another, Kalahn's voice filled his mind. *I want to kiss him, but I'm not sure if he wants me to.*

Ryven stood at a fork in the road. He could be noble, pretend he didn't hear her thoughts, and stick to his vow to train Kalahn before he pursued her.

But as he stared into her green eyes, with her heat and scent so close, he wanted the less noble path. For the first time in years, he was going to shirk his duty to do something he wanted.

He leaned down a fraction closer and whispered, "I want you too, Kalahn."

Her eyes widened. "W-what are you talking about?"

Lightly stroking the underside of her chin, he smiled. "You've been projecting again."

"That's impossible. My shields are strong."

"Then maybe you wanted me to hear you."

He waited to see how she'd respond.

Kalahn finally placed a hand on his chest, and he sucked in a breath at her touch. Physical strength meant nothing when it came to this female. A simple caress could probably fell him to his knees.

Her voice was low when she finally spoke again. "What I want usually doesn't matter."

"In this moment, it means everything. Take what you want, Kalahn. I promise I won't tell anyone."

Raising her face, her hot breath danced against his lips as she whispered, "You may regret those words."

"With you, I will regret nothing."

With a growl, Kalahn closed the distance between them and kissed him.

Ryven immediately opened his mouth and allowed Kalahn's tongue to tangle with his. Each caress and lick only made him groan harder at her taste. It was sweeter and more addictive than he remembered.

He hauled her body against his, loving the feel of her soft curves against his hard muscles. Everything about her, from the swell of her hip to the lushness of her breasts, made him want to toss her on a bed, rip off her dress, and worship her body.

As if reading his thoughts, Kalahn growled and dug her nails into his shoulders before she bit his bottom lip.

His princess was a little rough. And he liked it.

Her voice filled his mind. *More, Ryven. Show me more.*

Each syllable sent heat through his body, straight to his cock. When she added, *I-I don't know what I want, but I want something*, his lust intensified tenfold and his control snapped.

Ryven lifted her hips and turned to sit her on the counter. Kalahn opened her legs to allow him to stand between them. He rubbed her luscious thighs and wished he could feel her skin instead of the material of her dress.

I want that, too.

Since Ryven hadn't spoken, he must've projected. But he was too far gone to care.

Running a hand up under her skirt, he took a possessive hold of her calf and tugged her closer to him. Her skirt was in the way of what he truly wanted, to feel her hot center against his trouser-clad cock.

Maybe Kalahn would allow him to rip it in two.

A male voice boomed inside the room. "You might want to lock the door next time."

Ryven immediately broke the kiss and stood in front of Kalahn, to shield her from view. "Orvar, what are you doing here?"

The male didn't move from his place leaning against the doorjamb. "There's something you should see."

"Can't it wait?"

Orvar shook his head. "No. Otherwise, I would not have set foot inside this volcano." He stood upright. "I'll give you a few minutes to right yourself, but no longer. This is important."

The male disappeared down the hallway, leaving Ryven alone with Kalahn once again.

The realization of what he'd nearly done washed over him. He'd nearly tried to take a female that wasn't his bride, and with her sitting on a kitchen counter no less.

Maybe he was still that dishonorable youth who'd stolen and lied on the streets.

"You're not," Kalahn stated.

With a frown, he turned to face her. "What did you say?"

"You're projecting again." She scooted to the side, closed her legs, and righted her skirts. "And if you regret what just happened, then maybe it's a good thing Orvar interrupted us."

"Kalahn—"

She put up a hand. "Just go and cool off. We'll talk when you get back."

Ryven leaned forward and touched her cheek. "I don't regret it for the reasons you think."

"Later, Ryven," she murmured.

He wasn't sure if Kalahn was hurt or confused, not that he cared for either option. But he would give her time to cool off and then discuss their future at length.

There was one last thing he needed to do before he left, though. "Let me check your shields, just in case."

Before she could speak, Ryven looked inward. However, Kalahn was inside his mental space. *Have you been here the whole time?*

Of course I have. This is my area.

No, it's mine.

What are you talking about, Ryven?

He took a second to scan around and something seemed off with the dimensions. *I'll be right back.*

Exiting the small passageway through the mouth of the feline, Ryven searched for Kalahn's signature. She shouldn't be far from him.

But once his eyes found her signature, he was speechless.

What's wrong, Ryven?

After a few beats, he found his mental voice. *Come see for yourself.*

Kalahn's presence was soon next to him, and she finally saw what he did.

His signature of a feline and hers of the flower with thorns were melded together, with no space in between them. It appeared as one, oval-shaped signature.

Kalahn spoke again. *What does this mean?*

To be honest, I have no idea.

But whatever it was, it seemed Kalahn had been telling the truth earlier about being within her own mental area. Somehow their two places had become one.

And the hell if Ryven knew what that meant.

※ ※ ※

Kalahn had gone from the high of Ryven kissing and touching her in ways she'd only dreamed of, to him feeling guilty, and then eventually with her at his side, staring at his cat and her flower creating one oval-shaped signature.

Even being outside the shared space, she sensed his emotions of confusion mixed with fascination.

When they'd been kissing, she'd felt his every emotion as well, but had put it down to her own desire. After the fact, she started to wonder. *Can you tell what I'm feeling right now?*

He didn't hesitate to answer. *Yes. But I put it down to you projecting.*

I think it's more than that.

Retreating inside her—or, rather, their—shields, she used her voice. "I think, somehow, we're now telepathically connected."

He frowned. "There's nothing in the records about this happening with others, though. Maybe it's my fault, for coaxing out strong emotions before you had a firm grasp on your telepathic abilities."

She took his chin between her fingers and leaned forward. "My shields never cracked. Up until you stood between my thighs, I was constantly checking them to ensure I didn't broadcast my fantasies."

"Putting aside your fantasies for the moment, then it must've been something I did."

"Ryven, stop. Until we talk with a natural born, knowledgeable telepath, neither one of us will truly know what caused it."

He ran a hand through his short hair. "Kason will kill me for this."

Releasing his chin, she placed a hand on his chest. "Kason doesn't matter right now. What we need is to find a way to contact someone in the outside world and get answers from someone who understands what's going on."

He hesitated, and Kalahn did her best to hide her disappointment. However, Ryven's eyes widened and he said, "I'm not doubting your suggestion, Kalahn. But I must think things through." He switched to his telepathic voice. *I may have a way to reach someone at the settlement, but it's risky as unknown telepaths could be listening in. I'm skilled in secure transmissions, but there could always be someone better.*

When will you make a decision? The longer we wait, the greater the chance this might be permanent.

Ryven paused before saying, *I'll figure it out soon.*

A pounding on the front door made her jump. Orvar bellowed. "I didn't make the request lightly. If you wait much longer, it will be too late."

An idea struck Kalahn. *Go with Orvar and ask him to deliver a message to Syzel. He can then seek out a telepath inside the Jasvarian colony. I'm sure Taryn will know who to trust.*

Ryven grunted his approval. *And it will help to hide our tracks, as the request and inquiry will appear to be Syzel's.*

Exactly.

Pride at her suggestion emanated off Ryven, and she shifted her position on the counter. "It seems we're going to be sharing a lot with each other for at least the next little while."

"I'm sure we can reverse it. And you can still try to build your own wall within the space. That might lessen the intensity of the other's feelings. Because the best I can tell, you feel my emotions but don't hear all my thoughts, correct?"

She bobbed her head. "Words only come through sometimes."

"That's probably because I always keep up a set of inner shields, just in case. At least try to construct your own while I see what Orvar wants." At another pounding, Ryven sighed. "I'll be back as soon as I can." He leaned forward and gave her a gentle kiss. "Regardless of what happened, I don't regret kissing you, Kalahn. Remember that."

With a wink, Ryven left Kalahn alone in the kitchen. And although she knew he was out of sight, she still sensed his presence nearby.

While she wanted to know Ryven better, Kalahn wasn't quite ready to have him understand every emotion that flitted through her mind. It was almost more embarrassing than if out of the blue she dropped her dress and stood naked in front of him in full daylight.

Her best bet was to try and construct her own shield around herself and see if it worked.

She only had the few experiences and the information she'd read, but she would try her hardest. Because if she couldn't learn how to do this, she wouldn't be able to eventually help her family.

And so Kalahn closed her eyes and tried her best to construct a new type of shielding.

Chapter Twelve

Ryven was still trying to process the strange situation he'd found himself in with Kalahn when he exited their home and came face-to-face with Orvar.

The male eyed him a second before speaking. "I don't care what you do with the female, but I'm only here as a favor to Taryn. So if you take too long to heed my request next time, I may just leave."

Ryven took a closer look at Orvar. He'd had yet to see any lightness or joy in the male's eyes. And while Orvar had always been casual, relaxed, or even indifferent in the past, the male currently kept shifting his feet and glancing over at what was the bathing area.

If not for the monumental problem he had with his and Kalahn's mental signatures melding together, he might ask the male for more details. However, those would have to wait. All Ryven cared about for the moment was getting back to Kalahn's side. "You said this was time sensitive. So, let's get a move on."

With a grunt, Orvar turned and made a beeline for the exit. Ryven followed, attempting to reinforce the outer shields over him and Kalahn at the same time. He sensed her confusion, but held back on contacting her.

Ryven had never had a problem balancing a current task with a brief mental exchange in the past, but his and Kalahn's situation was much more complex. He wouldn't risk going into a telepathic trance and losing focus on his physical self, which he suspected could easily happen what with he and Kalahn being connected for the present.

Right before they exited the main entrance—the one covered by bushes—Orvar put up an arm. "What I'm about to show you is one of the deadliest predators on Jasvar. There's a rare flock of them not far from here."

"A flock? As in birds?"

"Yes, you'll see. I need you to be quiet and not step into any streams of sunshine. Their eyes are hypersensitive to changes in light levels, and one misstep could spell your death."

Ryven was tempted to raise an eyebrow at the possible hyperbole, but managed to keep himself in check. After all, Jasvar was a new planet to him. Maybe there were actual death birds waiting nearby. "I'll follow your lead. But what should I do if they attack?"

"Play dead. It doesn't always work, but unless you have a crew of hunters firing arrows and throwing spears at the same time, there's not much else you can do. But the predators do prefer to eat their prey alive, and usually walk away once their prey is dead."

Sadistic death birds might be a better title. "So why are we seeking out these predators in the first place? I imagine a picture and information on signs to watch for would be sufficient."

Orvar met his gaze. "A picture won't convey the noise or the smell they project. Both are important to memorize, because if you hear or scent them, you need to flee as soon as possible. They don't appear often, which is why we need to hurry."

The Forbidden

Under normal circumstances, Ryven would probably be fascinated with learning about a Jasvarian predator. However, he wanted to test the limits of his new situation with Kalahn and focus on fixing that problem instead.

Motioning with a hand to follow him, Orvar treaded lightly, careful to make as little sound as possible. It wasn't long before they were deep inside the tree cover. Ryven started to note a few cawing sounds in the distance. Unlike with regular birds, they were in a deep cadence. The louder it became, the more he wanted to follow it.

Yes, he should find what animal made it. No animal with such an addictive melody could be harmful.

Orvar put up a hand and whispered, "As you can tell now, their song attracts people to the source. You must resist it."

He blinked, the spell broken. "Why didn't you warn me before?"

"Because sometimes you need to experience something to truly make a warning stick. And I would've ensured you didn't get too close, either."

The brief conversation had brought back his wits, and Ryven committed the cawing to memory. If he ever heard it, he would plug his ears and turn around as soon as possible in the future.

Orvar motioned them onward again. This time Ryven was careful to notice any sounds or smells, and to analyze them rather than simply ignore them as part of nature. Although given how everything smelled different from his home on Keldera, it was borderline overwhelming to keep track of it all.

When the cawing was almost unbearable to his ears, a sweet scent bombarded his senses. Tapping Orvar's shoulder, he garnered the male's attention. Ryven touched his nose and raised his eyebrows. Orvar nodded.

So the flock of doom awaiting them both hypnotized with sound and tempted with scent.

Orvar halted them about ten feet from the edge of the tree line, to a spot hidden mostly by bushes and undergrowth. It was then Ryven saw them.

The iridescent feathers of the people-sized birds glinted in the sunshine, reflecting every color. If Orvar hadn't warned him of the danger, he would've thought the birds beautiful and harmless. After all, they merely stood on the ground, occasionally pecking at the dirt. Each time they did, the longer feathers on top of their heads flopped around as if it were hair.

The blue beaks and legs were the final touch to the beautiful predators.

The wind blew and Ryven was accosted with a sweet scent. At the same time, the birds began to sing in unison, almost as if they knew the wind would start to bring in their prey.

One pig-like beast tottered from the woods and into the bright sunshine. In a matter of seconds, the flock of eight birds surrounded it, pecked furiously as the beast tried to run away, and then retreated.

When they cleared, all that was left of the creature was bone.

Ryven had faced many dangers over the course of his life, but never an animal that could clean a carcass so quickly.

Orvar met his gaze and raised his brows. Ryven nodded—he'd seen enough and understood the dangers.

The male turned back and Ryven began to follow. However, after a few steps, large branches tumbled down from above and crashed into the ground. He'd barely jumped out of the way before Ryven realized he was no longer hidden by the undergrowth.

On top of that, the midmorning sunlight bathed him from head to toe.

The birds were on him in an instant. As sharp beaks torn his flesh, his every instinct was to scream and flee.

But somehow, he ignored the intense pain, gritted his teeth, and did his best to flop to the ground and play dead.

He swore some of the birds backed away and stopped ripping off his skin.

However, the world went dark before he could be sure.

✷ ✷ ✷

Kalahn barely finished her attempt at constructing an inner wall around her half of the mental area when pain, such intense agony, crashed over her.

She instantly crouched to the ground and screamed.

Almost as quickly as it came, the hurting ceased. Catching her breath, she dismantled her new wall and reached out to Ryven. *Ryven? Are you okay?*

Silence.

Please answer me.

Again, no response. She moved closer to his flickering presence in their shared space. If he were dead, she surely wouldn't be able to sense him. Right?

While she had a feeling it went against every rule of conduct for telepaths, she brushed against Ryven's presence.

Within seconds, a lifetime of memories rolled over her. To the point that Kalahn couldn't keep up. All she could do was lay there and experience them.

Ones of Ryven with his parents, laughing in the garden.

Another of him holding a motionless small girl in a dirty building as he cried.

Kason inviting him to the palace for the first time and Ryven feeling out of place.

His first kiss with Kalahn, and the guilt of his fantasies.

Kalahn brushing his mind for the first time.

A flock of giant birds descending on him as they tore at his flesh.

When the nothingness finally came, Kalahn opened her eyes and tried to catch her breath. She didn't remember laying on the ground, but she was content to remain that way as she tried to regain her own mind.

Because instead of just her memories, she now had Ryven's. That also meant his knowledge, too.

Timelines then warred with each other, each side wanting to take center stage as her own personal timeline.

As minutes ticked by, Kalahn curled onto her side and put her hands to her head. If she didn't learn how to control and manage her own thoughts, she would lose herself. While she cared for Ryven, she didn't want his memories to erase her own.

Gathering her mental muscle, Kalahn created an imaginary vault and slowly separated Ryven's memories from her own. She had no idea how long she sorted through them, but she was only partially done when a guard's voice broke through. "Princess, are you all right?"

With what remained of her waning willpower, she closed the mental vault and waited. When it looked to hold, she blinked her eyes open. It took a second to make her voice work. "Ryven's in danger. Help him."

The guard's brows came together. "How do you know that?"

"Just trust me. Find him."

"Not until I know you're well."

She put out a hand and he helped her sit up. Her head pounded, but she did her best to keep her markings a neutral color and emotion free from her face. "I'm well enough. Just please check on Ryven and Orvar."

"As you wish, your highness. But I will go alone. However, the other guard will stay and monitor the entrance. Shout if you need anything."

The guard saluted and left Kalahn alone once more.

Raising her knees, she laid her arms and head on them. She closed her eyes and returned to her and Ryven's shared mental space. While Ryven's presence was weaker, he was still there. *Ryven, someone is coming to help you. Please, hold on.*

There was no reply.

If his final memory with the birds was true, then Ryven was severely injured and he would need medical help.

Kalahn had only minimal first aid training.

But then an idea struck. No matter if she wanted them or not, she had Ryven's memories as well. It was worth sorting through them to see if she could find anything to help him.

Slowly, she opened and stepped inside her mental vault. Images came in quick succession, of not only first-aid training but field medic training. Ryven wasn't a doctor, but a video-like sequence played out of him staunching bleeding, sewing up a deep cut by hand, and a variety of other tasks using the Kelderan laser instruments.

When the pictures stopped, she took a deep breath, moved out of the vault again, and tried to process what she'd just seen. It was surreal to see things from someone else's point of view.

But while helpful, Kalahn had no idea of the extent of Ryven's injuries, and field medic training might not be enough. She might have to reach out to Syzel for help.

Even though she'd never tried to contact someone so far away, she now had the information via Ryven. However, she wouldn't risk the connection unless she had to. Kalahn had already used up an enormous amount of energy separating memories. Given what she'd read earlier, a telepath could overexert themselves to the point they burned out.

And sometimes that meant the telepath would be turned into a motionless vegetable.

No. She wouldn't allow that to happen. Ryven needed her.

Finally standing up, it took a few seconds to keep her balance. Once she had it, Kalahn quickly assembled as many items as she could find to help with first aid and triage. She was just about to race out and check the other buildings in the area when Orvar's voice echoed inside the extinct volcano's walls. "Princess Kalahn!"

Racing out of the house, she missed a step when she saw Ryven's body propped between Orvar and the guard's.

He was covered in makeshift bandages, most of them seeped with blood. His head lolled around, as if he were dead.

Orvar grunted. "He's alive. But I need medical supplies. Go get them."

At Orvar's order, she snapped back to the present. "I have as many as I could find in the kitchen. Come on."

The Kelderan male didn't blink twice at her statement. Either her brother Kason or Ryven must've shared her tendency to defy Kelderan female norms.

Still, she didn't have time to think much on it as she raced into the house and helped Orvar and the guard get Ryven onto one of the counters in the kitchen.

The next hour was a blur as Orvar barked orders and Kalahn fetched supplies. As often as she could, Kalahn murmured encouragement to Ryven via telepathy. He never responded, but she had to believe it helped.

By the time Orvar finally stepped back and surveyed his work, he, Kalahn, and the guard were covered in Ryven's blood.

The Forbidden

Orvar placed two fingers at Ryven's pulse. "It's slow, but steady. The next few hours will be the most dangerous." He met Kalahn's gaze. "I don't wish to leave you, but there are some medicinal herbs I need to find as soon as possible. Otherwise, infection and fever will set in."

As the adrenaline left her body, Kalahn struggled to stand upright, so she leaned against a counter and motioned a hand toward the door. "Go, Orvar. The guards and I can watch over him in shifts. When you get back, you can tell me everything that happened. Just one last thing before you leave—will reaching out to Kason and Taryn help at all?"

Orvar nodded. "Since the colony transport ship is still in orbit, the Kelderan medical supplies and devices could greatly speed up the healing process. However, I need to stabilize him first and then I'll race to the settlement."

"You get the herbs and I'll send the message," she stated.

Confusion flashed in Orvar's gaze, but it faded quickly. "Do as you wish. However, if you haven't been successful by the time I get back, I'm going to the settlement."

She'd barely bobbed her head before Orvar was gone.

Kalahn avoided looking at Ryven's face for a few more minutes, lest she cry in front of the guard.

Instead, she focused her attention on the male warrior. "I'll take the first shift. Come back in two hours and we'll switch."

The guard made a fist and pounded it over his heart before he left.

Once she was alone with Ryven, Kalahn took a deep breath and another before she looked at his face.

His normally golden skin was a sallow yellow, marred by numerous lacerations and bruises. The stitches on his cheeks, forehead, and chin would most likely leave scars if Kelderan technology wasn't used soon.

Fresh bandages covered most of his arms and legs,

concealing the gashes and cuts she vaguely remembered during the haze of fixing him up.

But it was the gentle rise and fall of his chest that she latched onto the most. Because as long as she saw that, Ryven was alive.

With the other two males gone, Kalahn pulled up a chair next to Ryven and took hold of one of his unharmed fingers. She didn't like the overly warm temperature of his skin.

Even now, infection could already be setting in.

All she knew about the attack was that huge birds had caused it. No doubt their beaks carried all sorts of bacteria.

Since there was nothing she could do for his physical body, she closed her eyes and looked inward. Ryven's warm, masculine presence remained at one side of the mental space. She came close but didn't brush against it. She'd already inadvertently stolen his memories. She didn't know what touching him unprotected again would do.

Still, she danced around him, letting him know she was near. *Pull through, Ryven. Don't you dare die on me.*

He didn't reply, not that she'd expected him to.

I know you wanted to talk about us earlier, but you've gone to extremes to put off the discussion.

Kalahn continued to chat with him, not caring that it was a one-sided conversation. She wanted to believe he heard her, and that her mental touches might convince him to hold onto life.

No, she needed to purge any doubts of him making it because Ryven might be able to sense her emotions, even while unconscious. Ryven *would* live. If that meant she had to stretch her telepathic muscles and reach out to Syzel, even if she didn't know what would happen if she burned out trying, so be it. For too many years she'd kept her distance from Ryven, citing every possible excuse. But no more.

The Forbidden

She wanted him as her own, and to do that, she needed to get to know him better. His memories were only part of who he was—she wanted more of the teasing, life experiences, and his kisses. In order to do that, it required him staying alive.

Chapter Thirteen

Almost an hour later, Kalahn struggled to keep her eyes open. Her stubbornness would only go so far in keeping her awake. If Orvar didn't return soon, she'd have to allow the guard to take her place.

And for some reason, she didn't want to. It was almost as if she knew that if she left the room, Ryven would die. The only time she'd even moved from his side was to change into the clean dress one of the guards had brought her.

Kalahn lightly slapped her cheeks. It was time to try reaching out to Syzel again before she fell asleep. She'd attempted to find him earlier, but hadn't made it far in the telepathic plane before losing her bearings. This time she had to reach him, end of story. Even if Orvar returned and raced to the settlement, it could end up being too late.

Closing her eyes, she first checked to ensure Ryven's warmth was still in their shared mental space, which it was. With that comfort, she moved to her hidden exit and out to the vast darkness.

From Ryven's memories, Kalahn knew that Syzel's signature was a starship fighter constantly changing in shape and color. She guessed it had to do with Syzel's career in the army as a strategist, but didn't think too much more on it. All that mattered was finding the blasted thing.

The Forbidden

She pushed on and on to the east, which was the direction of the settlement according to Ryven's thoughts, and saw nothing but blackness. One of the few good things about there not being many telepaths was that she didn't have to wade through signatures for hours, days, or even weeks to hopefully find the one she needed.

Each minute she reached further, the more effort it took to push forward. If not for Ryven's life hanging in the balance, she probably would've retreated to rest.

She had no idea how long she pushed on eastward when a faint light appeared in the distance. It didn't take long to reach it, but disappointment flooded her body at the giant stone fortress surrounded by a ring of rainbow color. Unlike any other signature she'd seen before, the colors surrounding it were strong and pulsating, which fascinated her.

But since she didn't want to be detected by the person behind the odd signature, Kalahn raced past. Any other telepath on Jasvar should be in or near the settlement, so she had to be close.

The second signature she spotted was incorrect, too—a mythical winged animal with four legs and a spotted hide running on the clouds. Kalahn swore she felt a feminine presence, but ignored it. She had to help Ryven.

Several minutes later, another one appeared in the distance. Kalahn released the breath she didn't realize she'd been holding when she saw Syzel's starship signature.

Her reading material had mentioned that approaching another telepath's signature too quickly could signal a threat. Since she didn't want to be on the receiving end of some sort of mental attack, Kalahn forced herself to move slowly and ignored the need to rush. Becoming incapacitated wouldn't help Ryven at all. It may even sign his death warrant.

Studying Syzel's signature, she scanned for the best place to mentally knock. However, she'd barely begun when a male presence approached her. *Princess Kalahn? What are you doing here?*

It was Syzel. *Can I speak freely here?*

Not yet. Wait a second. Syzel constructed something around them, no doubt a special kind of shield. Once done, he continued, *Now, what's wrong?*

It's easier to show you.

Kalahn steeled herself as she replayed Ryven's attack. When she finished, Syzel spoke again. *Please tell me he's alive.*

For now. But while Orvar did his best to patch him up, he needs Kelderan medical technology to help him. Please send someone with medical training.

I will. We'll also be moving locations, just as soon as Ryven is stable. Expect more guards. This will be the lead. Syzel flashed an image of a Kelderan male with magenta skin and silver hair. *And one last thing, you need to retreat to your space as soon as possible. While you've done a fantastic job for such a new telepath, you're flickering, and you don't want to be caught in the telepathic plane while unconscious and defenseless.*

I have no wish to delay. Ryven needs me.

If Syzel thought it odd that Kalahn spoke of the warrior in such a tender way, he didn't show it. *I'll contact your brother straightaway. Help should arrive within an hour. Until then.*

If help were coming that quickly, then most likely someone would fly a shuttle down from the colony ship.

Syzel lowered the shields and retreated. Kalahn put her remaining energy into backtracking her steps. She barely paid attention to anything but the almost beacon-like signal emanating from her own signature. She'd only just returned inside and patched up the entrance when she heard footsteps.

Despite her eyelids seeming to weight a hundred pounds each, Kalahn opened them to find Orvar at Ryven's other side.

Without a word, he took out some plants and a small mortar and pestle. As he began grinding them, Orvar barked, "I need hot water."

Ryven's makeshift bed was still the counter in the kitchen. Even though every cell in her body screamed in protest, Kalahn stood and raced to the nearby stove. After placing the kettle and stoking the wood to flare the flames, she turned back toward Orvar. "Anything else?"

The male never looked from his task. "Only that you should know that what happened to Ryven wasn't an accident."

Some of her fatigue faded as her curiosity took over. "What are you talking about?"

Orvar never looked up from his task. "The branches that fell and caused Ryven to jump into harm's way were cut with a laser knife."

She wanted to ask if someone knew Ryven was her telepathic trainer, but Kalahn didn't know how much Orvar knew of her situation.

Orvar finished grinding the herbs and motioned toward the steaming kettle. "Fetch me some water." As she did so and handed him a cup, Orvar added, "I know why Ryven is here, Princess. And somehow, some way, another person has figured out that Ryven is your trainer." He met her gaze. "Although if they know it's for telepathy or not, I have no idea."

"So Ryven's condition is my fault."

Mixing the pounded herbs into the steaming water, Orvar shook his head. "No. If anything, it's mine. I should've noticed the person trailing us."

"Excuse me for asking, but just how good are you at that? I have no idea."

He met her gaze again. "I'm one of the best. Only an empath and telepath have bested me on Jasvar in the past, and I suspect only because of their extra senses."

Pushing aside her curiosity at another telepath, Kalahn focused on the issue at hand. "Then I suspect the person following you had a leg up, probably thanks to Kelderan technology. The Jasvarians use axes and saws to cut trees."

"The cut was too smooth to be either of those. Regardless, I'm more curious as to why the army didn't do a better job of screening individuals and checking for illegal technology. But I worked with them enough in the past before coming to Jasvar to know the answer to that—corruption is more prevalent than the Kelderan Army will ever admit." Orvar held the cup out to Kalahn. "I'm going to raise his head and you need to make him drink this brew."

She took the proffered medicine without a word. Once Orvar had Ryven's head up, she looked inward and said, *Drink this, Ryven. It's going to help you.*

Silence was the only reply.

Undeterred, she drew on Ryven's medic training to put the cup to his lips, put a small amount into his mouth, and closed it. She waited to see if she'd need to take further steps to entice him to swallow, but his throat moved, telling her he'd drunk it.

Kalahn repeated the steps until the cup was empty and Orvar took it from her. He asked, "Did you contact the settlement?"

As Kalahn's head began to spin, she sat down. "Yes. Syzel is sending someone and they should be here in less than an hour."

"Then take a rest, Princess. I'll watch over Ryven while you sleep." She opened her mouth to protest, but he cut her off. "Don't argue. You can't help Ryven if you're exhausted."

She looked over at a stack of unused blankets. Orvar gathered them up and made a makeshift bed on the floor, not far from the counter where Ryven lay. "Sleep."

She didn't possess the energy to protest when Orvar helped her down to the pile of blankets. She managed to say, *I'll be back, soon* to Ryven before sleep claimed her.

※ ※ ※

An unfamiliar presence knocked on Kalahn's mental shields. She immediately woke up and fortified the inner walls she'd constructed around her and Ryven.

A male voice in accented CEL filled her ears. "I know you're awake, so open your eyes."

Her eyelids popped open and Kalahn tried to scoot away from the unfamiliar male with light green skin and yellow hair that stood a few feet away from her. However, she then noticed Syzel stood right behind the older male. If he were here, the green-skinned man couldn't be an enemy.

Syzel motioned toward the male in front of him. "Borzet can be trusted, Princess Kalahn. Don't be afraid of him."

Despite the cobwebs of exhaustion filling her brain, she said, "Forgive me if I'm being careful after what happened with Ryven."

At his name, she scrambled to her feet and searched for him. But Ryven still lay motionless on the counter except for his breathing. The only change was that an older human female and a Kelderan male, both of whom she didn't know beyond their faces being somewhat familiar, stood to either side of him.

Syzel moved to her side. "Jynkor and Matilda are doing everything they can to heal Ryven. While Kelderan technology will help a great deal, Matilda is the head medicine woman of Jasvar. Taryn insisted she come, too, in case there was a plant or herb that could help him."

Kalahn never took her gaze from Ryven's face. "Will he be all right?"

"It seems so when it comes to his body, although he has a lot of physical therapy in his future," Syzel said.

"What do you mean when it comes to his body?"

The unfamiliar male with light green skin named Borzet chimed in. "I sense Ryven's mind is raw and scattered. If we can't heal his mind with yours, and he remains a fractured individual for too long, he will change in ways we can't predict."

Kalahn nearly asked how he knew her and Ryven's minds were connected, but held back. She didn't know him well enough to possibly confirm one of his suspicions. Instead, she studied Borzet. "Who are you to speak on such authority regarding his mental state?"

Syzel motioned toward the male. "As I mentioned, this is Borzet. He's Matilda's lord and a natural-born telepath. Hirlanzian, to be exact."

Something sparked in her brain. "I've heard of that race before."

"Yes, but we'll talk about that later."

At Syzel's dismissive tone, she finally remembered that the female assassin was part Hirlanzian.

Which meant that Syzel didn't want to discuss the female in front of the new additions to Kalahn's household.

To better know who she was dealing with, Kalahn took a tentative peek outside her mental area and saw a familiar signature—a fortress with rainbow colors glowing from it.

Borzet spoke telepathically. *Yes, I sensed you nearby earlier. Since you are a made telepath and not a natural-born one, your power and level of control called to me.*

I-I don't know what you're talking about.

You will, in time. Borzet switched to speaking aloud. "Is he stable, Mattie?"

The human female looked up. "Nearly so. Give us a few more minutes. Then you can have him."

Kalahn interjected, "Wait, what are you going to do with him?"

Borzet answered, "More like what are *we* going to do. In order to save Ryven, I need your help, Princess."

She frowned. "I'm not sure how much help I can be with him. Nothing I've done so far has garnered a response, and it's definitely not from a lack of trying."

The alien male shook his head. "You underestimate your importance. You two have telepathically bonded. More than anyone, you have the power to save him."

"Telepathically bonded?" she echoed.

Borzet nodded. "Among the Hirlanzians, when two people are compatibly suited on every level, they automatically bond with their minds."

"But I'm Kelderan, not Hirlanzian."

He shrugged. "My guess is that between the Kelderans mimicking Hirlanzian DNA to give you the ability, as well as your own genetics, it was enough to initiate the bond. And before you ask, the other partner doesn't have to be Hirlanzian. While my Mattie isn't a telepath, she is bonded to me. While it means I can't connect and speak with her, I can always sense her emotions."

Kalahn tried to take it all in, but her mind kept going back to one thing Borzet said. "What do you mean my own genetics play a role?"

"I suspect somewhere far up in your family tree that there was at least a part-Hirlanzian ancestor."

Kalahn had never dug too deeply into her ancestry as it'd never interested her. But now she wondered exactly how she had alien blood, no matter how minute, running through her veins. Maybe her father would know. She'd have to find a way to ask him while she still had the chance.

The bigger issue was that Borzet knew more about signatures melding, or bonding as he put it.

Kalahn had too many questions and didn't know where to start. However, before she could voice any of them, Syzel jumped in. "Let's not overwhelm the princess with too much information." He moved his gaze to Kalahn. "Once Ryven is stabilized, all of us are going up to the colony transport ship. We'll stay there until Ryven is awake and mostly recovered. You'll also be learning as much as possible from Borzet at the same time."

Kalahn didn't hold back. "No offense, but isn't including more people in your circle of trust increase the chance of exposure? Someone already made an attempt on Ryven's life. I suspect it won't be long until they try to take mine, too."

Borzet spoke up. "If you're referring to your telepathy and training, the ship has technology to protect all of us from prying eyes down here on the surface. And honestly, if we don't get you up to the protective folds of the ship as soon as possible, every telepath on Jasvar will know about you. After all, if I could sense you merely passing by, others will feel your power soon enough."

"You keep talking about my power, but I haven't done that much."

Borzet raised his brows. "You've done more in the short time you've had the ability than most Hirlanzians accomplish in two or three years of training."

THE FORBIDDEN

She tried her best to hide her surprise. If she let Borzet's words stroke her ego, she might start taking things for granted. "Then I'll agree to the training provided it doesn't interfere with me helping with Ryven's recovery and that you teach me everything I need to know to help protect my family from future attacks."

Smiling, Borzet replied, "That's a tall order."

She raised her chin. "Now that I finally have something worthwhile to contribute, I want to hone it and help the best way I can."

"And I respect you for it." Borzet put out a hand. "I agree to the terms."

Taking Borzet's hand, Kalahn shook it and released. She turned her gaze to Syzel. "So us going to the colony transport ship must mean that Kason is delaying the return trip to Keldera?"

"Yes," Syzel answered. "This is more important than going home. Ryven could recover in the settlement, if need be. But we need your power harnessed and controlled. Given Borzet's initial assessment, you may end up being the most powerful telepath on the planet."

And with that power came great responsibility. Too bad she hadn't understood that earlier.

Kalahn's eyes moved back to Ryven's face. Not only had being near her ended up harming him, he was now bound to her mind because of some unknown talent. Yes, she wanted to claim Ryven, but he should have a choice in the matter.

Borzet said telepathically, *Beyond putting him on another planet, it would've happened eventually. The fact it happened so quickly means he was open to the bond.*

Once you explain more about what a mind-bond does, let me be the one to explain it to him.

Of course. But you must do it soon after he wakes. Otherwise, he may attempt to sever the connection, and that will end badly.

How so?

If one or both parties succeed in severing their melded signatures, both will live the rest of their lives in a vegetative state.

So one way or another, she and Ryven would be together. It wasn't exactly the solution she'd wanted when thinking of how to break the news to her brothers, but at least they couldn't make him disappear like her father had done with Keltor's love over twenty years ago.

Chapter Fourteen

Ryven opened his eyes, immediately noting the composite walls, computer units, and whirring medical devices.

He was inside one of the medical bays onboard the colony transport ship.

At first, he thought he must be dreaming. The last thing he remembered was being pecked to death by birds bigger than him.

But then Kalahn's voice filled the space. "You're awake."

Her face came into his field of vision. He tried lifting his arm to touch her face, but he didn't get more than a hairbreadth off the bed before stabbing sensations shot up his arm.

He definitely couldn't be dreaming. The pain was too overwhelming.

Kalahn lay a hand on his forehead, her cool skin bringing him back to the moment. She murmured, "Don't try to move. Your body is still healing. Even with Kelderan technology, it's going to be a few more hours before you can do more than lie there."

Since his throat was dry, he tried to use his telepathy. But he couldn't find anything inside his mind.

Kalahn's soothing voice washed over him again. "To ensure you heal properly, Jynkor muted your telepathy temporarily."

After having it for so many years, the lack of his telepathic abilities felt as if someone had cut off a limb. "When will it come back?" Kalahn bit her bottom lip and looked away. Since he couldn't turn her head, he used his voice. "Don't hold back with me, Kalahn. Whatever it is, I can take it."

It took her a few more seconds before she met his gaze again. "The doctor said I shouldn't cause any undue stress."

He managed to raise his brows and ignored the ache that followed. "Me not knowing the truth is stressful. Tell me, Lahn."

He expected her to scold him at the ridiculous nickname, but she smiled. "If you can provoke me, you must be doing okay."

"I've been better. Although I'll admit I look forward to being able to move again."

Her smile faded, and her markings flashed white—the color of worry or indecision. "About that. There's something you should know, Ryven."

Dread twisted his stomach. "What?"

"You'll be able to move, but there was too much damage to your muscles. You won't recover a full range of motion in at least your arms. In other words, your days of training warriors in self-defense and combat are over."

Ryven had trained warriors for so many years that he expected disappointment to flood his body.

However, he was alive. That was more than he had expected the last time he was conscious.

Besides, he hated the sadness in Kalahn's eyes. "As long as you don't mind a stiff old man, then I'll be fine."

She blinked. "Just like that, you're okay?"

What he wouldn't give to touch her. "Kalahn, I've enjoyed my years as a warrior trainer. But helping you with your telepathy has shown me that I enjoy other forms of teaching, too. Will it eat at me that I might not be able to protect you without a weapon? Of course. But to fall into despair about it means I'll miss out on any and all future memories with you entirely."

Tears filled Kalahn's eyes and Ryven wished he could stroke her cheek. She murmured, "You say that now, but you've lost so much. And all because you volunteered to help me."

"Kalahn tro el Vallen, stop doubting me. I was nearly pecked to death by a group of murderous birds. And as they ate my flesh and I teetered on the edge of consciousness, all I could think about was how much of a fool I've been. There are a million reasons why we shouldn't be together, but I want you as my bride one day. I'm sure it'll take time to build up trust and convince you that it's what I truly want, but that's my plan from now on. Either of us could be gone tomorrow, and I don't want to regret it and constantly live with a cloud of what-ifs hanging over my head."

Kalahn burst into tears and Ryven struggled with what to do. Hadn't he said the right thing? If so, why was she crying? Had she changed her mind about him, now that he wouldn't be strong enough to defend her in all ways?

Drawing on what strength he possessed, Ryven barked, "Kalahn." It took a few seconds, but she stopped crying and wiped away her tears. He softened his voice. "Talk to me and tell me what's wrong."

She sniffled. "What you said is beautiful, but once I fill you in on everything that's happened since your attack, you may want to rescind your words."

He searched her gaze for a clue of what she was talking about, but didn't note anything. "Beating around the bush is your brother Keltor's style, not yours. Don't keep me in suspense. Sit next to me and tell me everything."

She hesitated, and Ryven half expected her to turn and put distance between them.

However, before he could think of how to convince her further, Kalahn sat next to him on the bed and took one of his hands. The slight twinge in his arm was worth it to have her soft, warm fingers around his.

Just having her near helped him to forget about his injuries, too.

Kalahn stared at their clasped hands as she talked. "When Orvar brought you and you were unconscious, I was frantic and wanted to try out anything that I thought might wake you up, or at least keep you alive. The thought of losing you was too much." She paused, took a deep breath, and continued, "One of the things I did was brush against your unguarded mental presence. And..." He managed to squeeze her fingers, and Kalahn met his gaze. "I saw all of your memories, Ryven. I couldn't stop it. They just flowed uncontrollably. I'm truly sorry. I never meant to pry like that. It just happened."

He resisted blinking. "All of them?"

She bobbed her head. "But I did my best to separate them and store them inside a mental vault. While they all flashed through my head, I don't remember most of them. And if I can help it, I won't access them unless it's an emergency."

Ryven stared at their hands. He'd wanted Kalahn to know him better, but everyone had a few secrets they wished to keep.

Kalahn now knew every good and bad thing about him.

Her soft voice filled his ears again. "If it matters, nothing I saw changed my opinion of you, Ryven. If nothing else, I think even more highly of you. I hope you'll forgive me."

Before the attack, he might've retreated and brooded for a while. Maybe even sparred a few times to think things through.

However, while Kalahn might've unintentionally found out more about him than he'd intended, it didn't change how her warmth soothed his pain. Or how her smile stole his breath.

And even in that moment, the urge to chase away the tears in her eyes hadn't left him.

Holding her accountable for something not even he had known would happen was pointless. "Since I had no idea that brushing against an unguarded mental presence would give someone all of that person's memories, I'm not sure I can be angry about it. You were just trying to help me in a dire situation. However, just promise me that you'll keep them locked away unless absolutely necessary and merely ask me what you wish to know."

She nodded. "Of course. But there's more. It's the reason I could access all your memories so easily in the first place."

He wanted to frown, but resisted. "I'm not sure I follow."

Taking a deep breath, she finally explained, "We're mentally bonded, Ryven. It's why our signatures melded together. According to Borzet, if we weren't bonded, your mind would've stayed shielded even while unconscious due to your years of training. Only because we shared a space was I able to brush against your unguarded self and access your memories."

"Back up. Who's Borzet? And what does mentally bonded mean? No book I've read on the subject has ever mentioned it."

"That's because it usually doesn't happen with made telepaths. Borzet is Hirlanzian. He's married and bonded to Matilda, a Jasvarian human."

"So he's a born telepath. Still, that doesn't explain our situation."

She lightly stroked the back of his hand. "Somewhere in my family tree there must've been a part-Hirlanzian ancestor. It takes two recessive genes to create a natural born telepath, and Kelderans don't possess that characteristic. So it never manifested in any of the royal family. But when I was given the DNA-splicing operation, it must've reacted with the recessive gene that I did possess, meaning I'm not going to act or react like every other made Kelderan telepath."

He opened his mouth and promptly shut it.

He'd expected a lot of things upon waking up, but not that he was mentally bound to Kalahn.

Not that he hadn't enjoyed her presence with him in the past. But he had no idea what it really entailed. He needed more information. "Explain the bond to me more."

She touched his cheek and he met her gaze again. As she stroked his skin, a sense of calmness came over him. It was as if she had magical powers.

For all he knew, maybe the mental bond was somewhat similar.

He was about to demand more information when Kalahn spoke up again. "The bad first—the bond is irreversible. Anyone who's attempted to sever the mind-bond on Hirlanzia ended up in a perpetual vegetative state, never to wake again."

"Okay, now explain the benefits."

She studied him a second before replying, "Well, we'll always be able to sense each other's emotions. At least we will once your telepathy is no longer muted. I suspect that will help with arguments."

He smiled. "I'm sure many a male wishes he could gauge his female's emotions on any given subject. Even if sometimes it may not be what they wish to know."

She frowned. "How are you able to tease and take this in so calmly?"

The Forbidden

What Ryven wouldn't give to be able to shrug. "Delaying the information won't change it. If I'm to make any plans for the future, I need to know all the facts."

"To find a way to break the bond, I understand."

He wished he could take her face between his hands. "No, you don't, Kalahn. Will it make our relationship unusual and maybe a bit more trying at times? Even not knowing all the facts, I suspect so. But it would take a hell of a lot more for me to give you up. I've never felt as much at ease as I have around you, not even with some of my best friends. And there is no female in the universe more beautiful and determined than you. I'm not giving up on us, love. So don't dare give up on us when you've fought your whole life for what you wanted."

It was a tad presumptuous for him to say as much. For all he knew, Kalahn didn't feel as strongly about him.

But given the few glimpses he'd had of her dreams and thoughts, she wanted him too. This would be the real test to see how much.

So Ryven held his breath and waited. He may have thought when he woke up that he had a second chance to make Kalahn his, as he should've done for years. But Kalahn had the power to take it all away. He wasn't above being stubborn, but he wouldn't force her into a life she didn't want. No one deserved that future.

❋ ❋ ❋

Kalahn was torn between bursting into tears and curling up against Ryven's side and never letting go.

She'd had a feeling that Ryven could be romantic, but it was more than that. He seemed so determined and certain they could be together.

To even love each other.

And he did it all while barely being able to stay awake, lying on a bed, and being unable to move most of his body.

He was stronger than she'd ever realized.

She'd cared for him before, but she was falling for him. It would be easy to love such a male.

No. She couldn't allow those sort of feelings to bloom. At least not until Ryven understood the true extent of what their bond entailed.

Taking a deep breath, she finally replied, "I'm not giving up on us. From the moment Orvar brought you back and during the hour it took to clean you and stitch you up, all I wished for was you to wake up and smile at me. I think even without the bond there's a connection between us. But I don't want to kindle it until you know all the facts. After all, your life will be in danger as long as you're connected to me and my family."

He never broke their gaze. "Danger will always exist, Kalahn. It doesn't matter whether it's related to the royal family or something else. No one can protect against everything."

"But our case is different from everyday dangers, Ryven. If either one of us dies, the other half could become a walking ghost, barely able to survive. The effect will only be exacerbated as feelings grow and mature."

He raised an eyebrow. "Since when do you play it safe?"

She growled. "This isn't just my life we're talking about here."

"Kalahn, if I could, I would sit up, pull you close, and kiss you to show how I feel. But since I can't, won't you believe me? I was already determined to brave your brothers' ire before I knew any of this. Nothing you say will change my mind."

At the mention of his mind, Kalahn quickly checked his mental presence. Part of the reason Ryven's telepathy had been drugged silent was that he was still too weak to repair the damage that had been done from her brushing against his unguarded self. Not to mention some of the drugs the doctors had used to heal him had also weakened his mental state. Apparently, certain things affected telepaths differently than non-telepaths.

Assured he was still stable for the moment, she asked, "I'm tempted to wait until you're fully recovered before I take your word." He opened his mouth, but she beat him to it. "But I'm going to be selfish and do this."

Leaning down, she kissed him gently. As his lips moved against hers, Kalahn wished she could take it further. Memories of his wildness back in the kitchen on Jasvar filled her mind, and heat spread throughout her body.

It was only when she moved a little more toward him and he grunted that she remembered his injuries. She instantly pulled back a few inches, but never took her gaze from his eyes.

The heat and determination she saw there made her shiver.

Ryven grunted as he moved a hand to touch her thigh. "Kisses seem to make me stronger. You should definitely give me more of them."

The corner of her mouth ticked up. "I almost think that's an excuse."

"More like it's motivation." He lightly stroked the side of her thigh, each motion making her nerves overly sensitive. "And not just for me. I'm using my wiles to entrance you so that you'll do everything to make me whole faster. It'll be much easier to kiss you and try to make you my bride when I can move around freely."

"Ryven."

"I'm being honest. I want you, Kalahn. If you ever forget that, I may just have to kiss you senseless to remind you."

Since Ryven's chest was one of the most injured parts of his body and she couldn't touch him there, she traced his jaw. As she moved her fingers back and forth, Ryven closed his eyes with a groan.

She wondered if he were as affected by touch as she was by his. There was one way to find out.

A proper princess won't look, but Kalahn glanced down. The bulge under the sheets told her plenty.

Ryven's voice was husky. "Kalahn, don't. Your gaze only makes it worse."

Since she'd never seen a naked adult male before that she could remember—surely any she'd seen as a child didn't count—she was tempted to move aside the thin fabric to see her male.

Yes, she rather liked thinking of him as hers.

Ryven lightly squeezed her thigh, but she didn't move her gaze. Before she lost her nerve, she tossed back the sheet and gaped.

At Ryven's long, hard length, her nipples tightened and a tingle started between her thighs. She wanted him in ways she'd only ever read about.

She reached out a hand, but before she could touch him, Ryven whispered, "Anyone could walk in."

"No. Your next check-in isn't for about ten minutes." Somehow, she forced her eyes away from his hardness and to Ryven's eyes. "Are you in pain there? I don't want to hurt you."

"I'm in pain in a good way, love. But not from injuries. Males tend to guard their cocks above all else, and I wasn't about to let the birds get it."

Kalahn looked back at his...cock. She'd heard the word before, of course, but princesses weren't supposed to be vulgar.

However, she rather liked the term.

Running a finger down his length, she was surprised at how hard, yet silky his cock was. To truly test it out, she gripped his base and Ryven groaned. Before she could let go, he whispered, "Don't stop, love. Please don't stop."

At Ryven's words, confidence flared and she gently pulled up and down. Each time she did, Ryven made a variety of sounds, ranging from growls to groans. Each one told her more of what he liked.

She finally noticed a small drop of liquid at the top of his cock. Curious, Kalahn leaned down and licked it off.

The salty taste only increased the pulsing between her own thighs. Since she knew she couldn't bare herself to Ryven just yet, she'd just have to make him groan some more in other ways.

Opening her mouth, she sucked his cock in.

"Mm, yes, Kalahn."

The heady power she had, with Ryven at her mercy, was a new sensation. And one she rather liked.

Remembering how he liked her stroking him, she did that with her hand as she licked and sucked the top of his cock. With each pass of her tongue, she swore he grew harder.

Ryven moved his hand from her thigh to one of her nipples and plucked.

Kalahn cried out and released him.

Ryven's voice filled her ears. "What you're doing to me right now is exactly what I plan to do later with your nipples and between your thighs."

Images flashed, and Kalahn wished he could do it now.

But he couldn't, so she took him into her mouth again and increased her pace. She understood the basics of male orgasms, but she wanted to experience Ryven's.

After everything her male had gone through, he deserved it.

Tightening her grip slightly, she continued to stroke him as she tortured him with her tongue. She had no idea how long she licked, nibbled, and laved, but Ryven's strained voice eventually said, "I'm coming, love. Back away now."

Not one to take orders, she continued until Ryven shouted her name as hot, salty spurts filled her mouth. Only when she'd swallowed every last drop did she raise her head and meet Ryven's eyes.

At his half-lidded gaze, full of desire, a sense of accomplishment crashed over her.

He stroked her thigh again. "I could die a happy male now."

She frowned. "Don't you dare die, Ryven Xanna. You owe me."

He chuckled. "That I do, love. So that must mean you're stuck with me until I fulfill my debt."

Tossing the sheet back over him, she turned toward his face. "And to do that, you need to heal as fast as possible. Maybe if I left, you'd go back to sleep."

"If you laid next to me, I would doze right away knowing you were at my side."

"Is that a good idea?"

"Why? Are you afraid of someone finding us?"

She shook her head. "No. I was thinking of your injuries."

He grinned. "A certain princess's body heat would do wonders for my healing process."

She rolled her eyes. "You're never going to stop, are you?"

"Making you smile? No. I want my female to be happy as often as possible."

"Your female?"

"Yes. Because if you think I'm letting you go after the best orgasm of my life, you're crazy."

"They say men think with their cocks...I guess you're proving that true."

His grip tightened on her thigh. "I value your mind and spirit, too, Kalahn. Don't ever doubt it."

At the fierceness of his words, Kalahn shivered.

Ryven's voice softened. "And I miss your mental touch, too. When can I have it back?"

After everything she'd just done, Kalahn had forgotten about his mental self. However, she wasn't going to be a coward. Ryven deserved the truth from her. "That's a bit tricky to determine. Repairing yourself in the telepathic plane is going to take a lot of energy. However, the doctors seem more concerned about your physical injuries."

"But you're more worried about the mental ones."

She widened her eyes. "Yes. How did you know?"

"Just because I can't sense your emotions right now doesn't mean I can't still read you. You trust me enough to allow your markings to reflect your thoughts."

"I guess I'll just have to work harder at keeping them neutral, like you taught me."

"You can try, but once our mental connection is back, you won't be able to hide again." He paused and asked, "You keep asking and making sure I'm okay with it, but has anyone asked you the same?"

She took his hand. "No, but if I'm honest, I'm glad of the bond. I've wanted not only you but also closeness with someone else for a long time. I just never had the courage to go after it and came up with excuses as to why it would be a bad idea, especially regarding you."

The corner of his mouth ticked up. "Yet something else we have in common. I also made excuses."

Kalahn smiled back. "But since neither of us is walking away now, you know what that means, right?"

"Hm?"

"We get to irritate my brothers with the news. And before you say it should wait, etc., I think we have to decide now. Because the closer we get physically I think will also make us stronger mentally. That will help with the female assassin problem."

Frowning, Ryven asked, "So how will us being a better team help with the assassin problem? I must've missed something while I was unconscious."

Her male yawned and Kalahn hesitated. She'd kept him up longer than she should have. And no doubt making him orgasm had only exhausted him further.

As if reading her thoughts again, he grunted. "Yes, I'm tired. But how about you lay next to me and tell me what I need to know? Then I promise to get some sleep. Maybe I'll even dream of a solution to all of our problems as well."

"Right, because that's going to happen simply because you will it to," she drawled.

"You never know." He moved his hand to the empty space of the bed and patted it.

Unable to resist the invitation, she released his hand and gingerly moved to lay next to Ryven. Even though she couldn't rest her head on his chest or hook her leg over his, his warmth and scent put her at ease. Her eyelids drooped, and she had to blink them back open.

At this rate, she'd fall asleep before him.

So she focused on filling in Ryven regarding the assassin problem to help stave off sleep. "As for how us being a better team will help with the assassin problem, it comes back to the mind-bond. Apparently, I'm an extremely powerful telepath. Usually, it could create chaos without proper training in the beginning. However, that power seems to stabilize easily because of our bond."

"I like being useful…"

She sighed. "This isn't a joking matter, Ryven. Borzet mentioned I may unintentionally drain you to fuel my own power. That's why I don't want to allow you access to your telepathic powers too early. As long as they're dormant, I shouldn't touch them. However, once they're whirring again, I may draw on them before you're ready."

He grunted. "Regardless, it will be better to bring my telepathy back while we're still on the transport ship. Because of the security shields around the ship, it will give us a safe space to learn how to work together. After all, unless this Borzet person betrays you, there shouldn't be any telepathic threats up here. Especially since I doubt there are many telepaths onboard."

She shook her head. "Just Syzel."

"Right, then whenever I can speak to the doctor, maybe we can convince him to slowly take me off the suppression drug and begin testing out our limits. I know it's a risk to do it so soon, but over the years I've learned to test out abilities slowly with some of my trainees. This shouldn't be too much different. I think I can control it."

"Only if you promise me that you will be upfront about your condition. You will be telepathically weak for a while, and I don't want your pride to end up doing further damage."

"I'm not like most of the other warriors," Ryven stated. "If I need help, I ask for it. I vow to do it with you."

"Good. Then that just leaves telling my brothers about us. We shouldn't put that off for too long, either."

"Ask Kason to come here and I'll talk to him first."

"Why not together?"

Ryven grunted. "We can talk with him together, afterward. But Kason is my best friend, and I owe it to him to speak the truth, one on one. He will hold back with you in the room, and I don't want that. I hope to be able to keep him as my friend, which will require complete honesty."

"You're too important to Kason for him to dismiss you and never talk to you again."

"Maybe so, but there is a difference between a true friendship and tolerating someone out of convenience. I don't want to become the latter."

Kalahn kissed a patch of uninjured skin on his side. "You are truly an honorable male. Don't ever doubt it again."

He smiled. "I'll try, but it's not that simple. Just as you sometimes doubt your worth as someone of use, it's the same for me. We'll both just have to remind the other that those statements are mostly rubbish."

"Mostly?"

His gaze turned heated. "I have some dishonorable acts I'd like to try out with you, once you're my bride and in my bed."

A flush crept up her cheeks. "I would almost say you're trying to unsettle me on purpose."

"Maybe it's part of your training."

"If so, then I have some training of my own to do in the future with you."

Ryven chuckled. "My princess is a little dirty, too. I like that."

"Well, then you'll just have to woo me and convince me to accept you as my lord. Then I can show you some of my fantasies."

"That will be done as soon as I'm out of this bed."

As they smiled at one another, Kalahn wished they could be back in the kitchen on Jasvar, teasing one another and acting like a normal couple would.

But if she ever wanted that future, she had to overcome a few obstacles first. Namely, the threats to her family and to her male.

Ryven touched her rear, and murmured, "We can plot more of our future later. For now, it's nap time so I can heal as quickly as possible. Only then can we go after that slightly dirty future you dream of."

She snorted. "You're never going to let that go, are you?"

"No way." He yawned. "After all, as long as I'm alive, I'll always be teasing you, love."

"Good," she mumbled.

Her eyelids drooped and she stopped fighting it. As Kalahn drifted off, she wondered why Ryven kept calling her love. But she fell asleep before she could think too hard on it.

Chapter Fifteen

The next day, Ryven was able to sit up by himself but not stand. So as he waited for Kason to meet him, he tapped one of his fingers against the mattress pad.

He wanted nothing more than to have Kalahn sitting next to him, telling him more about her training with Borzet. It was still hard for him to believe she was such a powerful telepath, but it made sense. Especially since she'd picked things up so quickly and had even managed to reach out to Syzel after Ryven's attack with little more than his memories to rely on.

The attack. He shuddered. Another reason he wanted Kalahn at his side was to help stave off the memories of the blasted birds. He'd endured a lot over the years in both training and even battle, but a flock of birds ripping flesh off his body was definitely the worst thing to ever happen to him. It'd be some time before he stopped reliving those horrifying seconds.

The door chimed and Kason walked in. He scrutinized Ryven's face and bare chest before speaking. "You nearly lost to the Siren birds."

He raised an eyebrow. Leave it to Kason to ignore his injuries and focus on the defeat. "Thankfully I didn't."

The Forbidden

Kason crossed his arms over his chest. "While I'm glad to see you're alive and recovering, what's so urgent that Syzel had to bring me to the colony transport ship so quickly?"

Ryven had rehearsed a million times inside his head of what to say and finally blurted out the most simple one, "I care for your sister Kalahn and one day want to make her my bride."

Kason's expression remained neutral. As his friend stared at him in silence, Ryven decided he needed to use logic as well. "You, of all people, know that we can't always control who we fall for."

Kason finally grunted. "How long has this been going on?"

"Only recently. But I'm going to be completely honest and tell you we kissed once several years ago, too."

Kason's silence signaled he was thinking. Ryven had seen him use the tactic to unsettle warriors in the past. However, it was strange to be on the receiving end of it for a change.

Still, he refused to allow Kason's silence to dissuade him of anything. If he couldn't stand up to Kason, he didn't deserve Kalahn in the first place.

Kason's voice eventually filled the room. "My bride suspected Kalahn harbored something for you, but I dismissed it as nothing. Apparently, I was wrong." He uncrossed his arms and moved closer to Ryven's bed. "If you ever hurt her, shame her, or cause any sort of scandal around my sister, I will consider our friendship over and will probably toss you into a jail cell to rot for the rest of your life. Do you understand?"

He searched his friend's eyes. "I would rather face another flock of Siren birds and allow them to tear off my cock than hurt her."

"Considering Kalahn's unpredictable nature, she could've done worse than you," Kason muttered.

At the lightened tone, he smirked. "I'm not a teenage errand boy who follows her around like a pet. That would be much worse."

"And good thing, too, because Kalahn needs an occasional firm hand."

"But lightness as well," Ryven said. "If she were with a growly, overprotective male like you, she'd flout every order and make it her life's mission to defy him."

"So you do understand her," Kason stated.

"Of course I do. And not just because of the mind-bond."

Kason frowned. "The what?"

Ryven couldn't help but notice the confusion in Kason's eyes. "Kalahn didn't tell you?"

"No, so start talking," he growled.

"Your order doesn't scare me, Kason. I want to be on your good side, yes, but this is Kalahn's news to share, too. Not just mine. She needs to be here before I say a word. And keep in mind, I know all of your intimidation tactics, and they won't work on me, either."

Kason spoke aloud. "Computer, order Princess Kalahn tro el Vallen to come to this room."

"Understood," the computer said. After a few beats, it added, "She is en route."

Ryven sighed. "Couldn't you have waited until she was done with her training session? After all, she's working hard to help protect you and the others."

Kason shook his head. "I sense this is something I should know about and that it shouldn't wait."

The door chimed and Kalahn entered the room. She immediately met Ryven's eyes, and he nodded, letting her know he'd spoken to Kason about their relationship. The one upside to temporarily losing his telepathy was that he and Kalahn had to learn each other's body language.

Kalahn moved her gaze to her brother. "If you've called me in here to try to convince me to forget Ryven, it's not going to happen, brother."

Kason waved a hand in dismissal. "Ryven is a fine male and one that I trust. He's shown that further by not giving away your secrets, which is why I called you here. What is a mind-bond, Kalahn? I can't make plans if you keep important information from me, and I sense this is important."

Every cell in Ryven's body urged him to stand at Kalahn's side to support her.

However, since he couldn't stand, he waited to offer her support in other ways. Kalahn was a strong female and could handle her brother. Ryven just needed to trust her.

✵ ✵ ✵

Kalahn barely had time to process that Kason had accepted Ryven before he asked her about the mind-bond. She focused on answering him, since that might earn her favors. "I don't know how much you know about telepathy, but a mind-bond is when two telepaths suit each other and their mental signatures come together to form one."

"I know the basic definitions of telepathic signatures and shields, but not a whole lot more." Kason frowned. "Is the bond voluntary? How does it change things? Explain it to me, and quickly. I can't stay on this ship too long before someone notices that I'm gone."

She wanted to press Kason for details about his own plans to draw out the traitors, but resisted since he probably wouldn't tell her anyway. Besides, he was right. Her brother couldn't make plans if he didn't have all the information. "I would say it's similar to destined brides for the males of the royal family—it's predetermined by fate and genetics, but usually it takes some willingness for it to happen and connect."

Males of the royal family had been genetically engineered over the years so that they could find a female able to bear them children; a genetic defect meant few women could do so. The fated females were called destined brides, and the royal males found it hard to resist one. While it could be done, Kason's own bride was one of them, as was Keltor's.

Females of the royal line didn't suffer the same genetic defect that made it difficult to bear offspring, and thus didn't have the equivalent for a destined lord. Kalahn had been thankful for that, as it had given her choices.

Although she had to admit that forming a bond with Ryven had worked out. Well, provided they could control it and find a way to live without killing one another.

Kason moved his gaze to Ryven. "I've never heard of this happening with any of the warriors who've been spliced with telepathy."

"No, it's never happened on Keldera before, that I can tell anyway," Ryven replied. "Usually only natural born telepaths experience a mind-bond."

"Then how did it happen between you two?" Kason demanded.

Kalahn explained Borzet's theory about a Hirlanzian in their family tree and added, "I suspect the same would happen to any of the royal siblings, if they were given telepathy. But since you and Keltor each have a destined bride you love and cherish, you may want to resist. I have no idea if a mind-bond would form with the same female or not."

"I have no intention of gaining additional abilities," Kason said.

Ryven jumped in. "There's more than your distant ancestor in all of this, too. What Kalahn isn't telling you is that Borzet deems her a powerful telepath with a natural affinity for it, which is another factor for the bond."

Kason looked between them. "How will the bond affect Kalahn's abilities?"

Leave it to Kason to steer them back to the mission. She shrugged. "We still have to test it out, although Borzet and I have theories."

Theories that she could end up killing Ryven. Not that she was going to tell Kason that.

Kason asked, "Because time is short, let me be blunt—when will you be able to probe the female assassin and find out any information you can?"

Kalahn stood tall. The action had always given her the strength to stand up to her brother in the past. "I'd rather try to avoid probing her without permission." Kason opened his mouth, but she continued before he could say anything. "But I have a plan. If I can crack her shields, she'll broadcast automatically. So if someone questions her heavily and then puts her into a cell near me, I can weaken her defenses and hear her thoughts without violating her private space and possibly killing her. Given the intensive interrogation, I suspect her thoughts will be about her colleagues or her plans to attack us."

"And this is something you can do?" Kason asked, his voice a bit skeptical.

She shook her head. "Not quite yet, but I'm working on it. Borzet is a good trainer, but to accomplish something so powerful, I need to lean on Ryven via our connection. And I won't do that until he's mentally strong enough to lend me some of his power."

Kason looked at each of them in turn. "I don't want to push either of you too far too fast. However, my own plans are not going as well as I'd hoped. So if you could focus all of your energies on this project, it would help us all."

Kalahn glanced to Ryven. "I will do all the training I can, but I won't risk Ryven's life."

"Don't worry, love. We'll figure it out soon enough," Ryven murmured.

Kason cleared his throat. "Just make sure your energy isn't wasted taking advantage of my sister."

Kalahn frowned at Kason. "How about not discussing and dissecting my personal time with Ryven?"

Her brother grunted. "All I'll say is be cautious, Kalahn. If you end up pregnant before we can implement the plan, even I know that over-stretching your telepathic abilities can harm a babe."

Kalahn willed her cheeks not to flush and decided to embarrass Kason as he'd done her. "Not that it's any of your business, but I've started birth control hormone treatments. I'm far from ready for a child, no matter how cute they may be."

Out of the corner of her eye, she saw Ryven's grin. He was onboard with embarrassing Kason.

Doing her best not to laugh at her brother's wary gaze, Kalahn continued. "I'll update you in code with how things are progressing. But I'd rather not give too many updates, just in case there's a mole within your trusted ranks."

Kason crossed his arms again. "We're still trying to find the person who cut the branches down, with the intention of having the birds kill Ryven. Every precaution is being taken."

"Good." She finally moved to Ryven's bed and took his hand. "Then if there's nothing else, I need to tend to my male and then go back to training."

Kason's face softened. "Just be careful, Kalahn. I know you want to prove yourself, but just make sure not to kill yourself in the process."

Ryven squeezed her hand before saying, "I'll look after her. I know a thing or two about keeping a stubborn royal from pushing themselves too far."

Kason made a fist and thumped it over his heart. "Take care of my sister. Her life is in your hands."

"You know I'm standing right here, don't you?" Kalahn drawled.

Her brother raised an eyebrow. "Yes."

Ryven chimed in. "It's a male thing, Kalahn. And it's not meant to insult. It's almost a statement of approval concerning our relationship."

She blinked. "Really? There needs to be a manual on male behaviors. That would save me a lot of time."

Ryven snorted. "Maybe someday I'll try my hand at that."

After sharing a grin with Ryven, Kalahn looked back at her brother. "I'll be careful, I promise. I'm not about to lose Ryven after I finally have him as my own."

Kason nodded and murmured his goodbyes. Once they were alone again, Kalahn sat next to Ryven and gave him a quick kiss. "So I take it everything is going to be fine between you and Kason?"

He snorted again. "I think 'fine' is a long way off, but he's tolerating the idea. Especially after I hinted you could've done much worse, as well as far more scandalous, than me."

She stuck out her tongue. "If you weren't injured, I'd hit you for that."

He winked. "But I am and you can't. I need to make sure to live this up while I still can." He sobered. "On a more serious note, I'm happy to hear about the hormone treatments. It means I can claim you as soon as I'm well and you agree to be my bride."

She plucked at the sheet. As much as Kalahn wanted Ryven, she didn't think they'd be married when she finally let him claim her, given the laws and her own plans. She'd just have to think of a way to make that happen despite Ryven's honor. "I hope it's okay I started them. I'm just not ready for a child yet. I know you're older and maybe you are ready, but there's too much I want to do first."

He touched her cheek and she met his gaze again. "Kalahn, I want more than a baby with you. Would it be nice at some point to start a family? Yes. But I want some time with my bride first. After all, I have to make sure she gets the chance to live out each and every one of her dirty fantasies."

"I haven't agreed to be your bride yet," she pointed out.

"But you will." He brought her hand to his lips. "As much as I'd love to keep you all to myself for the day, I know Borzet is waiting for you."

She gently brushed his hair with her fingertips. Not being able to touch him wherever she wanted was killing her. Ryven couldn't heal fast enough. "I'll come back as soon as I can."

"And then you can assess my mental stability."

Searching his gaze, she looked for any doubt, but saw none. She only hoped Ryven's lack of concern was a signal that he would be fine. She asked, "Are you sure you're ready? It's still fairly soon after the attack, Ryven."

"I'm fueled by craving your mental touch again."

She smiled. "Just so you can project sexy fantasies into my head."

He grinned. "That's only part of it. In all seriousness, I want to explore the mind-bond and test the boundaries. After doing that, I can confer with Borzet and come up with some training exercises."

"Once a trainer, always a trainer."

He winked. "And just wait until I train you in the ways of the flesh."

Kalahn did her best to keep her markings a dark blue as thoughts of Ryven pleasuring her in different ways flashed inside her head. Her on her back, her side, even on her stomach.

He probably had other things she didn't even know about, either.

She was eager to learn, but there was no way she would share those visions right now, or she'd never leave the room. So instead she rolled her eyes. "The horny side of Ryven is out in full force."

"No, I just want to use every tool available to convince you to be my bride."

Kalahn wanted to scream yes, she'd be his.

And yet, she didn't want to put Ryven in harm's way again simply because of him being her lord. Once she took care of her mission surrounding the assassin and knew more about the threats to the royal family, then she'd claim him and never let go.

She just had to hone her skills first.

After kissing Ryven goodbye, Kalahn exited the room and headed back to Borzet. She'd been having a hard time concentrating before because of Kason coming to visit. However, now that her brother had accepted them—if only tentatively—she could flex her full mental muscle and get to work.

Chapter Sixteen

Five days later, Ryven's mind was finally cleared and he was slowly brought off the drugs suppressing his telepathy.

His body was nearly healed as well due to Kelderan medicine techniques, and as a result, Kalahn currently curled against his side and snored softly. He gently rubbed her back, more than aware that he'd become attached to her scent and heat at his side. To be honest, it was hard to imagine falling asleep without her next to him.

Her training was, by all rights, going well. And provided Ryven was strong enough to help her, she could be ready to go back to Jasvar and implement their plan regarding the assassin in less than a week.

And according to Borzet, after a few years of training, she might even become the strongest telepath in their galaxy.

As Ryven watched her face slack in sleep, he wished he could whisk her away and protect her. Every day she told him of another way she could die via a mental attack, and each time it became harder and harder to be supportive.

And yet, he knew that if he put his foot down and forbade anything, fire would flare in her eyes and she'd defy him. Maybe even leave him, bond or no bond.

The Forbidden

So the only thing he could do was support her and do his best to grow stronger. Oh, and try his best not to die when it came time to lend his mental power to amplify her own.

With each passing minute, the fogginess of his mental space lessened. Since Kalahn had been training so hard, he would only wake her once he had a clear mind again. Although as he was able to see his mental presence clearer and clearer, it took every bit of restraint he possessed not to instantly reach out and call to Kalahn.

Even with her asleep, her emotions were starting to filter through because of their bond. Happiness, mixed with excitement, came through. Maybe she was dreaming of another adventure near a waterfall. He'd already promised to make that dream a reality as soon as they could.

To be honest, almost all of his plans now included Kalahn. Their lives would never be easy, but he didn't care. His princess was worth any trouble. He just needed to ensure they had a future first, and then he could spend his life wooing and making Kalahn happy.

She murmured something in her sleep and nuzzled his chest. The brush of her cheek against his skin sent electricity racing through his body and straight to his cock. As her breath tickled his chest as well, he tried to keep memories of her mouth on him at bay, too. Otherwise, he would be nothing but a distraction to Kalahn; she'd feel his desire when she woke up and probably act on it.

Not that he didn't want to be inside her, but they needed to protect her family first.

So he thought of every mundane training manual he could muster to deflate his cock once more. His princess deserved romance and laughter for her first time, and not a crude awakening in a hospital bed.

He contented himself with stroking her back and committing her soft form to memory. Eventually he could see his—no, their—mental space clearly, and he stilled his movements.

And if he were talking, he would've been rendered speechless.

Gone were the haphazardly constructed walls on Kalahn's half and in its place were some of the most complex shields he'd ever seen, tightly woven into a pattern he'd never witnessed in the past. At first glance, he wasn't even sure how to go about dismantling it. He also noticed that the barrier even extended inside his own walls, to encircle them both.

Some males might balk at a female protecting them, but Ryven wasn't one of them. After all, Kalahn's skill meant she could better protect herself when the time came.

If her barrier wasn't enough of a surprise, gone was the empty space of light. Instead, images of both back home on Keldera and scenery from Jasvar danced on different sections of the walls. The floor was in a traditional Kelderan pattern, usually reserved for rugs. There were even plants spaced around the room, too.

And to think, Kalahn was able to maintain all of it while deep asleep. Maybe she was ready to complete their assignment after all.

Kalahn's mental presence swirled around his own. *You're back.*

I never left, love.

You know what I mean. She circled him more slowly this time. *And the small signs of mental rot are gone, too. I think you might be healed.*

So now you're an expert on telepathic health?

Not exactly an expert, but it's another thing that comes naturally to me—judging a person's weaknesses on the telepathic plane.

He retreated from his mind and lightly pinched her bottom. Kalahn opened her eyes and squealed. "What was that for?"

"I had to ensure you weren't completely invincible in your physical self, too."

Her gaze turned wary. "Are you intimidated?"

"Truthfully? Yes." Her face fell, and he turned to face her and take her head between his hands. "But that's not a negative. Don't hide your true strength, Kalahn. It's one of the things that's always drawn me to you."

The worry fled from her eyes. "I was concerned you might not want to work with me, once you saw all that I did. But there was no way I was going to hold back. After all, the stronger I become, the better protected we both are."

He gently kissed her and pulled back a fraction to whisper, "As long as you help train me and include me in your plans, we'll be fine."

She smiled slowly, and his breath hitched at how beautiful she was.

He should put desire to the side and focus on business. But after nearly a week of being careful and holding back, he closed the distance between their lips and kissed her.

❋ ❋ ❋

Even though Kalahn had done her best to improve her and Ryven's mental space and make it more homey, she'd always had a thread of doubt running through her. She'd seen fights and even brawls break out between males over who was the strongest, richest, or most powerful. And those were just inside her father's conference rooms.

Every day, she'd hoped that Ryven would be different.

So when he praised her abilities and told her to never hold back, she fell a little in love with him.

Not that she had much time to think about it, because as soon as his lips touched hers, every thought fled her head.

With each nip, nibble, and caress, Ryven became rougher. Gone were the gentle kisses and caresses.

He now pulled her close and rolled on top of her. Kalahn moved her hands to grip his rear. When she dug in her nails, Ryven broke the kiss with a growl. "We should stop."

Her breathing was as ragged as his. "Don't you dare stop, Ryven. You owe me."

The corner of his mouth ticked up. "I won't claim you yet, but I'll repay the orgasm without hesitation."

She rubbed her foot against the back of his leg. "Then what are you waiting for?"

"Gah, you're like my every fantasy thrown into one, Kalahn."

Before she could tease him, he kissed her jaw, her neck, and finally kissed her nipple through her dress. The heat of his mouth through the fabric only tightened her nipples further, and wetness rushed between her thighs.

When he took her tight bud between his teeth and gently nibbled, she cried out his name.

"Just wait for what's to come, Princess. I'm just getting started."

He laved his tongue against her, moving the fabric and creating delicious friction against her sensitive nerves. She was torn between asking him to remove the material and letting him make her orgasm just like this.

His hair was long enough now that she could thread her fingers through it and gently tug. With a growl, Ryven released her and met her gaze.

Her heart skipped a beat at the heat and desire there.

Never taking his gaze from hers, he traced the neckline of her dress up to her shoulder. Hooking his finger under the material, he slowly slid it down her arm until her breast popped free.

But Ryven didn't immediately take her into his mouth. He stared at her face as the cool air caressed her breast.

Each second that ticked by only heated her skin more. Who knew that a look could drive her crazy and make her want to pluck her own nipples until she came.

"Do it," Ryven murmured.

Crap, she must've been projecting again.

While Kalahn had brought herself to climax on her own, a brief flash of embarrassment washed over her. She hated being so inexperienced with men.

Ryven reached down and placed his hand on her knee, slowly running his fingers up to her inner thigh. As he rubbed his rough palm against her, Kalahn squirmed her hips like a wanton.

His husky voice filled the room. "Never be afraid to take or ask for what you want, love."

He continued stroking her thigh while he stared, never reaching her core or even touching her nipples again.

Her breasts ached to be touched. With a word, she could have Ryven's mouth on her again.

But as she slowly brought her fingers to her exposed breast and began to roll and pinch her tight bud, approval and desire emanated from Ryven via their bond and washed over her.

The combination of his desire and her own nearly made her come right then and there.

As pleasure built, Ryven gently ran a finger between her thighs and Kalahn bucked her hips.

Ryven's mental voice filled her head. *Tell me to stop, and I will.*

No, no don't stop.

He continued his ministrations and finally leaned closer to her breast. "Let me make my princess come."

Her hand fell to the side, and Ryven instantly sucked her tight bud between his teeth. As he worried her flesh with teeth and tongue, she raised her hips, inviting Ryven to touch her there, too.

One of his long, thick fingers entered slowly. As he moved it, he increased the pressure and pace of his mouth on her nipples.

Her thoughts were too scattered to talk to him, with a voice or her telepathy, so she moaned and groaned as the pressure built. Ryven touching her was more intense than anything she'd done to herself.

When lights finally flashed before her eyes, ecstasy crashed over her and she cried out his name.

After Kalahn finally came down from her high, she smiled at Ryven. He quirked an eyebrow. "So have I paid off my debt?"

It was hard to concentrate since Ryven still gently moved his finger inside her, but she managed to reply, "I don't think so. You'll be paying it off for years."

"Good." He removed his finger and brought it to his lips. Watching him slowly lick her wetness off his skin made her insides flip. He finally added, "Because one taste of you will never be enough."

The way he said it, as if it would be pure ecstasy to taste her, made her shiver.

She wanted to be bold enough to ask him for more, but settled on spreading her legs. "You could work on your debt a little more."

After he took her lips in a slow, rough kiss, he murmured, "I will, but not today, Kalahn. I want you in a proper bed, where I can take you as many times as I can before we both collapse with exhaustion."

He kissed the side of her breast, her chest, and her jaw. His breath whispered against her skin. "My bride will be treasured as she deserves."

He was all but asking her again to be his bride, and Kalahn hesitated. Whether through body language or the mental connection, Ryven must've noticed and instantly met her gaze and searched it. "What's wrong?"

She could dismiss it as nothing, curl up next to him, and merely enjoy the moment.

However, if she kept trying to hide things from Ryven, it would probably backfire. And just the thought of never seeing her male again squeezed her heart.

So she took a deep breath and let the words spill from her lips. "I don't want to hurt you, Ryven. I want to be your bride, I do. But I don't want to say yes until I'm sure we're out of danger."

He cupped her cheek. "I don't remember asking."

"Well, no, but you all but have."

The corner of his mouth ticked up. "I might have a solution, then, to put your mind at ease."

Her hands went to his shoulders. "This had better be good news."

"Oh, it is. I'll wait for you to ask me to be your lord."

She blinked. "That's highly unusual."

He raised his brows. "And we are a usual couple? I'm not sure many males capture a princess's attention, let alone form a mind-bond with one."

She searched his gaze for any negative emotions. "Are you really okay with that? To be honest, I keep waiting for you to run the other way at something I do."

He took her face with both of his hands. "You are a brilliant, talented female, Kalahn. Kind, funny, and plenty stubborn. I'm here because of all those things. I love you."

Her breath hitched. "You love me?"

"Yes, I do. Maybe I should've waited to tell you, so as to cause less of a distraction. But you left me little choice, what with you talking about how I'm going to leave. I'm not going anywhere. And not just because of the mental bond, either. You're the only female I think of when it comes to my dreams and my future. So, Kalahn tro el Vallen, you're stuck with me. And I'll be waiting for your proposal when you're ready."

Nothing but love emanated from Ryven's mental presence.

He told the truth.

She fell a little more in love with him, but Borzet's warning rang inside her head: *The stronger the bond becomes between you and Ryven, the greater the chance you may kill him during such a delicate assignment. You require more training to protect him.*

So rather than say anything, she pulled his head down and distracted him with kisses until it was time to leave for their first joint training session.

Chapter Seventeen

On the sixth day of their joint training sessions, Ryven projected a small tendril of his mental self out toward Kalahn. Borzet was nearby, observing everything they did. While it was odd to have a third person inside his and Kalahn's shared space, it was nothing more than a precaution. If needed, Borzet would step in and coax Kalahn to stop drawing power from Ryven.

Because if she took too much, it could kill him.

Not that the risk deterred him in any way. After all, not only did he trust her not to hurt him, he was also pretty sure she'd never propose to him until her mission was complete.

Kalahn finally brushed against his tendril and said, *Let me know as soon as you feel weak.*

As I tell you every day at practice, I will. Now, go.

Kalahn's objective was to smash through an outer barrier Borzet had constructed around his fortress signature. If she could crack Borzet's multilayered, complexly woven shield, Kalahn would be ready to tackle the female assassin's. While part Hirlanzian, she wasn't as skilled as Borzet, at least according to Syzel's observations over the past few weeks.

While he had faith in Kalahn's abilities—it was hard not to after every new thing she did to amaze him—it was still difficult for him to watch Kalahn as she gathered her strength and sent some of her mental energy outside of their signature. Especially while he did nothing.

However, he was intelligent enough to admit that while he was skilled in many things, Kalahn was superior in this. He needed to hold back.

He didn't know how long Kalahn took scouting out weaknesses in Borzet's shield, but her mental presence eventually brushed against the tendril he'd offered. *Brace yourself.*

Even though he'd experienced the same power draw several times before, it was still a shock. It was as if someone punched him in the stomach repeatedly and all he could do was try to catch his breath.

Focusing on his love for Kalahn, Ryven dug deep and managed to offer her more. He could sense her gratitude through the bond.

Several moments passed and he wondered if Kalahn would ever attack. He only had about ten more seconds before he'd have to sever their connection and rest his brain until the next day.

Sending encouragement through their bond, he placed his trust in Kalahn and continued to give her every bit of strength he possessed.

Kalahn hit Borzet's shield with a direct hit, the boom vibrating through even Kalahn's mental walls. Light blazed at the contact, and for a few seconds, Ryven couldn't see anything. Had she succeeded? Was today yet another failure?

Kalahn ceased drawing energy from Ryven as the light dimmed. He had just enough energy left to peer out toward Borzet's mental signature.

From his vantage point, he couldn't tell if the shield had cracked or not. Since it was a specially constructed target and not Borzet's own protection, no thoughts streamed outward as they should do with the female assassin.

But as soon as joy emanated from Kalahn, he knew she'd done it. His mental voice was weak as he said, *Good job, love.*

She sent him an image of a closer look at the crack, which was a good eight feet in length. More than long enough to allow thoughts to escape and be projected to those nearby.

Kalahn should be ready to do the real thing.

Before she could say anything, Borzet jumped in. *Retreat and let's discuss outside the plane.*

Outside the plane meant talking with their mouths instead of their minds.

Once Borzet was gone from their shared space, Kalahn quickly patched up the opening to the outside, gave a quick, comforting swirl around Ryven's presence, and then said aloud, "Even you can't deny I succeeded this time, Borzet."

The male nodded. "Yes, but I think you're celebrating a little prematurely."

Kalahn frowned. "Why?"

Borzet answered, "Because there are still some mental booby traps that I need to show you how to disarm."

The training session had been set up to emulate the real-life scenario, so Kalahn was physically on the opposite side of the room; she and Ryven wouldn't be together when Kalahn finally went after the female assassin. Otherwise, he would've given her a reassuring hug. He said, "It's still a big step, Kalahn. And I'm still alive, so that's something."

"Don't joke about that, Ryven." She closed the distance between them and cupped his cheek. "Did I take too much?"

He placed his hand over hers. "No. I will tell you when it's too much."

As she stared into his eyes, Ryven wished Borzet wasn't in the same room as them. He wanted nothing more than to draw Kalahn into his lap, hold her close, and forget about everything else for a little while. He trusted in her abilities, but Ryven knew firsthand that sometimes the most skilled individuals still didn't come back from a battle or assignment. Too many of his fellow warriors had never returned, despite many of them being the best of the best.

Which meant he wanted to treasure every moment he had with Kalahn that he could.

Borzet cleared his throat, the usual signal to remind them that the training session wasn't over yet.

Kalahn stroked his cheek, mentally whispered to him alone, *Don't worry*, before turning away to face Borzet again. "Tell me exactly what else I need to learn. Because I'm starting to think you have orders from my brother to keep devising new items to tackle so that I'm never ready."

"I wouldn't do that," Borzet stated. "However, I won't risk you before you're ready. Your mind is too powerful to waste. With it, we might be able to form treaties with nearby planets that have telepaths and further protect everyone on Jasvar. We all need you to come out the other side unscathed."

Ryven suspected that the male knew more than he had told them about his homeworld of Hirlanzia, and that they might be one of the ones Borzet wished to form a treaty with. Once everything was sorted with Kalahn's mission, Ryven would have to find out more.

His female sighed. "While I'm all for creating a peaceful galaxy, I want to protect Jasvar and Keldera first before engaging in intergalactic diplomacy. So I repeat: How many more things must I learn before I can tackle this assignment?"

Kalahn never moved her gaze from Borzet until he finally replied, "Only two more essential items remain. If you can manage to stay apart from your bond-mate during the day, then we could probably be finished by the end of the week."

Hirlanzians called the person they formed a mind-bond with their bond-mate. Ryven wasn't too sure of the term as he would much prefer calling her his bride.

Kalahn nodded. "I can do that. Give me half an hour to rest and say goodbye, and then teach me everything I need to know, Borzet. The longer we wait, the greater the chance the female assassin becomes out of the loop with regards to information."

It was possible the assassin communicated via telepathy, but no one had been able to determine if she did so or not. Especially if she were bonded with another telepath, then their communications would be undetectable inside their shared signature.

Even though Ryven played a supportive role, Kalahn had insisted he know everything she did.

Borzet moved to the door. "Thirty minutes. And I warn you, it won't be easy, Kalahn. The less distracted you are, the better."

He exited the room, and Kalahn sighed as she sat next to Ryven. He instantly put an arm around her. "What distraction is he talking about?"

"Caught that did you?" she murmured.

"Kalahn, whatever it is, just tell me."

✵ ✵ ✵

For a split second, Kalahn wished she were just a normal female, able to lounge about all day in the arms of her male. In such a scenario she could speak her mind and not worry about causing possible pain to Ryven.

But then she remembered her family, especially Kajala and her unborn baby, and the wish faded away. They needed her protection and it was time to stop being a coward.

Sitting up so she could look into Ryven's eyes, she finally answered him. "The distraction on my mind is that I might kill you."

Ryven frowned. "There's a low chance of that, especially given all the training we've done."

"No, there's more to it."

He raised his brows in question, staring her down. Ryven would never brush things aside and leave her alone.

Which was exactly what Kalahn needed after a life of her father and brothers doing exactly that. True, they were trying to make amends for never asking her what she wanted, but Ryven would always be the male to demand the truth, even when she didn't want to give it.

Placing a hand on his chest, she brushed her fingers against his warm skin a few times. She finally murmured, "There's something about the mind-bond you need to know." Taking a deep breath, she met his eyes again. How a male had eyes such a beautiful shade of teal, Kalahn would never understand. "As two people start to care more about each other, the bond becomes even stronger."

"Isn't that a positive?"

"With most people, yes. But with us, it's dangerous."

He stroked her lower back. "Explain the details to me, because right now you're not making a lot of sense."

There was no going back now. "As corny as this is going to sound, the more we care about each other, the greater our signatures will meld and eventually, we'll appear as one to everyone else."

He smiled. "Even though having a thorny flower constantly swirling and appearing to prick my cat in the butt isn't the most intimidating, I think I can handle that."

"Ryven, be serious. It also means I can take as much power from you as I wish, with or without permission, let alone any realization that I'm about to kill you."

He shook his head. "I find it hard to believe you'd ever do that."

"Borzet says many telepaths of my level have done it to their bond-mates by accident in the past. And usually the couples more in love were affected the most because of their bond being the strongest."

He stilled his hand a second. "This information itself isn't the distraction, is it?"

"Am I projecting again?"

"No, I'm just relying on my powers of deduction."

In any other situation, she would probably lightly hit him and ask him to tone it down. However, Ryven's teasing nature had already helped her body relax a fraction, alleviating some of her stress at least. "Couldn't you be a little bit awful? That way I could get this over with quicker," she muttered.

He spoke in an overly dramatic voice. "Oh, Kalahn, you're such an awful, weak person. I can't stand you at all. I'm trying not to vomit as we speak." Rolling her eyes, she did hit him, and he grinned. "See? You don't want me to act any differently."

"No, I don't."

His gaze turned serious. "Then talk to me, love."

At his endearment, she found the courage to speak the truth. "I love you, okay? And I've been trying to keep it to myself so as to keep our bond weaker. But it's proving more of a distraction than I'd bargained for."

He grinned wider than she'd ever seen before. "You love me?"

"Didn't I just say that?" She hid her face against his chest. "I may as well have just signed your death warrant."

"Kalahn tro el Vallen, look at me." When she met his gaze, the fierceness there stole her breath away. He continued,

"I've witnessed many a male resist love, thinking it would make them weak and vulnerable, including your brother Kason. But in every instance, it only made them stronger. It will be the same for us, love. I guarantee it."

She shook her head. "But you can't guarantee it, and none of them had a mind-bond, either."

He raised his brows. "So that's it? You tell me you love me and then give up? That's very un-Kalahn like of you."

She growled. "I'm just trying to protect you, you infuriating man."

He cupped her cheek. "Then trust that I will protect you, too, even if it means telling you to hold back. If you think I'm just going to let you drain the life out of me without a peep, then you don't know me at all. You might be the stronger telepath, but I'm strong in my own right, too."

Covering his hand with hers, she asked, "You think you could stop me, if it came to it?"

"I'm sure you can give me pointers, but I won't let you kill me, because then that means I'll never be able to do this again." He kissed her gently and pulled back a fraction. "Not to mention that I can't let myself die before I fulfill as many of your dirty fantasies as possible."

She groaned. "That again."

"Yes, that again." He kissed her once more. "I'm going to use every motivation available to protect our future."

As she stared into Ryven's eyes, all she could think about was how much she loved him. Maybe, just maybe, that would help her protect him instead of hurt him. "Then maybe I need some more motivation, just in case."

He chuckled. "You're getting as bad as me, love."

She moved to straddle his hips and looped her arms around his neck. "Are you really going to decline an open offer to kiss me, and more?"

His gaze turned heated. "I'll kiss you and make you orgasm, but I won't claim you until after you complete the mission. That should be good motivation for you."

He moved his hips under her, his already hard cock brushing against her center. Kalahn sucked in a breath. "You play dirty."

"Always, love, always," he murmured before he kissed her, fondled her, and did everything but claim her with his cock. By the time she screamed his name, Kalahn had added quite a bit more motivation toward her will to succeed.

Chapter Eighteen

Kalahn paced the small room inside one of the Jasvarian mountains, her skirts flying with each turn. All she wanted to do was get started, so where in the world was Kason?

Ryven said from across the room, "Your brother will be here soon."

She stopped in her tracks. "He's late, and Kason is never late."

"Stop surmising the worst. He does run the Kelderan colony after all."

She growled. "How are you so calm?"

Ryven shrugged. "I meditated earlier, not to mention that this isn't the first battle I've gone into." He moved close enough to take one of her hands. "Every warrior acts like you do the first time, love. But worrying and fretting won't help you in the end."

She glanced to the side. "Don't you think I know that? But there's so much at stake. And if I fail…"

She could lose some of the people most important to her. Maybe even all of them if the traitors succeeded in their plot to assassinate every member of her family.

He placed a finger under her chin and gently forced her gaze up. "I have faith in your abilities. However, if something does go wrong, there will be other options, love. And I'll be here to help you find them, if need be."

She sighed. "I know that. I'm just not the most patient person in the world."

"You don't say?" he said with a grin.

She stuck out her tongue. "You're supposed to be on my side."

He pulled her up against his chest. "I am on your side. But if you think I'm going to lie to you and sugarcoat things, then you're in for a rude awakening."

Leaning against him, she said, "No, don't ever do that. I've had enough of that over the course of my life."

He nodded. "That's what I thought."

He pressed his lips to hers, and Kalahn worked on memorizing the feel and taste of her male.

She'd barely gotten started when Ryven broke the kiss to murmur, "I'm not going anywhere, so don't treat this like it's the last time."

Before she could reply, he kissed her again and took it deeper. Kalahn lost all sense of place, completely consumed with Ryven's heat, taste, and touch.

She had no idea how much time passed before her brother's voice filled the room. "I may not be against Ryven as your future lord, but I'd rather not see him kissing my little sister."

Kalahn turned to face the voice. Kason stood there, with his bride, Taryn, grinning at his side. Taryn leaned against her male. "It's still the new period when it's all about stealing kisses. Don't take that away from them."

Kason grunted. "They've had far more time alone than we did. They should be able to control themselves."

Taryn rolled her eyes. "Ignore him. I've had morning sickness the last few days and it's put him in a sour mood, imagining the worst-case scenarios for what will happen to me and our daughter."

Taryn's demeanor helped Kalahn relax a little. "Just wait until she's born. He'll be even worse."

"Don't remind me," Taryn muttered. "So, are you ready?" She lifted a parcel in one of her arms. "I have all of the appearance transformation goodies needed from the Kelderan ship."

Since Kalahn's face was well-known among the Kelderan people, her eldest brother Keltor had suggested that she try some of the makeup tricks he'd used to go incognito on Keldera. If it worked for him, it should work for her, too.

"Just about." Kalahn turned back toward Ryven and looked up into his eyes. "I love you."

Happiness and love filled his eyes. "I love you, too."

Not caring about her brother, she stood on her tiptoes and kissed Ryven.

Eventually, Ryven broke the kiss and laid his forehead against hers. "But that had better not be goodbye. After all, I'm still waiting on a certain question. And if this succeeds, I fully expect you to ask it soon."

She raised her brows. "You know that if a female said that to a male, it would send him scurrying the other way?"

"I don't think you're going to run, so I should be safe."

She battled a smile and lost. "Cocky warrior."

He raised an eyebrow. "Says the stubborn telepath."

She laughed and kissed him once more before turning away from the male she loved. Squaring her shoulders, Kalahn nodded. "I'm ready. Let's go."

✺ ✺ ✺

Several hours later, Kalahn no longer had golden skin and blue hair. Instead, she temporarily had purple skin and black hair, all thanks to the special Kelderan cosmetics.

Between her new looks and a dress more suited to merchant's employee, no one questioned her being brought into a cell inside the Kelderan jail.

While putting her into a cell right next to the assassin would be suspicious—she'd been isolated for weeks, after all—Kalahn was put farther down in the same wing.

While the cell wasn't cold, it was small, with three walls and a door. All she had inside was a bed, basin, pitcher with water, and a bucket to be used as a toilet.

Since plumbing was still being developed, most Kelderans were learning to rough it. Still, being confronted with it in a small room only reminded her of how different things were from life back on Keldera with its fancy technology.

She probably wouldn't miss it so much if it weren't for the people trying to kill those she loved. Her brothers suspected Kelderan technology had been stolen to aid in their tasks. So until they were neutralized, the colony transport ship might never be able to return to Keldera.

And considering she hoped to bring Ryven's mother to Jasvar, Kalahn wanted her plan to work and set off a chain of events to end the threat. Ryven had lost his parents as a child; he shouldn't be separated from his second mother, too.

In other words, she couldn't fail.

So Kalahn focused on reinforcing the cloaking barrier around her and Ryven's signatures. While she couldn't keep up the complicated barrier that would hide them from other telepaths on the plane indefinitely, she should be able to maintain it long enough to complete her mission.

Borzet had assured her that the assassin wasn't as skilled as he was, let alone at Kalahn's level. However, Kalahn wasn't going to allow herself to be overconfident. One mistake could tip the balance of power instantly.

Someone knocked on her cell door before a slit opened at the bottom and a tray was pushed inside. Kalahn retrieved it and searched the food until she found the small capsule containing a message. Taking out the paper and unfolding it, she read: *Interrogation is over. Prisoner back in cell.*

This is it. Crumpling the paper, she lay down on her bed and closed her eyes. While she usually didn't need to perform either action in order to use her telepathy, Kalahn didn't want to waste any unnecessary energy by standing or sitting. That meant less she'd have to take from Ryven.

Speaking of her male, she felt Ryven's encouragement through the bond and drew strength from it. After a few seconds of soaking in Ryven's love as well, she exited their shared space and maintained a cloaking barrier around her mental self in the telepath plane.

There were only two signatures nearby—Syzel's starship and the one she'd been shown before, a circle of stone trees surrounding something no one could see.

The tree ring signature belonged to the female assassin.

The further Kalahn went from her own place and toward the tree ring, the more she started to draw energy from Ryven. While she'd love to stay and study her opponent's signature for hours, she didn't have that option. Especially since the female could detect her presence at any time, and that would compromise the mission.

Kalahn, Borzet, Ryven, and Syzel had discussed the best place to attack the female's signature. They'd decided on the top, where the circle of trees protected something.

As Borzet had taught her, Kalahn gathered energy into a ball and imagined compressing it as much as possible. The more confined the energy, the bigger the resulting blast should be.

She could feel Ryven weakening through the bond, but did her best to ignore it. She trusted him to let her know when to stop.

When she finally amassed enough energy, she took a few steadying breaths. This was it. She would only have a few seconds to grab some thoughts before the female could patch up her defenses again. While it was possible to kill another person this way, Borzet had taught her how to avoid it. Kalahn wanted to protect her family, but she didn't want to kill anyone in order to do it.

Matching her actions to her next exhale, Kalahn hurled the energy at her target. A blinding light filled the space and Kalahn rushed closer to the female's signature. A few thoughts drifted out.

I miss them so much. But I must protect them. He'll raise them well.

After a beat, more came. *I've been attacked. I'm sorry, but I can't allow any of them to be discovered. The secrets will die with me. I love you. Goodbye.*

Kalahn decoded her words—the female assassin was going to attempt to kill herself.

Kalahn had a split-second decision to make. But in the end, it all boiled down to one thing.

She couldn't let the female die.

Pushing aside morality, she dropped her invisibility barrier and dove into the crack in the assassin's signature. She quickly dismantled the female's inner shields and touched her mental presence.

Much like what had happened with Ryven, memories flew through Kalahn's mind. However, before she could contain them, she needed to do something else. Wrapping herself around the female's mental presence, Kalahn squeezed until the female fell unconscious.

She would no longer be able to commit suicide.

Just as Kalahn was about to pull back, Ryven's weak voice came through the noise. *Kalahn. Stop.*

She wanted to stop, but the rush of memories made it impossible for her to concentrate, let alone leave the female assassin's mental space.

If she wanted to get back to Ryven, Kalahn needed to contain the memories. Only then could she pull back.

Working as quickly as she could, she finally reached a point where she had most of the memories contained and she could concentrate on something besides the mental vault.

Kalahn left and headed back toward her own space as fast as she could. However, when she arrived, she instantly looked around for Ryven.

But instead of the warm, glowing presence she'd come to expect, there was barely a flicker of light.

He was dying.

And it was all her fault.

No. She wasn't going to let him go. She needed to save him by any means necessary, even if it meant sacrificing herself.

Kalahn wrapped herself around Ryven's spark and channeled as much energy through the mind-bond as she could. She couldn't lose him, not now. He'd trusted her and she'd let him down. She said sternly to him, *Live, Ryven. You need to live.*

He never replied, which worried her further, making her transfer even greater amounts of energy to him.

She had no idea how long she both tried to save him and tried to coax a reply, but eventually her own consciousness faded and she blacked out.

Chapter Nineteen

Ryven woke up some indeterminable time later, opened his eyes and was greeted with a dark room filled with medical equipment.

Recent events flooded his mind and he instantly checked inside their mental space. He finally found Kalahn's presence. However, the usually large, round form was a tenth the usual size. *Kalahn? Can you hear me?*

Silence.

He turned to try to sit up, but that's when he noticed he wasn't alone in the room. Kalahn was in a bed next to his. There was also a doctor standing near her, but Ryven didn't pay him any attention as he slowly stood and moved to Kalahn's side. Taking her hand, he brought it to his cheek. "Kalahn? Wake up, love. I need you to wake up."

The Kelderan doctor, Merctor, spoke. "She won't be waking up anytime soon."

If ever was left unsaid.

Never taking his gaze from Kalahn, Ryven demanded, "What happened to her?"

"The best we can tell, she overstretched her powers. And when she saw you were dying, she transferred her own energy to save you."

He took in Kalahn's pale face and wished he knew of a

way to bring her back. "There has to be something you can do, Merctor."

The doctor shook his head. "Telepathy is beyond my sphere of knowledge, especially for someone on Princess Kalahn's level."

He met his friend's gaze. "Where's Borzet? Maybe he can tell me how to give her some of my energy."

Merctor replied, "Borzet already told us not to try that. Passing energy back and forth will eventually kill you both. It's up to Kalahn to wake up."

He looked back down at Kalahn, smoothed her blue hair back from her forehead, and kissed her temple. He whispered, "Don't you dare die on me, Princess. I still have debts to pay."

He willed for her to wake up and tease him, but Kalahn remained motionless save for the rise and fall of her chest. His heart constricted. Kalahn should be the one alert and lively. She shouldn't have sacrificed herself to save him.

He retreated inside their mental space and swirled around Kalahn's small, flickering presence. *Kalahn. Wake up, love.*

Still silence.

Remembering how she had reached out to him when he'd been injured, Ryven carefully directed a thread of his mental self outward. He wouldn't consume Kalahn like she'd done with him, but he let a small part of himself wrap around Kalahn's light.

He then sent every loving thought he could toward her, including memories of their first kiss years ago. Him kissing her jaw to see if she could keep her marking colors dark blue. Her making him come with her mouth. The endless teasing of her fantasies.

Ryven had no idea how long he stood there trying to coax Kalahn back, but eventually, Kason's voice filled the room. "She'll wake up, Ryven. Kalahn isn't one to give up lightly."

He met Kason's gaze. "At least tell me her sacrifice was successful."

"Yes and no."

He sighed. "I'm in no mood to drag information out of you, Kason. My soon-to-be bride almost forfeited her life to help you. So tell me exactly what you've discovered."

Kason crossed his arms over his chest. "The assassin fell unconscious and mumbled a few things about her children and protecting them. Some other ramblings gave us the location of her mate. Guards are bringing him and their children back here as we speak."

"The female had children?" he asked.

"Yes. There must be a specific reason why she was going to such extremes to kill the royal family. Thanks to Kalahn, we should be able to find out why."

Ryven grunted. "I sense Kalahn learned more, but I'm not sure what."

"I have no doubt she'll wake up to share it. She's always wanted to be useful."

Ryven looked back at Kalahn's sleeping face. "Just make sure to tell her that when she regains consciousness. You have no idea how much she wanted you to notice her as more than a sister to be married off, Kason."

"I can't change the past, but Kalahn has more than earned her place in my inner circle. If she reaches out telepathically, ensure she knows that I'll have other assignments for her. Provided she wants them."

Ryven smiled. "She'll want them."

Kason grunted. "Good. Keep me updated on her status. I need to help with the incoming arrivals."

"I will. And normally I'd offer to help you, but I'm not going anywhere until Kalahn wakes up."

Kason put a hand on his shoulder and squeezed. "I

wouldn't expect you to. Just make sure to take care of yourself as well. Borzet will be along shortly to see if he can help heal Kalahn's mind, and having you awake will probably make that situation go smoother."

Ryven paused, but decided he had to know. "Will there be permanent damage?"

"It's too early to tell. But knowing Kalahn, she'll find a way back to us."

After a few more seconds, Kason murmured his goodbye and left.

Ryven pulled up a chair and sat next to Kalahn's bed. Not knowing what else to do, he sang her some of the lullabies and songs his adopted mother had sung to him. They had always had a way of soothing his soul and bringing him out of a fever in the past. While it probably wasn't sound medical advice, it couldn't hurt to try everything he could to bring back the female he loved.

❋ ❋ ❋

Thorin Jarrell stared at the little girl with red skin and did his best not to gawk.

The daughter of the female assassin was part-Brekvan. Not from her mother, who was part Hirlanzian, but rather from her father's side.

He didn't understand Brevkan females as well as males since he'd never met one. At least, he'd never met one that he knew of. According to his bride, Vala, there were many who lived pretending to be full Kelderan, much like he'd done for most of his life.

But the little girl was important because she was a sign of what his bride had been suggesting to him. Namely, that there were other part-Brevkan Kelderans inside the Jasvarian colony.

The Forbidden

He'd wondered as much when Syzel had told him about the security breaches and the faked information concerning the passengers and their genetics. But seeing the little girl's red face was undeniable proof. No Kelderan had skin that color, and a DNA test had confirmed her heritage.

Her older brother sitting at her side had light blue skin, which hid his non-Kelderan heritage. Blue was one of the skin tones that Kelderans, Hirlanzians, and Brevkans all shared.

As he watched the boy play with a wooden starship and the little girl attempt to draw something on the paper in front of her, Thorin wished he could interrogate the father instead. But Kason had asked him and Vala to talk with the children, and he wasn't one to turn down a request from the leader of the Kelderan colony. He and Kason had never gotten along earlier in their lives and only recently had learned to work together, but they both wished to protect the colony and their respective brides above all else.

Vala sat across from the little girl, drawing her own picture. When Vala finished, she turned it toward the girl named Arvia. "Can you guess what this is?"

The girl glanced up. "A flower."

Vala snorted. "It's a bird, actually. What are you drawing?"

Arvia didn't answer but continued sketching her picture. It was her brother who finally spoke. "It's one of her nightmares."

Vala leaned forward to get a better look and gasped. Glancing over her shoulder, she met Thorin's gaze and said, "You should see this."

He'd never been good with children, but he would do anything for his bride. So Thorin squatted down at the low table and studied the scribbles.

While abstract, he saw a field of people lying in what had to be pools of blood.

The picture answered his question as to whether Brevkan females had rage visions or not.

He moved his gaze to the young female's face and wished he could protect her from such dreams. Thorin had nearly gone crazy from trying to contain similar visions for almost thirty years. He didn't wish that fate upon anyone.

Which meant his and Vala's plans to seek out the other part-Brekvan individuals and learn as much as they could about their whereabouts, so that they could help all of them, would have to be accelerated.

Vala touched his shoulder and he met her eyes. "We have to help these children, Thorin. Once the dust settles down with Kason and his family, I think it's time to ask for his help. I can't bear to watch these children go through what you did, especially if there's a way to calm it."

He nodded. "I think it's time to find the other hidden individuals, starting with those on Jasvar."

Thorin and Vala went back to watching Arvia. He understood why the female assassin and her lord would want to protect their children. However, he wasn't entirely sure why killing the royal family would help their situation. There had to be someone out there spreading misinformation. He needed to discover from where and try to stop it before it only made things worse. Because if extremist groups became the norm on Jasvar, Keldera would stop sending colonists.

And if that happened, who knew what might happen to the Kelderans who already lived on Jasvar. After all, the Earth Colony Alliance sent observers to the planet. If they saw the Kelderans as a threat, they'd be forced to leave.

Which meant they would have to return to Keldera. The thought of his Vala being forced back into the shadows as a Barren stoked his anger. Only because of his bride's presence nearby did he not fall into a rage.

No, he wouldn't allow the anger to take over. Vala deserved better.

It seemed Thorin's list of duties on Jasvar kept growing. But he'd only recently found love and happiness. He wasn't about to give it up. He'd do whatever it took to hold onto them.

Chapter Twenty

Ryven looked at each of the people standing in Kalahn's room and wished he knew anything about most of them.

However, all he knew was that the group of people consisted of all the telepaths and empaths—people who could sense and possibly manipulate emotions—from inside the human colony. They had also all been vetted and vouched for by Taryn Demara.

And they were here to help Kalahn.

It'd been almost two days since she'd fallen unconscious and with each passing day, her inner light dimmed a little more.

He'd been tempted every second of the last two days to try transferring his energy to save her, even if it meant losing his life.

If not for Borzet and the doctors arguing with him to let them try one more thing, he would've done it, too.

Borzet stood in the center of the dozen people. He and the male at his side were the leaders of the group. The other male had blue skin and metallic silver hair, which easily identified him as Gerzalt, Nova Drakven's father.

Ryven gently squeezed Kalahn's hand in his and asked one more time. "Are you sure this is a better idea than mine?"

Since Ryven and Gerzalt had both been given ear translator devices, Ryven easily understood Gerzalt's reply. "I sense your worry and fear, son. But this wouldn't be the first time empaths and telepaths have teamed up together to save someone."

"But it's never been done on Jasvar," Ryven stated.

Gerzalt shook his head. "No. However, my people can possess a variety of abilities, including empathy and telepathy. Anyone who possesses an extraordinary ability on my former planet is trained in its uses. Working with a telepath to heal an injured mind is one of the many things I studied."

Borzet spoke up. "While Hirlanzians only possess telepathy, Gerzalt has been training me almost nonstop over the last two days in how to work in tandem with the empaths. I believe we will succeed."

So the fate of his female was in the hands of a few tired individuals.

Taryn Demara spoke up from the corner of the room, where she stood with Kason. Thanks to the device in his ear, Ryven didn't need any help understanding her today. "I know you hate the unknown and any sort of risk. But Kelderan medicine isn't very effective at treating telepathic-related conditions. I trust both Borzet and Gerzalt implicitly. I believe this is the best chance we have at bringing Kalahn back to us, Ryven."

Ryven looked back at Kalahn's face. While they weren't married yet, Kason had taken into account Ryven's doubts when it came to Kalahn's treatment. The final decision about what to do had been given to him.

Brushing the hair from her forehead, Ryven retreated inside their shared mental space and examined her light. There wasn't much more than a flicker to Kalahn's presence.

And if that weren't worrying enough, her barriers were gone, as were all of her improvements to their area. Ryven was singlehandedly protecting their minds from outside influence and harm.

The telepaths and empaths could possibly fail and end up killing her, but she wouldn't last much longer without some sort of help. While there could always be a miracle, he preferred doing anything rather than sitting by and doing nothing.

In other words, the combined telepathic and empathic healing procedure was his best bet.

Ryven came back to the outside world. Standing, he leaned down and kissed Kalahn's lips. He murmured, "Fight for us, love. Whatever energy you have left, make sure to lend it to them. You need to pull through this."

Kason placed a hand on his shoulder. "You need to stand back and allow them to do their work."

After one more kiss, Ryven slowly released Kalahn's hand and allowed Kason to guide him to the side of the room. The dozen people of various races formed a semicircle around Kalahn and joined hands.

Ryven knew they'd do some sort of combination of power, energy, and emotions to try to heal Kalahn. However, the details fled his mind as he stared at Kalahn's pale face. All he cared about right now was seeing her eyes open and for her to smile at him again.

As the people forming the semicircle began to chant in a specific rhythm—for something related to keeping time—Ryven forced himself to retreat and look back on the telepath plane again. It was up to him to allow the other telepaths inside his and Kalahn's mental space. After dismantling a small entrance, Ryven stood back as the seven telepaths came in. With any other situation, he would note each person and try to memorize the shape and colors of the mental presences.

But he only had eyes for Kalahn's flickering light.

Once the telepaths formed a ring around her, a blast of positive emotions filled the space. Hope. Happiness. Gratitude. Love.

And a multitude of others he couldn't even identify straightaway.

Energy swirled around Kalahn, the different colors of the telepaths forming a sort of rainbow. While he couldn't see it, the positive emotions moved away from him and he knew they'd be joining the ring of light around Kalahn.

If all went according to plan, the mental energy combined with the positive emotions would help feed Kalahn's mental self to the point she could heal on her own.

There was probably a complicated scientific explanation for how it worked, but he didn't care what it did as long as it was successful.

The swirling ring of rainbow light intensified, moving closer and closer with each pass to Kalahn's flickering presence. While rationally he knew it needed to engulf her, his protective instincts shouted for him to go and guard the woman he loved.

As if sensing his desires and possible protection, the rainbow light immediately engulfed Kalahn, hiding her mental self from everyone on the telepath plane.

The seconds ticked by, the light around her growing dimmer and dimmer, until it eventually evaporated. At the same time, a force pinned him to the wall of the shared space.

At first, Kalahn's flickering presence was unchanged in appearance or intensity. However, Ryven didn't give up hope yet. He needed to do his part to give her the final push.

Sending love through their mate-bond, he said telepathically, *I love you, Lahn. Wake up so I can show you how much.*

The light remained unchanged. He was about to say something else when Kalahn's mental presence doubled in size, and then again, until her light was nearly as bright and large as before the attack. True, it was slightly dimmer than he remembered, but it was far from dying out.

A weak voice filled the space. *Don't call me Lahn.*

He smiled. *Lahn, Lahn, Lahn. Wake up and tell me to stop.*

Ryven waited to see if Kalahn would open her eyes. Some might say that goading his female would be the wrong way to go about it. But he knew Kalahn, and irritation was a strong motivation for her.

Kalahn's eyelids fluttered open. Her voice was so low he could barely hear it. "Don't call me Lahn."

He pushed past the telepaths and empaths to Kalahn's side. He kissed her before laying his forehead against hers. "You're awake." She grunted and he grinned. "Kalahn."

"Better," she whispered.

Merctor pushed to the other side of the bed and stated, "I need to examine her, Ryven."

All he wanted to do was crawl next to Kalahn in bed, hold her close, and never let go. However, he settled on taking her hand and never breaking eye contact with her. Since Borzet had told him that he couldn't use telepathy with Kalahn until she was deemed fully healed, he contented himself with conveying emotion with his eyes and his markings.

When his markings turned pink, the color of love, Kalahn's did the same.

Merctor finally finished and said, "Physically, her vital signs are stronger." He looked to Borzet. "Can you judge her mental state?"

Borzet moved around his and Kalahn's shared mental space. In all the commotion, Ryven had forgotten the other male was still there. But at least the other telepaths and empaths had exited the mental area and left them alone.

After a short while, Borzet finally spoke aloud. "Princess Kalahn is stronger and out of immediate danger. However, she needs to heal and take it slow for a little while; otherwise, she might regress."

Ryven jumped in. "I'll ensure she takes it easy, even if it means strapping her to a bed."

The green-skinned male shook his head. "It's not just physically she must rest. She came extremely close to a telepathic burnout. I'm confident she'll regain her strength in time, both physically and telepathically, but she mustn't overstretch herself. So apart from emotions through the mind-bond, you must refrain from speaking to her via telepathy."

Ryven cupped Kalahn's cheek. "I've spent most of my life talking to her only using my mouth. I'm sure I can manage it once more."

Kalahn gave a weak smile. "I want to be witty, but my mind is foggy. So you'll just have to put up with a boring version of me until I can think straight again."

"You'll never be boring, Kalahn." He kissed her lips. "You being here is all that matters."

As he stared into Kalahn's eyes, Ryven put every bit of love he had for the female into his gaze. Kalahn whispered, "I'll soon have a question to ask you."

Even though he wanted to make Kalahn his bride right then and there, he replied, "Whenever you're ready, I'll be here. And just so you know, I expect romance. Lots of it. Flowers strewn about the floor would be a good start."

He winked, and Kalahn snorted. The sound helped to erase a fraction of his built-up stress.

His semiprivate reunion with Kalahn was short-lived, however, as Kason and Taryn took Merctor's place on the other side of the bed. Kason took Kalahn's other hand and said, "It's good to have you back, sister."

Kalahn moved her gaze to her brother. "I agree. But since I don't have unlimited amounts of strength, we can share relief later. Will you fill me in on what happened after I blacked out?"

Taryn snorted. "Stubborn as your brother, that's for sure. Here you are, back from nearly dying, and you want to know how your mission went."

Kason spoke before anyone else could. "She has a right to know. After all, without Kalahn, we never would've found out what we did."

"What did you discover?" Kalahn asked.

Kason glanced at Merctor. "Does she have the strength for this?"

"Keep it brief. I suspect hiding it from her will only prevent the princess from resting."

Even the doctor understood Kalahn well.

Kason signaled and waited for all of the telepaths and empaths to leave before he focused back on his sister.

Ryven resisted growling and telling Kason to hurry up. He, too, had been kept in the dark about what Kason had discovered.

Kalahn's sacrifice had damn well better have been worth it.

❇ ❇ ❇

Kalahn struggled to keep her eyes open. Her body and mind demanded rest, but she needed to make sure her family was at least somewhat better protected first. Because if her mission had been successful, it meant she could finally ask Ryven to be her lord.

Maybe they could even retreat to an isolated place for her recovery and get to simply be together without any other prying eyes or expectations.

So while probably only seconds had passed for Kason to answer, it felt like years. Her brother finally spoke again. "The female assassin, Pelryka, is alive. She's also led us to her lord and children, which are the key to everything."

She barely noted that it was the first time Kason had used the female assassin's name before focusing on the bigger picture. "Which is?"

Taryn jumped in. "Kason will drag this out, so let me tell you. As we suspected, Pelryka is part-Hirlanzian. However, the interesting part is that her husband is part-Brevkan."

"Like Thorin," Kalahn stated.

Taryn nodded. "Yes. The pair have two children. While the son can pass as Kelderan, the little girl has red skin and will instantly be identified as something else. The female was trying to protect her children. And through a warped sense of reasoning, she believed getting rid of the royal family would make it easier to change the laws surrounding the halflings inside Kelderan society. Especially those with Brevkan parentage, like her son and daughter."

The Brevkan wars had devastated Keldera, and no doubt many would still blame, not to mention harm, anyone who could be linked to them.

Ryven jumped in. "But the royal family can't change the laws without the commoners' representatives. So why go after the royal family?"

Kason answered, "We're still working on extracting information, but the best we can tell, there is someone or a group of someones spreading lies and misinformation to help target the royal family. Keltor has information on one such group, but nothing was ever said about the rights of those with some Brevkan heritage. He and I are trying to determine if they are the same group with two factions, or if this is another group entirely."

Even with Kalahn's tired brain, she put some of it together. "The female was trying to assassinate us so her children could gain rights?"

Taryn bobbed her head. "Yes. It doesn't excuse her actions, but I at least understand them now." She placed a hand on her lower belly. "My child isn't even born yet, and I would do anything to protect her."

Ryven leaned forward. "So what's being done about all of this?"

Kason grunted. "Thorin and Vala have an idea, one that may help discredit the person advocating that the only way to gain greater freedoms is to kill the royal family members. There are more part-Brevkan individuals on Keldera than I had been aware of. The Barren, apparently, take care of them when younger and some may be willing to reach out to their now-adult charges and convince them to talk with Thorin about going public. While outing them and protecting them on Keldera is too great a step right now, Thorin and Vala are going to search for them here on Jasvar. Maybe if they cooperate with the colony's administrative council and show they are just like anyone else, then the news will spread back home and give hope to those living in the shadows."

"And the female, Pelryka?" Kalahn asked.

"She will remain imprisoned," Kason stated. "However, if she and her lord break their silence and share the information we need, then she may get probation. Either way, her children will be guaranteed protection for as long as they are on this planet. I won't let innocents suffer because of crimes committed decades ago. They are not to blame for their Brevkan ancestors' actions."

Despite the heaviness of her entire body, Kalahn drew on what little strength she had to say, "When I saved Pelryka from suicide, I unintentionally obtained all her memories. Once I'm stronger, I can look for anything we need, to help your search."

Ryven caressed her cheek. "Are you sure? You don't have to. I know it's not easy reliving other people's pasts."

She shook her head. "No, I need to do this. And it won't be so bad this time since I'm not planning on marrying her."

Ryven filled in the others about Kalahn accidentally taking his memories before adding, "Then Kason can use what you find against Pelryka's information to gauge how well the female is cooperating."

Kason said, "It can also give us more information about how and why Pelryka felt she needed to kill us."

Ryven stilled his fingers on her face. "Yes, but later. For now, Kalahn needs to rest."

Kason frowned, but Taryn placed a hand on his arm. "Let's give them some privacy, Kason. They've earned it."

After Kason and Taryn murmured their goodbyes and exited the room, Kalahn looked over at Ryven. "There's so much I want to say, but I'm struggling to stay awake."

He gently laid down next to her and put an arm over her waist. After kissing her neck, he whispered. "Sleep, love. We have the rest of our lives to talk."

Snuggling closer against his body, she reveled in his heat and scent. Love also emanated from their mind-bond.

All of her doubts and worries about what still needed to be done to protect her family fled her mind, and she fell asleep in the arms of the male she loved.

Chapter Twenty-One

Kalahn watched Ryven's sleeping face, taking in the small crinkles at the corners of his mouth and at his eyes. She almost traced them, but held back and listened to the slow rhythm of his snores.

Some might be bothered by his soft snoring, but to her, it only reinforced that he was alive.

She'd come close to losing him when she'd drawn too much power from him during her mission. And when faced with Ryven's death, it'd been unbearable. So much so that she hadn't hesitated to risk her own life to save the good-humored, fierce warrior currently lying next to her.

To say she was happy they were both still alive and together was an understatement.

He stopped snoring right before his lips curled up. He whispered, "Had your fill yet, Lahn?"

"Of your snoring? Yes, yes I have."

Chuckling, he opened his eyes and tightened his arm over her waist. "Someone's feeling better today. And I didn't even have to use my magical lips to cure you."

She rolled her eyes. "Most people would be nicer to someone who's recovering from nearly dying."

"Yes, they would. However, admit it, it'd only irritate you if I did."

"I would argue, but unfortunately you're right."

He winked. "See, there's a reason you love me."

She caressed his jaw, running her fingers through his short stubble. "There are many reasons, but irritating me isn't high on the list."

He placed his hand over hers, stilling her movements. "Irritation should be one of the top ones. After all, it's how I coaxed you back to me."

As she stared into Ryven's eyes, Kalahn couldn't help but smile. "It did, although I hope that's not how you plan to solve everything with me. Because one day you could wake up with no hair and some rather interesting skin concealer colors. I'm thinking of making you a rainbow warrior."

He pulled her closer, until her body was up against his chest. "Cheeky princess. But no, once you're healed and cleared by the doctor, I'm going to use my lips for much better things than talking and irritating you."

Ryven closed the distance between them and kissed her gently. Kalahn sighed and Ryven took advantage, slipping inside her mouth and caressing her tongue with his own.

He took his time tasting her, letting her know how much he'd missed her. And even though they should both be safe for the foreseeable future, Kalahn committed every lick and caress to memory. She would never take her time with Ryven for granted ever again.

When he finally pulled away, he said, "Now that you understand how glad I am to have you back, we need to talk."

"Uh-oh. That doesn't sound good."

"Kalahn, I'm serious." He stroked her cheek with his thumb. "While I'm ecstatic that we're both alive, promise me that you won't risk yourself to save me again. I couldn't bear to be here, knowing I was the reason for your death."

She absently traced one of the markings on his chest. "Silly man, I can't promise such a thing. I love you, which means it's my duty to protect you."

Ryven growled. "Duty has a time and place, but not in this."

She quirked an eyebrow. "Let's reverse the situation. Would you sit by and let me die?" His silence was her answer. "Exactly. So how about we both just try to avoid getting killed? That will make things a lot easier for everyone."

"We'll see how that goes." He searched her gaze. "I sense worry through the bond, love. What's wrong?"

Kalahn didn't hesitate. "I'm worried about the female assassin, Pelryka. On the one hand, she was part of a plot to kill my family. On the other, she was protecting her children. I wish her case were more black and white rather than gray."

"You aren't sorting through her memories yet, are you? It's too soon."

She sighed. "I know it is, and I'm not. But the instant I'm cleared, I'm going to look. I also need to see if I can find out who tried to kill you by cutting those branches."

She traced one of the scars on his chest, a permanent reminder of the Siren bird attack he'd endured. While Ryven was getting stronger every day, he'd never be able to fully raise his left arm again.

Not that it changed him one bit in her eyes.

Ryven captured her hand and brought it to his lips. "There are other things you can do in the meantime. After all, I'm still waiting to be swept off my feet."

She fought a smile. "You're incorrigible."

"I never said I wasn't."

It was on the tip of her tongue to ask him to be her lord, but something held her back. "You know I still haven't received word about either Keltor changing the law successfully or the council approving you as my choice. Until they do, we can't marry anyway." He opened his mouth, but she beat him to it. "And before you say you'd gladly sit in a jail cell to show how much you care about me, I refuse to accept that. Honor has a time and place, but not if it means you'll be kept away. So, I'll ask when I can."

"Someone has become a little less impulsive," Ryven stated.

She shook her head. "Not entirely. If I were stronger right now, I'd surprise you with a few things and be impulsive enough to live up to my reputation."

His gaze turned heated. "Maybe I should be the one to surprise you."

Kalahn kissed him as a response. However, before he could do more than stroke her back with his hand, the door chimed.

Since they were temporarily staying inside one of the shuttles from the Kelderan colony transport ship, and they moved around often to keep their location a secret, it could only be someone they trusted.

So she said, "Computer, open the door."

The door slid open. Kalahn expected to see her brother, but it wasn't him.

She sat up and said, "Kajala!"

Her sister waddled inside the room, appearing even more pregnant than before. Kalahn was well enough to get up and hug her sister. "I'm glad to see you." She pulled back. "But are you sure you should be here? You look about ready to pop at any second."

Taryn emerged from the hallway and spoke in CEL. "Kajala demanded to see you, and Kason finally capitulated after a little convincing on my part. After all, just because she's pregnant doesn't mean she's an invalid."

Kalahn suspected Taryn was setting the standard for her own pregnancy.

Kajala spoke up in Kelderan before she could. "They told me what happened to you and I just needed to see you for myself, to make sure you're okay."

"I'm on the mend." She searched Kajala's eyes. "But how are you holding up? Are you okay, or have enemies found you again and tried to attack?"

Kajala shook her head. "No one has gotten close to me like before. Kason and Taryn have been taking good care of me." She paused before adding softly, "Although I still mourn what happened to the honorable warrior who protected me."

At the sadness in Kajala's eyes, Kalahn gave her another hug. "I'm sorry you had to go through that. But give us a little more time and the worst of the danger should be over."

Ryven came up behind her and Kalahn released her sister. Kajala searched her gaze. "It's not the danger but rather that someone died trying to protect me. I know it's not much and it won't help bring the male back to his family, but I'm going to honor the warrior's memory by naming my son after him. That way, my baby will know and appreciate the male's sacrifice."

"Jala," Kalahn whispered.

Her sister stood a little taller. "But you're right, I can't change what happened." She took Kalahn's hand. "I'll do my best to appreciate what I still have. I know we haven't known each other long, but I've missed you and can't wait to have you around again."

As Kalahn studied her sister's face, she couldn't help but notice the circles under her eyes or the paleness of her skin. "I've missed you, too. However, I'm a little concerned about your health. Shouldn't you be resting?"

Kajala rubbed her belly. "My son has been giving me a little bit of trouble lately, and the stress of recent events haven't helped, but the doctors haven't found anything to be concerned about. They said a short visit wouldn't hurt either of us."

Kalahn guided her sister to a chair. "Still, you should sit down." Once Kajala complied, she sat beside her sister. "Now that you're here, there's something else I want to tell you while I have the chance."

"Let me guess, it has to do with Ryven?" Kajala asked, amusement dancing in her eyes.

She blinked. "Wait, how do you know that?"

Kajala waved a hand at Ryven, who hovered at Kalahn's side. "He's been following you around the room, almost like he's afraid you'll die at any moment. Also, given that Ryven is a warrior and he's allowing his markings to flicker, it tells me it's more than a duty. He cares for you." She glanced between them. "I'm glad it worked out, Kalahn. I like him."

Kalahn smiled. "That's good, because I love him. Well, most of the time."

As she shared a glance with Ryven, Kajala cried out. Kalahn whipped her head back around just as liquid hit the floor below her sister.

It looked like her nephew was ready to come out and greet them all.

✹ ✹ ✹

After sixteen hours of labor, Kajala Mayven tried to remember to breathe.

She'd read about labor and had known that on Jasvar, she'd have to forgo any sort of Kelderan medical advancements.

And even with some medicinal herbs to help with the pain, it still felt as someone kept gripping her insides and twisting.

When the most recent contraction finished, she slumped on the bed. Even though she was anxious to meet her son, someone was painfully absent from what should've been one of the happiest events of her life.

Davrel.

No. She couldn't think about her dead love. Their son needed her now, and that's what she had to focus on.

So she continued to breathe to pass the time between contractions.

Matilda, the head medicine woman on Jasvar, looked up from between Kajala's legs. "With the next contraction, push, my fierce fighter. I think he's finally ready to come out and say hello to his mother."

Kalahn squeezed Kajala's hand. "I'm here, Jala. And I know you can do this."

While she knew her sister was being supportive, she wanted to snap that it wasn't so easy to push a person out of her.

Thankfully she managed to keep her thoughts to herself.

She lost count of her breaths until the next pain gripped her and she cried out.

"I know it hurts, but push, Jala," Matilda ordered in a gentle yet stern voice.

Gripping Kalahn's hand in hers, Kajala pushed with every bit of strength she still had left, ignoring the way her body stretched. If her nerves could scream aloud in pain, everyone in the room would be deaf by now.

The contraction ended, and she tried to catch her breath. She barely heard Matilda's voice. "One more should do it, Jala. He has a lovely head of white hair."

Just like Davrel had had.

Tears filled her eyes and she couldn't stop them from flowing. Davrel should be in the room with her, loving and protective as always, and just as anxious as she to meet their son.

Kalahn brushed away her tears. "You're nearly done, Jala. You can do this."

Not wanting to correct Kalahn's assumption for her tears, Kajala gave a slight nod.

In less time than it should have, another contraction hit. She pushed and pushed, more than ready to meet her son.

A baby's cry filled the room and Matilda held up her boy. Even not cleaned up, she could see that her baby had her golden skin and Davrel's white hair.

The perfect combination of him and her.

The tears threatened to fall again.

Matilda quickly wrapped him up, which stopped his cries, and brought him to her. Once her son lay on her chest, Kajala kissed his forehead and murmured, "Nice to finally met you, Tyden."

Her son moved a little, but didn't cry.

Staring at the product of her and Davrel's love, she finally gave in and let the tears flow again.

Davrel should be alive to help raise their son. No doubt, her boy would then become the same strong, honorable male that Davrel had been.

Instead, Tyden would have to face a constant wave of pity and maybe even resentment unless she found a way to change things and lessen the stigma attached to unmarried Kelderan mothers and their children.

Maybe that would be her new purpose. She'd been trying to forget about her love every day, and she doubted she ever would. But fighting for her son's future might be the thing she needed to finally heal.

Tyden moved again, reminding her he was there. Yes,

he was a piece of Davrel she'd always have, and one she'd protect with her life.

Closing her eyes, she breathed in his scent. It reminded her that she had another person to care for now.

Kajala couldn't let her grief surrounding Davrel take over her life. She would always love him, and miss him every day, but her son needed to become the new center of her world.

Opening her eyes, she kissed Tyden again. Kalahn finally spoke, "He's beautiful, Jala."

She smiled up at her sister. "Thank you. Would you like to hold him?" Kalahn hesitated, and Kajala added, "You'll be fine."

Kalahn gingerly picked up Tyden and cooed soothing words to him.

Watching her sister only reminded Kajala that even though Davrel was gone, she wasn't alone. Between her family and Tyden, she should be able to carve out a good future for herself.

Chapter Twenty-Two

Ryven double-checked the rucksack he'd packed and resisted pacing.

Kalahn was with the doctor and would find out if she were physically cleared and deemed recovered. While he knew it would be some time yet before he could talk with her via telepathy, he had a surprise for his female. One that required the doctor to approve of her resuming physical activities.

Before his mind could wander to the physical activities he wished he could do with Kalahn, which involved both of them naked, his female walked out. He tried to read her expression, but couldn't find anything. Even her markings were a dark blue.

He tried his best to hide his apprehension. If anything were truly wrong, Kalahn wouldn't try to hide it from him.

Merctor came out after her, nodded, and said, "I'll be back tomorrow for your physical therapy evaluation, Ryven."

Before Ryven could do more than bob his head, the doctor exited the Kelderan shuttle he and Kalahn were currently staying in.

Focusing back on his love, Ryven closed the distance between them and gently took hold of her shoulders. "Well?

What did he say?"

She stared another second before she laughed. "I was trying to imitate Kason, but I have no idea how he does it. Anyway, I'm physically fine. I just can't use telepathy yet."

Ryven smiled slowly. "Good, because I have a surprise for you."

"A surprise?"

He kissed her quickly before stepping away to pick up the rucksack. He held out a hand to her. "Come with me and you'll find out what it is."

Kalahn didn't hesitate to place her hand in his. "Okay, but this surprise had better not involve me hunting or gathering my first day back on my feet. I'm content with replicator fare for the present."

"Says the woman who complains about the artificial taste every time she eats it now."

She stuck out her tongue. "It's still better than hunting. I have many other qualities to offer. Someone else can do the killing and meat preparation part."

"And the cooking?"

"Hey, I've been a bit busy to learn how to cook. You know, what with protecting my family and saving your life."

He motioned his head toward the exit. "Then let me start to repay that debt with this."

Kalahn sobered. "Ryven, you don't owe me anything. That's not what I meant."

Winking, he squeezed her hand in his. "I know. It's called teasing. Whenever I stop doing that, then begin to worry." He tugged. "Come. I already scouted the area and had Kason confirm it was safe."

He left out the part about Kason accusing Ryven of being a fool. However, a quick reminder of what Kalahn did whenever she was caged up quickly garnered Kason's attention. He didn't like forcing his friend's hand, but

Kalahn needed this excursion. Not only because she sometimes had nightmares about accidentally killing him and could use some new pleasant memories to push away the bad, but also because they'd both been mostly cooped up inside the shuttle. Ryven was fine with that if he was on duty, but lounging around with a fidgety Kalahn was rubbing off on him.

Kalahn's voice filled the shuttle's corridor. "Fine. Then let's go. The sooner you show me your surprise, the sooner I can celebrate no longer being confined to this shuttle in my own way."

He raised his brows. "You can't say that and not tell me what you mean."

She grinned. "See? Surprises can be awful, can't they?"

Chuckling, he guided them out of the shuttle and down the stairs to the ground. "Unlike you, I like surprises. I would say taunt me all you like, but that would only invite trouble."

"You do know me too well, don't you?"

He glanced over his shoulder. "I suspect what I do know is just the beginning, love." Kalahn looked away and bit her lip, no doubt remembering how she had his memories. He stopped walking and waited until she met his gaze again. "Kalahn, this will never work if you keep feeling guilty about my memories or taking too much power from me. None of that matters if it means I have you by my side."

"Ryven."

He adjusted the rucksack over his shoulder and cupped her cheek with his free hand. "I love you, Kalahn tro el Vallen. Just as you are."

Closing the distance between them, she kissed him gently before murmuring, "And I love you as you are, too. Well, 99.99 percent of the time. That other 0.01 percent is when I'm impatient to find out about a surprise."

He snorted and kissed her gently. "I'm sure you'll find another 0.01 percent to add to that over time. No one is perfect, after all."

"Good thing you realize that now."

Shaking his head, he walked once more and Kalahn followed. "I think I'll hold back on my reply, lest I get into trouble."

Touching his arm, she murmured, "No, don't. I may not always like it, but I want to hear whatever you want to say."

"As you wish. Talking with you requires a lot of give and take, and I'm starting to see why Kason locked you up sometimes. He isn't very good at negotiating with females, at least until he met Taryn, and that was probably the only way he knew how to handle you."

She raised her brows. "Try to lock me up and see what happens."

"I'm not your brother, Kalahn. Unless you're unconscious or otherwise unable to defend yourself, I'm not going to lock you up." The sound of roaring water grew louder. "And today is the opposite of locking you up. Come on, we're nearly there."

Ryven trekked the path he'd visited several times over the last week. It wasn't long before they came to a tall line of undergrowth and he released Kalahn's hand. "Do you trust me?"

"Of course."

"Then close your eyes."

When she didn't hesitate, happiness swelled in his heart.

He covered her eyes with one hand and guided her through the underbrush. The sound of the water was almost deafening, so he shouted, "This is for my slightly dirty princess."

He removed his hand and Kalahn opened her eyes. He took in her features as her mouth dropped open and her eyes widened. He asked, "So, what do you think of the first part of your surprise?"

※ ※ ※

Kalahn stood next to Ryven in front of a giant waterfall, one that fell at least a hundred feet before hitting the pool of water at the bottom. Light yellow and teal flowers grew around the edges, highlighting the purple tint of the water, which was a reflection of the purple stone at the shallow bottom.

It looked remarkably like the one from her dreams, when Ryven had morphed into her dream version of him to wake her up.

He'd lived up to his promise to make her dreams a reality.

She finally tore her eyes from the water to look at Ryven. "How did you even know this was here?"

He shrugged. "My best friend has Jasvarian connections. I merely asked Kason to find the closest waterfall to our present location."

"I have a hard time believing Kason would help you locate this," she drawled. "If my brother had his way, I'd be confined in that stupid shuttle until further notice."

"I didn't ask him. I asked Taryn, who was able to persuade Kason."

She snorted. "Taryn has him wrapped around her finger, doesn't she?"

He winked. "Usually, but only because he allows it." He waved toward the waterfall. "But I'd rather stop talking about your brother and how his bride seduces him and instead go for a swim."

She raised an eyebrow. "Since I don't have a swimsuit, you must mean we're going to swim naked. It seems I'm not the only one with dirty fantasies."

Heat flashed in his eyes, and Kalahn did her best not to let it affect her. At least not until she knew the full extent of his surprise. Then she would embrace her desire and hopefully jumpstart her plan. The waterfall was the perfect location for it.

His voice was gravelly as he said, "That wouldn't fit with your dream." He reached into the rucksack and produced two small bits of white material.

A memory of Kalahn wearing a bathing suit that barely covered her body flashed into her mind.

At first, embarrassment sparked. She could refuse him and the skimpy swimming outfit.

But the thought of wearing so little in front of her male stirred heat low in her belly. Maybe she could convince him to do more than kiss or fondle. After all, Kalahn wanted her male to claim her now that she was physically strong again. That had been her plan ever since the doctor had cleared her.

And since Ryven was honorable and would state never until they were married, she needed every trick she could get to change his mind. She might want to marry him eventually, but not until things were safe and the law was changed.

And there was no way she wanted to wait that long to be claimed.

Decision made, she took the bathing suit and twirled the top piece around her forefinger. "Face the other way and let me change."

Ryven raked her body from head to toe slowly, each inch making her body flush and her markings flash red. Desire coursing through their shared mind-bond only made her hotter. By the time he reached her feet and then met her gaze again, the smirk on his face told her he knew exactly

The Forbidden

how much he affected her.

Well, two could play that game.

Once his back faced her, she quickly put on the swimsuit. The entire time the spray from the waterfall caressed her warm skin, which made the fabric cling to her body.

Good. Maybe it would make Ryven's jaw drop. "I'm ready."

Ryven turned. But unlike before, his gaze never wavered from hers.

Kalahn frowned. "You all but undressed me with your eyes earlier. Why the chivalry now?"

His voice was tight as he said, "Because if I see your beautiful body mostly bare, I may never allow you to jump into the water. I'll be too busy holding you close and making you orgasm with my hand."

Her breath hitched. However, she found her voice again, otherwise she'd never carry out her plan. "I wouldn't mind that, except that you have too many clothes on." She moved toward the edge of the pool. "Join me when you're ready."

Since the air was warm, Kalahn dove right into the pool, the cool water brushing against her skin. She wondered what it'd feel like to have Ryven inside her while they were still in the water, the sound of their lovemaking rivaling that of the waterfall.

Maybe she was a slightly dirty princess after all.

After stroking forward a few times under the water, she surfaced and looked for Ryven. But he was nowhere to be found.

He would never abandon her, and there weren't any negative emotions coming through their bond. If only she could reach out to him via telepathy to discover where he'd gone.

Before she could debate whether or not to defy the doctor's orders, something grabbed her waist from behind.

She squeaked as Ryven whispered into her ear, "I think we still have a lot of defense training to do. I snuck up on you far too easily."

She tried to turn, but Ryven pulled her back against his front and held her there. Judging by his erection against her lower back, he was naked.

Good. One less obstacle for her to overcome and convince Ryven to claim her.

Looking over her shoulder, she said, "I may not be able to use my telepathy right now, but if there were a threat with you near me, I'd feel your concern through the mind-bond. Since there wasn't any, I had no reason to worry."

"You and your logic." He took her earlobe between his teeth and worried her flesh. Rational thought fled her mind and Kalahn resisted a moan as she rubbed her rear against his cock.

Ryven finally released her earlobe and spoke again. "I may have to find someone else to help with your training then because I see now that you'll never be able to concentrate when I do something like this." He moved a finger to one of her breasts and lightly moved the fabric against her taut nipple. Kalahn bit her lip and tried her best to focus on Ryven's words as he spoke again. "But I'll have to lay some ground rules because if any other male ever tries to touch you like this." He tweaked her nipple. "I will kill him."

A fierce protectiveness flowed through their bond and Kalahn smiled. "Good. Because if any female tries to do the same and touch your marvelous body, I will find a way to harm her."

With a growl, Ryven quickly turned her around and possessively placed his hands on her rear. "You're the only one who can touch me, Kalahn. You're mine as much as I'm yours."

He closed the distance between their lips and kissed her. Between his licks and nibbles, as well as the love coming down the mind-bond, Kalahn surrendered and pressed herself as close as she could against Ryven's muscled body. She wanted him more than ever before.

To give Ryven some encouragement, she moved her hips. However, Ryven immediately broke the kiss. They both breathed heavily as he growled, "Stop, Kalahn. I'm too close to the edge."

She cupped his cheeks and ran her thumbs against his late day whiskers. "But I don't want you to stop, Ryven."

He shook his head as much as he could with her hands on his face. "No, I can't. We should be married first. That's the honorable thing to do."

"And what if it takes years before the law changes? What then?"

"Then I'll wait."

"No."

Ryven frowned. "Why are you so persistent in this, Kalahn?"

"Why? Oh, I don't know. Maybe because we both came close to death recently. And that being cautious and holding back may be honorable by Kelderan standards, but we're no longer on Keldera, Ryven." She searched his eyes. "I want you. Isn't that enough?"

He leaned closer, but then moved his head back again. "If I have you once, I'll want you over and over again. And the longer we go unmarried, the worse it'll be for you. The colony may include more open-minded Kelderans, but not everyone will accept an unmarried female living with a male."

Ryven's thoughtfulness was one of the things she loved about him, but sometimes he took it too far.

Shaking her head, she replied, "I don't care about that.

And since I'm on hormone treatments, there's no chance for a child, either, if that's another of your concerns." She moved her head closer to his. "I love you, Ryven. Won't you claim me properly right here, right now, and make my fantasy come true?"

Indecision warred in his eyes and via the bond. For a second, she worried she'd pushed him too far. Ryven may be open-minded about many things, but sex before marriage might not be one of them.

Then he growled and ran a hand up her back to tangle his fingers into her wet hair. "Never doubt how much I want you, Princess. And now I'm going to show you just how much."

He easily lifted her butt with his other hand, thanks to the buoyancy of the water, until her core was against his waist. Kalahn hooked her arms around his neck and wrapped her legs around his middle. She expected him to kiss her, but instead he ordered, "Hold on, but lean back."

His voice brooked no argument, and she obeyed, the action making the water brush against her body. The odd combination of the heat of her own body and the coolness of the water only made her nerves more sensitive.

Ryven took his time, but finally lowered his gaze to her breasts. She had no idea if the material were see-through or not, but she didn't care. The longer he stared, the more her nipples tightened and pulsed with desire.

Ryven finally lowered his head and took one of her tight buds into his mouth. The contrast of his hot mouth with the coolness of her skin made her cry out. Taking the sound as encouragement, Ryven nibbled and swirled. Every caress made her lean her head back a little more and rub her hips against his erection, the water adding a third caress to her actions.

Yes, this was definitely a dream she had wanted to become reality. She'd have to ask Ryven for more of them in the future.

However, Ryven bit a little harder and she groaned. Other dreams could wait. Right now, she simply enjoyed Ryven's attentions on her nipple. When she was close to crying out in pleasure, he released her and moved to her other breast.

The man had a talented tongue and knew how to use his teeth. Each nibble and stroke pushed her a little closer to the edge.

At that thought, a little reason returned to her brain. If she didn't do anything, he'd probably make her orgasm and resist claiming her.

Ryven increased the pace of his attentions, banishing her last coherent thought. Ryven's evil yet delicious nibbles and licks continued unabated. Within seconds, she crashed over the edge and dug her nails into his neck as she came.

※ ※ ※

Ryven did his best to ignore his pulsing cock and simply watched Kalahn's face as she orgasmed. Her soft cries and surrender were better than any dream he'd ever had.

And he was only getting started.

Once Kalahn opened her eyes and smiled at him, he kissed her gently before murmuring, "Ready for more, love?"

She purred. "Yes. I was hoping you wouldn't back out." She moved her hips and he hissed at the friction. "It's your turn now."

He kissed her jaw, untying her top as he did so. He met her eyes again. "Soon. First, I need to prepare you."

"Yes, yes, I know it'll hurt at first. But don't take forever about it, Ryven. I want all of you."

While Ryven had never bedded a Kelderan virgin, he'd heard a few horror stories of how the female ended up in so much pain upon penetration that she sobbed.

No. He wouldn't lose control and rush things. Besides, even if Kalahn tried to keep it from him, her emotions would filter through the mind-bond.

Once her top was off, he undid the ties on either side of her bottoms. Rubbing slow circles on her butt, he kissed the side of her neck, her jaw, and finally took her lips in a quick, rough kiss. "Hold on to me, love. I don't want you to float away."

Playfulness danced in her eyes. "Maybe not now, but just think of all the things we could try in this pool."

A picture of Kalahn sucking his cock under water only made more blood rush to it. "Later. Right now, I want to come inside you."

Kalahn adjusted her hold on his neck and tilted her head. "Then do so. I'm waiting."

All the males who'd dismissed Kalahn for being outspoken and rash clearly didn't know what they were missing. Which suited him fine, because Kalahn was now his.

He kissed her as he untangled his one hand from her hair and inched it down her chest, her belly, and finally to her hot center between her thighs. Never ceasing his kisses, Ryven gently thrust one finger in and out, both loving how tight she was and afraid of what he might do to her.

Kalahn broke the kiss and murmured, "Don't worry about me. I'm stronger than I look."

As if to prove her point, she moved against his finger and squeezed. Ryven groaned. "You're so tight, though."

"Not for long. I'm sure my thick, long warrior will stretch me out with lots and lots of practice."

"Kalahn," he murmured.

"If you're going to say princesses don't say such things, keep it to yourself. Because this princess does."

At her bold, confident tone, Ryven decided to trust her and added another finger. Kalahn made a little noise of pleasure, and he lazily moved his fingers. "And I'm glad she does, and hopefully she tells me every dirty little fantasy she has so I can fulfill them all." Her markings flashed red, and Ryven added, "But before we get to those, let's finish this one, first."

Removing his fingers, Ryven took his cock and positioned it at her hot entrance. "Ready, love?" Kalahn nodded without hesitation. Taking a deep breath, he kept his eyes trained on Kalahn's and slowly entered her.

Damn, she was tight. As he inched inside her, it took everything he had not to close his eyes and start thrusting.

He reached her barrier and stopped. "Last chance, love."

She cupped his jaw. "I want this. I want you. I love you, Ryven. Don't stop."

He sometimes wondered how he deserved her. "I love you, too." Clenching his jaw, he pushed through her barrier. Pain radiated down the mind-bond the same time as Kalahn cried out. He kept still and rubbed her back, kissed her lips, and murmured, "As long as I live, I'll never hurt you again."

She answered through clenched teeth. "I know. Just give me a minute and I'll be fine."

As Kalahn curled against him, he contented himself with holding her close. The realization that Kalahn was his now and forever crashed over him, and a sense of rightness came over him. Woe betide anyone who tried to take her from him in the future.

He didn't know how much time had passed before Kalahn raised her head and nodded. "I'm ready. Make me forget all about that, Ryven. And don't you dare hold back."

Taking her lips, he moved his hips slowly at first. But with each moan and groan from Kalahn, he increased his pace, loving how she gripped him tightly.

Later he would find the strength to last and take his time. In the present, he could barely hold on. Merely being inside his princess was enough to drive him crazy.

As if reading his thoughts, Kalahn also joined him with her own motions, the water splashing around them. The sound created a memory he'd never forget.

Pressure built at the base of his spine. When Kalahn gripped him tighter than before, he cried out and stilled, spilling his seed inside her.

After the last spasm of pleasure wracked his body, Ryven release Kalahn's lips and laid his forehead against hers. Kalahn was the first to speak up. "So what do you think? Was it worth it to defy tradition?"

He smiled. "I want to say I should've waited, but you're addictive in so many ways, love. This is just another one." He kept her pressed against his body and he moved to shallower waters. When the water was low enough that he could sit down without it covering more than his shoulders, he did so. "But while we may have defied one tradition, I'm not going to eschew them all. You deserve the ritual cleaning after the first time."

He half expected Kalahn to protest, but she slowly backed off his cock and turned to sit on his legs. She spread hers, and she raised her eyebrows. "Be quick about it, though. I have a few more ideas to try while it's still warm out."

Chuckling, Ryven gently washed between her legs. Even though the pool of water should've done it already, he wanted to take care of his female. No one would ever say he didn't think of her needs even with his cock hard. With her scent surrounding him, it made him more than raring to go another round.

Finished with his task, he cupped her cheek and kissed her once, twice, and three times. He asked, "So what does my princess have in mind to do next?"

She grinned and glanced at the waterfall. "We've done it in front of it, let's do it behind."

"As long as we can do it a third time, with you floating on your back and me between your thighs."

Her markings turned red and stayed that way. "My warrior has a dirty mind, too."

He winked. "Good thing, as we'll never run out of ideas."

Ryven kissed her once more before they made their way to behind the waterfall and he had the chance to treasure her all over again and again until they were both exhausted.

Chapter Twenty-Three

In the coming weeks after Kajala had given birth, Kalahn did her best to rest and resist looking into Pelryka's memories. She couldn't help anyone if she hurt her mind again and never fully healed.

So far Keltor and Kason hadn't been able to find a link between the antimonarchist groups on Keldera and the one on Jasvar. However, thanks to Kason and Taryn making a joint statement that all people on Jasvar, regardless of heritage, were welcome as long as they followed the rules and laws of the respected colonies, the female assassin's lord had begun talking a little.

Of course, Kason and Taryn needed more than one person's cooperation if they were to ever neutralize the threats to the royal family. As a first step, the pair had even gone as far as having a public signing within each colony, to solidify the offer of acceptance and show they meant it.

In the beginning, no one else had come forward. But as soon as Thorin Jarrell stood up at the Kelderan colony meeting and announced his half-Brevkan heritage, others had slowly come forth as well.

Kalahn doubted all of the non-full-blooded Kelderans had come forward, but even a handful doing so was a move in the right direction.

However, while the public statements were a good start, there were still too many unanswered questions for Kalahn to rest easy. Especially when it came to who was driving the campaigns to kill the royal family.

That was something she hoped to rectify as soon as she could sort through the memories she'd collected. While Pelryka's lord had begun to share information, his female was still keeping quiet. Mostly because she'd been unconscious a great deal of that time, ever since Kalahn had interceded and stopped her suicide attempt.

Maybe with time, Pelryka would be forthright as well. Although the window for any sort of deal was closing. As soon as Kalahn could sort through the female's memories, her cooperation wouldn't be required.

Not that Kalahn wanted to have anyone else's memories inside her head. If she never had to do that again, she'd be happy. However, if the female assassin didn't talk, it was their last option to find out what they needed.

Kalahn adjusted her position on the bed for the tenth time and let out a sigh. She couldn't wait to do something, anything, to help. Borzet clearing her and deeming her mind healed enough to use telepathy again couldn't come soon enough.

Ryven lay next to her in the bed and began rubbing her upper arms. His voice filled the room. "Fretting to the point you don't get enough sleep will only make your recovery take longer."

She met his gaze. "I know that, but I can't help it. Besides, I don't know if I even need to rest much longer. I think I'm strong enough to use telepathy again."

"You have your final test with Borzet the day after tomorrow. Don't even think of using it before then, Kalahn. The risk is too great."

She sighed. "I know, but I wish I could move it up."

He tucked a section of hair behind her ear. "You know that's impossible, love. Tomorrow is Keltor and Azalyn's formal claiming ceremony. There's no way Kason would allow you to spend the day inside a training room and miss the viewing."

She traced one of the markings on Ryven's neck. "I'm happy for Keltor and Azalyn. However, I could be so much more useful if I could use my telepathy again. Even a day sooner could mean everything when it comes to ensuring he and Azalyn, as well as both their older twins and their unborn child, have a happy future."

"Since I know you won't stop thinking about this until you're cleared for telepathy again, I think I need to distract you."

Before she could do more than open her mouth, Ryven rolled on top of her and pinned her hands above her head with one hand.

Rationally, she should scold him. But with his naked, muscled body on top of her own naked one, she admitted that she wanted his brand of distraction.

He nipped her neck and soothed the sting with his tongue. Each stroke against her skin relaxed her more against the mattress. His hot breath danced across her skin as he whispered, "What does my female want tonight?"

She was more than aware that he wanted to call her his bride. However, Kalahn still hadn't asked him to be her lord yet, even though they had been living and sleeping together for weeks.

She could just imagine the talk if anyone back on Keldera had heard of it.

Pushing aside her guilt at not giving Ryven what he wanted just yet, she smiled and said playfully, "How about you surprise me?"

He nipped her neck again, sending a thrill through Kalahn's body. "That almost sounds like you're granting me the right to live out one of my fantasies rather than give you one of yours."

She wiggled her lower half and Ryven's cock hardened even more against her lower abdomen. Good. He was as distracted as she was now. "I'd like to think we can have shared fantasies from time to time. You doing what you want with me is one of mine, after all. And probably one of yours."

Keeping her hands pinned above her head with one hand, Ryven moved the other one to her cheek. "Then I know exactly what to give my female."

Holding her breath, she waited to see what Ryven would do. However, he merely stared into her eyes, never moving his body.

With his heated gaze never wavering, anticipation gathered in her belly, making her wet between the thighs.

He finally ordered, "Keep your hands above your head."

Releasing her, he moved both of his hands to her shoulders, down to her breasts but careful to avoid her aching nipples, and finally resting them on her lower belly. As he stroked her soft skin with his thumbs, she opened her legs in invitation.

Rather than touch between her thighs, Ryven moved his hands over her hips, down her outer thighs, and pressed her legs to bend them upward.

Spreading her legs wider, his gaze zeroed in on her core.

Even though they'd been intimate more times than she could count by now, his eyes on her never failed to make her body flush and heart pound.

Ryven ran a finger between her folds and she nearly jumped. He smiled slowly, leaning his head down to lick her slit up, down, and back again. Kalahn watched Ryven's head as he moved, tasting her, and dug her nails into the mattress.

All too soon, he raised his head and licked his lips. The ache between her thighs intensified, and she bucked her hips. It was almost as if she needed Ryven inside her to tame her heart.

His husky voice caressed her ears. "You'll get that soon enough, love. First, I need to make my female scream in orgasm."

Since Kelderan females primarily came from nipple stimulation, hers grew even tighter. If only he tweaked them a few times, she'd probably crash into a thousand pieces.

His hand ran up her belly, her waist, and finally to the undersides of her breasts. Never taking his gaze from hers, he pinched her nipples between his forefinger and thumb, tweaking and tugging in the way she liked.

If his fingers weren't making her melt enough, the heat in his gaze shot straight to her sensitive nerves.

The pressure built, and Kalahn dug her nails deeper into the bed. Every time Ryven was a little rough, ecstasy surged through her body and also thrummed through the mind-bond. He took pleasure in giving it to her.

Her male growled, and with a gentle twist gave her the final push over the edge.

Lights danced before her eyes as spasms wracked her body.

And with Ryven's heated gaze watching her, she fell even harder, screaming his name and losing all semblance of rational thought.

When she finally came down from her high and slumped against the bed, Ryven moved up and kissed her lips.

She moved to place her hands on his back, but he whispered, "No time for breaks. The fantasy isn't done."

After another lingering kiss, Ryven flipped her on her stomach and raised her hips. He ran his hands up and down the outside of her thighs before moving to her inner ones and spreading them apart.

Again, Ryven did nothing. As the seconds ticked by, the cool air against her core nearly made her moan.

She was empty and wanted, no needed, Ryven inside her. She moved her hips back, but he steadied them with one hand. She turned her head at the same time he ran his hard, warm cock against her. The tease was taking his time.

He was going to drive her crazy.

And that was just the way she liked it.

❋ ❋ ❋

Brushing his cock against Kalahn's hot, wet folds, Ryven's balls tightened and he threatened to come all over her beautiful backside.

Even though he'd had her probably over a hundred times by now, every time made him feel like a novice, ready to come at the first contact with her core.

So he took a second to breathe, pushing back the feeling. He wanted Kalahn's body to remember him in the morning and to do that, he needed more than a few, quick thrusts.

He lazily stroked her hip and moved his hand to her breasts. Kalahn sighed as he fondled her, her head dropping forward.

If he wanted to surprise her, this was the time to do it.

Positioning his cock at her entrance, he thrust into her. Kalahn groaned, leaning her hips back, urging him to do more.

He was a lucky male to have found a female so open when naked and gripping him tightly. Kalahn was unique. And his.

It was time to ensure she remembered that.

Gripping her hips, Ryven began to move, increasing his pace with each thrust. He loved the way Kalahn moved with him without any coaxing, unafraid to take what she wanted and increase her own pleasure.

Maybe next he'd ask her to pleasure herself and let him watch.

However, that was later. In the present, he positioned her hips up a little and the change in angle made both of them groan. When she squeezed him with her inner muscles, he lightly slapped her backside.

Which made her do it again.

Damn, he loved her.

Since his female liked it rough, he moved faster and faster, loving the way his balls slapped against her and filled the room with the sound of their lovemaking.

Kalahn's little moans and squeaks only encouraged him to try harder.

Moving a hand, he tweaked one of her hard nipples. She tightened her core in response and Ryven nearly came right then.

The minx was waging a war, but he would be the winner this time around.

He continued to tease her breasts, tweaking and twisting the way that made Kalahn all but melt into the bed.

Keeping her hips high with his one hand, Ryven changed his angle again and Kalahn screamed his name. Since he'd found the spot that would drive her crazy, he kept at it, the pressure building at his spine again.

Gritting his teeth, he held back, waiting for Kalahn. He would take care of her in all ways, and he took pride in making her come.

When she finally gripped his cock and released in spasms, Ryven allowed himself to fall over the edge, filling his female with his seed, branding her as his own.

Once she'd milked all he had, he collapsed to the side, taking Kalahn with him. He kissed her shoulder and murmured against her skin. "I love you."

Turning her head, she smiled. The pink color of her markings, combined with the feelings emanating from the mind-bond, told him all he needed to know. Still, he reveled in every syllable as she said, "I love you, too."

He pulled her close and closed his eyes, reveling in her slightly damp skin and delicious feminine scent that was uniquely Kalahn. He would never tire of holding her close and feeling her skin against his.

She completed him in a way he'd never known he'd needed.

Indeed, the forbidden female had turned out to be his perfect match.

After a few minutes of them lying in silence, Kalahn sat up and he slid from her body. He was about to reach for her again when she straddled his stomach and placed both of her hands on his pecs. Her long, blue hair tickled his skin, but he didn't brush it back. Instead, he put his hands on her bum and rubbed in slow circles.

Kalahn's markings tinged yellow, which signaled nervousness. He stilled his movements and searched her eyes, unable to judge what she was feeling. "What's wrong?"

She shook her head, her hair dancing around her face. "Nothing is wrong."

"Your markings suggest otherwise."

"Markings can be deceptive, as you've often told me."

He raised a brow. "Are you trying to trick me?"

"No, but that doesn't mean I couldn't do it if I wanted to."

He snorted. "Noted." He rubbed her behind again. "Then tell me."

"Wait a second and you'll see."

Before he could say a word, she jumped off the bed and ran into the bathroom of their temporary housing. Even though only seconds passed, it felt like hours. His curiosity was anxious to know what was going on.

When Kalahn finally returned to the room, she had her arms behind her back.

Ryven sat up as she closed the distance between them. When she reached the bed, she presented him with a bouquet of flowers. "I'm trying to romance you."

He laughed as he took them, and then tugged Kalahn to sit next to him. "It's working."

She grinned. "I hope that's enough romancing because the only other thing I have to offer is words." He raised his brows, afraid to hope for what he desperately wanted. Kalahn continued. "I thought I needed a guarantee of safety, to protect my heart and ensure I never lost you. But with each passing day, it becomes clearer and clearer that the future will always be uncertain. And if I ever lose you, it will break my heart. But protecting my heart isn't worth delaying what we both want. I want to be your bride, Ryven. Will you be my lord?"

He could tease her and draw it out.

But Ryven didn't want that. He answered, "Of course," before he pulled her close and kissed her.

While every kiss with Kalahn was unforgettable, he nipped and nibbled harder, as if to answer her again with actions.

Tossing the flowers aside, he rolled until Kalahn was under him. He broke the kiss long enough to murmur, "I love you, my bride. And I'll be out to prove it every day, so you never doubt it."

The Forbidden

As Ryven took his time to make Kalahn orgasm more times than he could count, happiness coursed through every cell in his body. Kalahn was his forever, and he was never letting go.

Epilogue

Many months later

Kalahn resisted pacing and instead used up some of her excess energy by changing the pictures on the walls of her shared mental space with Ryven. The purple forest of Jasvar became the mountains of Keldera. And another, displaying her and Ryven's favorite waterfall on Jasvar, changed angles to show it from behind rather than facing it.

They tended to spend a lot of time inside their shared space, as it was easier to talk with each other and still pay attention to others around them. Her siblings seemed to not understand how comforting it was to be able to reach out to Ryven at any moment. No, they balked at the closeness. However, after a lifetime of forced distance with her family, Kalahn reveled in it.

Indeed, their shared signature displaying a pair of green *cerrak* felines standing over a waterfall suited them well. After all, *cerraks* mated for life and always traveled or hunted together, working as a team, much like she and Ryven did now. What with all the work she had reaching out to nearby planets via telepathy, she needed Ryven's support and presence. Otherwise, she'd probably fail.

The Forbidden

Which she couldn't do and still protect her ever-growing family. Even though Kalahn still wasn't ready for children, all of the marriages, births, and pregnancies in her family had grown the tro el Vallen slash Mayven clan quite a bit.

In the next hour or so, it would grow by one more on Jasvar.

Ryven stood at the side of the reception room being used for the latest arrivals from Keldera, his arms crossed over his chest, and sighed. The sound garnered her attention. "You have nothing to be nervous about."

She faced him. "You can say that as she's your mother. I haven't even had the chance to talk with her via a video conference. For all we know, she might hate me."

He raised an eyebrow. "I didn't think you cared about people liking you."

She growled in frustration. "Usually, no. But she's important to you, so she's important to me."

His expression softened and he reached for her. Kalahn allowed him to pull her close. He nuzzled her cheek and murmured, "Because I love you, she will love you, Kalahn."

She finally melted against him and hugged him close. "Deep down, I know that. It's just hard to believe it will be that easy, given everything that's happened recently."

Such as with Kajala's surprise that had ended up breaking and then mending her heart again.

Not that she expected Ryven's mother to break her heart or hurt her in any way. Still, Kalahn was wary of anything going as planned anymore.

He rubbed her back. "I know it's been hard with your father's recent death, and the drama with your siblings. But while my mother may have a limp, she is one of the healthiest individuals I know. She'll be around for a long time. And she most definitely doesn't create drama. If anything, she helps stop it in its tracks."

She smiled. "I think we could use a little of that here on the colony. Pair her with Vala, and they'll have the Barren running everything but the colony's council before long."

He snorted. "Maybe hold off on mentioning that for a few days at least. Because my mother will try to do that as soon as it's mentioned."

She looked up into Ryven's eyes. "Even if I don't say anything, I'm sure Taryn will give her ideas."

Ryven opened his mouth to reply, but a bell hanging next to the door rang, signaling that someone was approaching.

Ryven shook his head. "I'm sure she will. However, you should worry about something else."

"What?" she asked slowly.

"While I'm content to wait for children, she's going to be asking nearly every day about when she's getting grandchildren."

Considering Ryven's mother was one of the Barren, Kalahn imagined that her having grandchildren was a gift she wouldn't ever take for granted. "I can handle that. Besides, all I have to do is steer her toward ruling the colony and she'll forget about it. Then it becomes your problem."

"You haven't even met her, and yet you're all but scheming with my mother already."

"Of course." She kissed him. "I imagine it'll be a regular thing, so you'd better get used to it."

"As long as I get some time alone with my love, I can deal with it." Ryven's mental presence swirled around her own, projecting images of their latest trip to their secret waterfall, when he'd laid out a picnic in front of the falls before making love to her in the water.

She met his gaze and spoke outside the plane. "Yes, yes, I know that you're romantic. I half expect music to start playing and flowers to be thrown into the room. I already asked you to be my lord. You don't need to romance me further."

"Ah, but that's where you're wrong, Lahn. Romancing you is part of my long-term plan." He nuzzled her cheek. "Making you scream in pleasure is another major tenet."

She lightly hit his chest. "Ryven, your mother could walk through that door at any moment."

"I already did," an unfamiliar female said.

Kalahn extracted herself from Ryven's embrace and whirled around. A female with light blue skin and purple hair stood in the doorway, the amusement dancing in her eyes a stark contrast to her stern expression.

Maybe some of Ryven's humor had come from his mother.

Kalahn curtsied. "It's nice to finally meet you, Gosarra."

Gosarra closed the distance between them, took her hand, and squeezed. Only once Kalahn stood upright again did she speak. "There's no need to curtsey. You're about to marry my son, and it's plain to see how happy he is, so there's no need to impress me."

Kalahn resisted blinking. Ryven's mother was extremely honest and straightforward for any Kelderan female, let alone a Barren.

Gosarra chuckled. "No, judging from your expression, you can tell I'm not conventionally what you'd picture for a Barren. But then again, this is Jasvar, is it not? And I'm not about to hide my true self from my future daughter-in-law."

"I didn't mean—" Kalahn began.

Gosarra put up a hand. "Since everything I've heard about you isn't exactly what I'd expect out of a Kelderan princess, I think we're even when it comes to preconceptions. Just be who you are, Kalahn. And that's good enough for me."

Ryven sighed. "Couldn't you save the life lessons until later, Mother?"

Gosarra opened her arms and Ryven stepped into them. "Of course not. I didn't do it with you, and I'm not about to do it to your future bride." Gosarra leaned back and touched her son's cheek. "I can't tell you how happy it makes me that you two waited to have your proclamation ceremony until I arrived."

Kalahn jumped in. "It was the right thing to do. I don't have any parents alive anymore, but I wanted at least one there. Even if you're only a parent through marriage, that means a lot to me."

"I'm sorry about the late king," Gosarra answered. "He was as fair to the Barren as he could be, given the law. If not for his help after the Brevkan wars, I'm not sure what would've become of the Barren."

Her eyes filled with tears, but Kalahn held them back. "Thank you for your kind words. You'll have to tell me more about my father from back then, as he never really talked about it with me."

"Many of us don't talk about the wars, but some good came from the bad."

As Gosarra smiled at her son, Kalahn's nervousness faded. Part of her had wondered if Ryven's mother would hold a grudge against King Kastor for not doing more for the Barren. But it seemed she recognized the good allowed, despite the limitations.

However, the present wasn't the time to talk about the past. Kalahn stood a little taller. "Now, how about we take you to your quarters to rest before the ceremony?"

Gosarra shook her head. "I've been resting the entire journey from Keldera. I'd much rather meet your family."

"Are you sure?" Kalahn asked.

Ryven moved so that he had his mother on one side and Kalahn on the other. "Don't argue with her, Kalahn. It's easier to do what she says."

Gosarra snorted. "I've trained you well."

Kalahn leaned forward and met Gosarra's gaze. "Once everything settles down, I hope you'll tell me some stories of Ryven. The more embarrassing, the better."

Ryven shook his head, but Gosarra spoke. "I have quite a few. However, I want some stories about you growing up in return."

She and Ryven had decided not to tell his mother about Kalahn having Ryven's memories, let alone Pelryka's. After all, Kalahn did her best to leave them alone. And when it came to Ryven, a mother's perspective was always different from a child's.

Ryven grunted. "You two can discuss embarrassing stories later. Right now, there's not a lot of time before the claiming ceremony. And since Kason saved several days' worth of energy to have enough to broadcast it to Keltor, Azalyn, and their family, we'd do best not to upset his plans. Otherwise, we'll never hear the end of it."

Kalahn leaned against Ryven's side. "Then let's show your mother her quarters so she can change." Kalahn peeked her head around again. "I had a dress made as a welcoming present. I hope that's okay."

Gosarra motioned toward her brown, flowing dress; the same one all Barren wore on Keldera. "As long as it's not brown, I'll gladly wear anything."

Kalahn tamped down the anger that flared. Her eldest brother was doing his best to change things on Keldera, but it took time. For the present, the Barren were still required by law to wear brown dresses outside the citadels.

Thankfully things moved quicker on Jasvar. "No, it's not brown. I thought silver trimmed with dark blue would suit you."

"Then what are we waiting for? The sooner I can take off a brown-colored dress for the last time, the better."

As Ryven guided them out of the room and down the corridor, Kalahn wanted to run and give Gosarra her newfound freedoms even quicker.

But Gosarra had a lame leg and limped slowly. Of course Kalahn and Ryven slowed their own pace to match hers.

She was just happy the first meeting had gone well with Ryven's mother. Kalahn had a lot more surprises in store, but would share them in time. First thing's first, she needed to officially take Ryven as her lord.

❋ ❋ ❋

A few hours later, Kalahn stood at the edge of a dais, waiting for her brother Kason to arrive and let her know it was time to come out.

Originally, Kason had wanted the ceremony to be a small, private affair. However, she and Ryven had had a different idea.

By sharing their ceremony with anyone on Jasvar who wished to attend, they were not only proving things were changing by a princess marrying a warrior, but it also showed that the monarchy were people like anyone else. Even they fell in love. And by having Taryn and Kajala attend, it showcased that they had and raised children, too.

What they didn't highlight was how the royal family wasn't completely free of danger just yet.

Yes, they'd made progress on tracking down the traitors, thanks to Pelryka's help, among others. The female was still under heavy monitoring and probation, but at least hadn't been separated from her lord or children.

They'd even found the half-Brevkan male who had been responsible for following Ryven and cutting down the branch. But Kalahn and everyone else who worked with the colony's security teams knew that something was bubbling under the surface, which would either be the last showdown or the start of a war.

No. While there were many things she wanted to accomplish to protect those she loved, the present was for her and Ryven. Soon enough she'd finally marry the male she loved, and then they could work on preventing future wars or catastrophes.

Love pulsed through their mind-bond, and Kalahn smiled. Unlike most brides-to-be, she could tell if her male was nervous. Ryven wasn't.

Kason and Taryn entered the side area of the dais. Taryn was the first to engulf her in a hug, doing her best to hold Kalahn close despite her pregnant belly. Her sister-in-law spoke in CEL. "I'm so happy for you, Kalahn. Ryven is quite the man, and he makes you happy."

Kalahn pulled back to look Taryn in the eye. "I know. And at least now Kason can't keep saying we should save our affections for our marriage. Because in a matter of minutes, we'll be married. If you think we've been caught making out before, just wait."

Kason sighed. "I'd rather not see my sister and my best friend kissing and fondling in a hallway."

"We're not fondling," Kalahn stated. "I do have some decorum."

"Since when?" Kason drawled.

Taryn snorted. "Enough. Kason is happy, too, even if it's hard for him to say so. Now, we'll go take our seats and you come out in a minute. Ryven should be waiting for you."

Her brother and Taryn exited, leaving her alone.

Kalahn smoothed the simple white fabric of her dress. Another concession, to show how much she differed from traditional royal weddings, was for her to wear a white wedding dress designed by the humans of Jasvar. A Kelderan one would've gone up to her neck, to her wrists, and to the floor. The human one was low-cut, exposed her back, and while it went to the floor, it was form-fitting.

She gave one last peek out to the audience, noting Taryn and Kason sitting near Kajala and her male, Thorin and Vala, and Ryven's mother. Her other family should already be watching the live feed.

Well, everyone but her father. But he was free of pain and had given his blessing before he passed.

Sadness must've carried through her mind-bond, because Ryven said inside their shared mental space, *Are you okay?*

Fine, fine. I was just thinking of my father. But that doesn't matter now. I'm coming out.

Taking a deep inhalation, Kalahn stood tall and walked out onto the dais.

Ryven stood in the center, wearing his formal warrior attire of tight pants, a sash across his chest decorated with his accomplishments, and boots that went to his knees. She didn't like that everyone could see his chest but knew that she was showing more skin than he liked as well, so they were even.

As soon as she reached him, Ryven took her hands in his. While her brother Keltor had stared down the council to get them to approve Ryven as her lord, the law still required her to speak first in the ceremony. So Kalahn said, "Ryven Xanna is my lord, and he has chosen me. Do you recognize my claim?"

Cheers went up in the room. They'd cleared the first hurdle.

Ryven winked and Kalahn did her best not to laugh. "Yes, I do as well. Now, Kalahn tro el Vallen is my bride and has chosen me. Do you recognize my claim?"

Another round of cheers echoed in the big room.

The Forbidden

Traditionally, they'd face the crowd and descend the stairs. However, before Kalahn could move, Ryven tugged her up against him and murmured, "I love you," before kissing her in front of everyone.

No doubt Kason was frowning, but Kalahn didn't care. She kissed her lord back, their tongues tangling much like how their mental presences twirled around each other inside their minds.

Love had a funny way of coming together for them, but Kalahn wouldn't have it any other way. She and Ryven were bonded in both hearts and minds, and she was never letting him go.

Author's Note

I hope you enjoyed Ryven and Kalahn's story! Theirs is the most probably the most light-hearted so far of the series, but Kalahn needed that. A stubborn male who ordered her around would've gone no where, lol. This story did set up the next two books: 1) A follow-up novella about Thorin and Vala and 2) Kajala's book. Thorin and Vala's story will be called *The Hidden* and should be out in 2019. As the title suggests, it will be about other partial Brevkan individuals and bringing them out of the shadows of Kelderan society. Kajala's book is tentatively called *The Survivor*, but I'm unsure of the exact release date. However, you can always sign up for my mailing list at www.JessieDonovan.com to stay in the loop of release dates and more.

With that out of the way, there are a few people I'd like to thank:

- My editor, Becky Johnson, of Hot Tree Editing. Without her, there wouldn't be a Chapter 22. She's amazing at calling me out when I'm lazy, and that chapter most definitely needed to be there.
- My cover artist, Clarissa Yeo of Yocla Designs. As always, she captures my stories so well, down to the little smile on Ryven's face on the cover.

- My awesome beta readers: Iliana G., Sabrina D., Sandy H., Alyson S., and Donna H. These ladies do a great job of spotting lingering typos and minor inconsistencies.

Thanks so much for following my sci-fi romance series! We're slowly heading toward the end I envision, but it's going to take another five or so books to get there. I hope to see you at the end of the next book. Thanks for reading!

About the Author

Jessie Donovan wrote her first story at age five, and after discovering *The Dragonriders of Pern* series by Anne McCaffrey in junior high, she realized people actually wanted to read stories like those floating around inside her head. From there on out, she was determined to tap into her over-active imagination and write a book someday.

After living abroad for five years and earning degrees in Japanese, Anthropology, and Secondary Education, she buckled down and finally wrote her first full-length book. While that story will never see the light of day, it laid the world-building groundwork of what would become her debut paranormal romance, *Blaze of Secrets*. In late 2014, she became a *New York Times* and *USA Today* bestseller.

Jessie loves to interact with readers, and when not reading, attempting to tame her yard, or traipsing around some foreign country on a shoestring, she can often be found on Facebook.

And don't forget to sign-up for her newsletter to receive sneak peeks and inside information. You can sign-up on her website:

http://www.JessieDonovan.com

Lightning Source UK Ltd.
Milton Keynes UK
UKHW040348130219
337212UK00001B/12/P